ISBN: 979-8-9891040-5-5
E-ISBN: 979-8-9891040-6-2
Library of Congress Control Number: 2024934574
Big Sister Books
Pittsburgh, PA

THE DREAMER

THE DREAMER

SIMEON HARRAR

Big Sister Books

For Bibi, the one who first helped me fall in love with stories

CHAPTER 1

Beyond the Bunker

Somehow, Joseph managed to gobble up his breakfast slop—the family's name for his father Abba's porridge—despite the nervous excitement whirling in his stomach. It was his sixteenth birthday, and he was finally getting out of this bunker and going topside. He'd woken early this morning and had already been up for hours when his little brother Benjamin toddled out for breakfast followed by his ten older brothers. Patience had never been Joseph's thing, and he knew they intentionally moved in slow motion to annoy him. For years, he'd badgered them with questions and begged to be allowed to join the outside expeditions. His curiosity and persistence knew no bounds. Clearly, they were getting back at him for his years of nagging.

But today he'd join them in the sacred realm of manhood. At long last, he'd be allowed to leave the family bunker to roam the wilderness landscape. For years, he'd listened to his brothers' tales of the strange world beyond their underground hideout with its thick metal walls. Soon he would have his own stories to tell.

He'd read every book in the bunker from cover to cover, memorizing most of them, but the world his brothers spoke of was vastly different from the one described in his beloved books, which all predated the Great War of 2052. Their tattered pages spoke of lush forests, sprawling cities, and blue skies. It was difficult to fathom that all those things had been destroyed, and yet it was true. Abba had regaled him with the tale of "the war that broke the world" many times.

On November 11, 2052, hopes were high after the signing of an international peace treaty. Everyone breathed a sigh of relief.

Then the world exploded.

Nuclear missiles rained down out of the morning sky, angels of death striking their targets with pinpoint accuracy. In a matter of seconds, Armageddon had descended upon Jerusalem. Mushroom clouds taller than skyscrapers blossomed on the horizon. The entire city went up in flames. The peace had been a lie.

And that was only the beginning. Clouds of deadly gasses poisoned villages, volcanic eruptions and tsunamis took out others. Crops failed. Animals died. Technology was destroyed. Civilization crumbled. The entire world fell into chaos in the gray, blistered aftermath of the apocalypse.

At this point in the story, Abba always took Joseph's hands and said, "It was into this broken world that you were born, my son. You brought me hope. A new life emerging from the ashes."

A new life who had spent his entire sixteen years as a bunker rat with nothing better to do than read about a majestic planet that no longer existed. Still, Joseph couldn't wait to see it with his own eyes, even if it was just a shadow of its former glory.

Before breakfast, while his brothers slept, Joseph had slipped into Abba's study. The man seemed to have been chiseled out of the rock in which the bunker was hidden. Joseph's older brothers all had Abba's short legs, bulging shoulders, and thick, brooding eyebrows. Meanwhile, Joseph was tall and slender for his age with dark curly hair that hung around his shoulders, but he had yet to grow even a wisp of a mustache. His brothers mocked him, saying he had a woman's build and a woman's hair. Joseph often told them they looked like cavemen. That always went over well, right before they pinned him to the ground and pummeled him.

But his brothers weren't here right now, and Joseph admired Abba's broad shoulders for a moment. Abba sat in a hand-carved chair with his eyes closed in quiet meditation. He blinked them slowly open and turned to Joseph.

"Happy birthday, Son." His voice was slow and deep, like a wide river, and Joseph felt it wash over him, but even his father's calming presence couldn't curtail Joseph's excitement today.

Joseph grinned. "Thank you, Abba. Today is the big day."

Worry lines creased the old man's forehead. "I know, you've spoken of nothing else for months." Then his features softened. "You have the power to choose your own path, Joseph. I see your mother in you as well, all her goodness. You were our little miracle."

Joseph knew his mother had been certain she could never have children while her sister Leah bore Abba ten sons. Joseph knew he was Abba's favorite, and his older brothers, while not the brightest bulbs in the box, knew it, too, and they hated him for it.

If that weren't enough, there were also the dreams. From as far back as he could remember, Joseph had vivid dreams. He loved how annoyed his brothers got when he told them his dreams, which made him want to tell them more. It was a vicious cycle, especially since the dreams usually involved Joseph saving the day somehow. They were a constant source of annoyance in the bunker.

But now, finally, Joseph was getting out of this bunker. His brothers ate at a snail's pace, but when all the bowls of slop were finally empty, it was time. Joseph leapt from his lowly seat at the foot of the family table and strode boldly to where Abba sat propped up with cushions. He knelt before him without speaking a word, although everything in him wanted to shout at them to hurry up.

The room was quiet. The silence stretched long and full until Joseph feared his father would not go through with the ritual. At last, Abba spoke in his most solemn voice. "My son, why do you come before me this day?"

Joseph couldn't get the words out fast enough. "Abba, the time for my blessing has come. I stand before you as a man. I am ready to protect and provide for our family and go out into the world. I ask your blessing to join my brothers."

He looked up into Abba's brown eyes glistening with tears. "As you have requested, so shall it be, my beloved son. On this day, the sixteenth anniversary of your birth, I receive your request."

Then he laid his calloused hands on Joseph's curly brown hair. Joseph could feel strength and warmth flowing from them like a river. "Receive these words, for they are the words of your Maker. 'Behold I will never leave you or forsake you. I will bless you and keep you and cause my face to shine upon you.' May the God of our ancestors look upon you with favor all your days and fulfill the promises of old through you."

The words poured over Joseph like oil and seeped into his soul. He was the descendant of an ancient family line—a family whose roots went back to the dawn of time itself when the Creator breathed life into the first humans. Their blood flowed in his veins.

After the blessing, Abba stood and handed Joseph a package wrapped in old newspapers and carefully tied with a thick piece of twine. This was not usually part of the ritual, and Joseph looked around at his brothers. He could see the surprise on their faces, probably wondering what sort of special treatment Joseph was about to receive this time. Joseph couldn't help the smirk that curled at the edges of his lips. He enjoyed being the favorite.

"This gift I give to you, my son," Abba said. "Let it be a constant reminder of my love for you when you venture from home. Know that I am always with you."

Then he wrapped Joseph in a mighty embrace and wept over him. Embarrassed, Joseph stiffened. He'd never seen such an outpouring of emotion from his father. When Abba finally let go, Joseph opened the package and gasped as he pulled out a brown leather jacket. He knew from his reading that it was a bomber jacket, the kind popularized by the old fighter pilots in the first great war more than a hundred years before. He ran his hands over the surface of the coat. The dark leather was smooth and pristine with no holes or patches like the other clothes he and his brothers wore. None of them owned anything half as nice as this. It was magnificent.

Joseph slipped on the coat. It was a little big, but it was the most comfortable, most luxurious thing he'd ever worn. He loved it. Words to express his gratitude fizzled out, which was highly unusual for him, but he managed to pull himself together and turn to his father. "Thank you, Abba. This is a most splendid gift!"

Abba beamed with pride. "You wear it well. It was mine when I was young, and it is one of the few things I still have from the olden days. I've kept it all these years just for you. Wear it proudly."

His words reverberated around the room and reminded Joseph that he and Abba weren't alone. When he looked up, he was met by the scowls of his ten older brothers. Simeon spat on the ground. Reuben started to walk out, then apparently thought better of it and turned his icy gaze back on Joseph. The others contented themselves with glaring at Joseph, but none of them dared to confront their father. There would be no formal complaint, but there would certainly be retribution. There always was.

Joseph's heart sank. Today was supposed to be the day when he joined their ranks and became one of them. Looking at them now, he knew that was impossible. He'd been an outsider his whole life, and nothing would change that. No ceremony, no magical sixteenth birthday, and certainly not his father's precious jacket.

CHAPTER 2

Into the Great Unknown

Joseph zipped up his birthday jacket and played with the zipper to release some of his pent-up energy. He could barely contain himself as he followed his oldest brother, Reuben, out of the main bunker.

His other nine older brothers had conveniently found other things to occupy their time, making it clear they wanted nothing to do with Joseph. But he refused to let their snub ruin his maiden voyage to the great outdoors.

His excitement got the better of him, and he pushed past Reuben and dashed down the final stretch of tunnel and out into the world beyond. He was finally free of the bunker!

The rugged landscape that met him was abrasive, all rocky outcrops and steep hills. Joseph squinted as a mixture of sand and ash blew into his eyes and throat. Above, a pale gray sky gazed down. Joseph shuddered at the chill in the air, but he knew it wouldn't last long. He was in sensory overload as he tried to take everything in. All he'd ever known was the sterility of the bunker. Reuben emerged from the tunnel and stood stiffly behind him.

"It's a lot, but you'll get used to it."

"It's amazing," Joseph said, not taking his eyes off the land.

Reuben followed his gaze. "It has a strange beauty to it, but don't let it fool you. This is dangerous territory. One wrong move out here can be the end of you. Just follow me and do as I do. Now let's go."

"Sir, yes Sir." Joseph saluted him.

Reuben narrowed his eyes. "Don't be snarky. You're lucky I volunteered to take you. I can just as easily un-volunteer."

"Abba wouldn't like that." Joseph smirked. He knew exactly which of Reuben's buttons to push. The "try hard to please Abba" button was always a good choice.

Reuben flinched. "Not all of us can be the favorite, Joey. Now shut up and walk."

Joseph scowled. He hated when his older brothers called him "Joey." But if he complained, Reuben might find some way to ruin the day. So, he ducked his head and followed his brother.

They trekked for hours through the desolate sea of blistering sand and shattered rocks. Joseph was drenched in sweat and his mouth was dry as cotton, but he refused to ask for a break. Finally, they stopped atop a large dune. Joseph stared at the shadowland spread out below. An eerie silence hung over everything. He could just make out the battered skeleton of an ancient mining town, now partially buried in ash and sand. It was the first real sign of civilization they'd seen. An old oil drill that had once tirelessly sucked the black lifeblood of the desert now stood motionless, rusted still for all eternity.

The few scrappy souls who'd once called this godforsaken place home had long since disappeared. Joseph knew from Abba's preparatory briefings that it was rare to see other settled humans this far from one of the major city centers. Nearly twenty years after the Great War, human society was still struggling to recover—still fighting over the few surviving resources the wounded earth had to offer. There were no more cell phones for easy communication. The magical thing that Joseph read about called the internet was gone, and with it died the never-ending stream of mindless entertainment that humans used to waste their lives watching. You couldn't press buttons on a screen and have food delivered to your doorstep with drones. Most of the people who survived the initial nuclear attacks died of starvation or dehydration within months. Those who made it past the initial extinction event had formed alliances and created gangs. Numbers were the key to survival.

Abba had drilled it into Joseph to always be on the lookout for roving bandits and scavenger teams who haunted the main roads. They preyed on those foolish or desperate enough to travel in search of resources or look for lost loved ones. But out here, where the highways and interstates had been swallowed by the desert, they were less frequent. Only those with a death wish ventured this far out. There were also the occasional doomsday cults who'd predicted the end of the world and escaped civilization before the apocalypse happened. They'd built underground bunkers, stashed rations and guns, and managed to survive on prayers and solar panels.

Joseph thought of the stories he'd heard about Abba's father, Grandpa Laban. Along with being a terrible father and an unscrupulous goat herder, the man had been a full-fledged end-times survivalist. Overprotective to a fault and a die-hard pessimist, he'd prepared for the worst and built a bunker on the far corner of his property. Tucked right on the edge of the Negev Desert, he'd stocked it with munitions, food, seeds, hydroponic equipment, and more. There was even room to house animals. Grandpa Laban had hated humans, but he made darn sure his old goats were taken care of. The bunker was the only reason Joseph and his family were alive today. That, and strict adherence to safety protocols to make sure they weren't detected.

It was a strange feeling to be kilometers away from the safe haven. Out here he was exposed with no reinforced doors to protect him. But Joseph liked the feeling of freedom welling up in his chest. He felt like shouting. The chances of there being people amidst the rusted rubble was almost zero.

Reuben leveled a gaze on him. "You've got that look in your eyes that makes me think you're about to do something stupid."

"What? Me? I would never."

"Yes, you would. Now show me that you know the scouting protocols."

Joseph unleashed an aggravated sigh to let Reuben know exactly how he felt about the protocols. "Are you going to tattle on me if I don't know the protocols?"

"No, I will do my job and inform Father of your negligence and obstinance."

"That won't be anything new."

"But in this case, his knowledge of your character flaws may actually lead him to punish you."

That wasn't a risk Joseph was willing to take. "All right. You don't need to lecture me. I know the protocols."

"As Father often says, 'Knowing and doing are different things.'"

Joseph had no doubt that Reuben would report back to Abba. If he stepped out of line or forgot something, he'd hear about it later. His brothers loved to remind him of his shortcomings as much as he loved to remind them that he was smarter than they were. It was a vicious cycle.

Joseph stuffed a small wad of goat jerky into his mouth and began to chew. The stuff was tougher than leather, but it did sate his hunger. He rummaged around in his pack for infrared binoculars. "Step one of protocol: always check for human life forms," he said in his most annoying voice possible.

Reuben ignored his insolence. "Do you know how to use those properly?"

"Of course. They're so straightforward even Simeon knows how to use them."

Reuben stifled a laugh. "Better not insult Simeon. He makes up for his shortage of brains with his brawn and shortage of self-control."

"Yeah, yeah. For once he's not around to pound me. Just let me just enjoy it."

"That's fine, but I'm not going to get myself killed because you're too proud to ask for help. Show me that you know what you're doing."

Joseph ignored him and stood up. He put the binoculars to his face and started scanning for signs of life. He was silhouetted against the ashy sky that had once been a gentle blue, according to his beloved books.

As he stood there, a strange sensation came over him. His entire body began to shake uncontrollably. His vision blurred, and the sky and sand and hills all swirled together like a churning whirlpool. Then the next thing he knew, he was falling through the whirlpool, head over heels, trying to find something to grab onto.

CHAPTER 3

Visions and Dreams

Joseph fell for what felt like a long time until his body hit the ground. He landed hard but strangely, felt no pain.

When he opened his eyes, he was staring out at a vastly different landscape. Everything was green and lush. There were no clouds of ash blocking out the sun. The world felt strangely alive, as if the very air was bursting with life. He looked around and saw his brothers seated near him in a big circle. They were lounging in thick grass, and there wasn't a grain of sand to be seen. Beside each brother, including Joseph, was a hefty backpack. Somewhere nearby, a stream gurgled like a contented child. The world was at peace; shalom.

Suddenly the shalom was shattered with a piercing siren. At the sound, Joseph's bag rose into the air and hovered high above him and his brothers. The siren morphed into the sound of trumpets. The brothers each stood and walked toward Joseph.

One by one, they emptied the contents of their bags at his feet as if he was their master and they were paying tribute. Food rations, bottles of clean water, medicine, and other supplies poured out. Then they knelt before him in submission, even Simeon. Joseph felt a rush of power spread across his body until his very fingertips throbbed with it. There was a sudden flash of light, and the next thing he knew, Reuben was shaking him.

"Joey, are you okay? Joey, can you hear me?"

Joseph opened his eyes, momentarily confused to find himself back in the gray wasteland. "I'm fine. I'm not sure what happened though."

Reuben sat down beside him with a concerned look. "You passed out. Scared me half to death there for a second."

"I didn't pass out," Joseph said defensively as he sat up.

What in the world was that? thought Joseph, trying to look calm and collected.

"Oh really? What would you call it, then?"

Joseph paused to gather his thoughts. "I think it was a vision. It was like my other dreams, only stronger. More real. It felt like I was transported away from here. I'm telling you, I didn't pass out."

Reuben rolled his eyes. "You've been telling us your silly dreams for years, Joey. You can't use that as an excuse. Those of us who have been outside the bunker call what just happened 'heat stroke.' You should have been drinking more water." He handed Joseph a canteen. "Before you fainted like a little girl, did you at least scan down into the valley?"

A burst of anger coursed through Joseph's veins. Reuben thought he was weak. They all did. He'd be the brothers' laughingstock at dinner tonight when Reuben told them he'd passed out. This was not how today was supposed to go. Joseph balled his fists. Someday he'd be the one laughing.

"I scanned all right, and the place is deserted."

"Good, let's get down there and start scavenging." Reuben paused. "That is, unless you can't go?"

Joseph scowled. "I'm fine, don't treat me like a child." He bumped Reuben intentionally with his shoulder as he ran toward the ruins without looking back. He knew he was violating safety protocol number two—stay together at all times—but he didn't care. He'd show Reuben he wasn't a scared little boy.

He slowed as he approached the ghost town. There were a handful of houses with corrugated iron roofs. The windows were busted, and walls had caved in all over the place. A few rusted cars were strewn about, and a massive oil tanker truck was flipped on its side. Joseph was about to enter the first house when a strong hand grabbed his shoulder and yanked him back.

Reuben was breathing hard. "What in the world are you thinking? Are you trying to get us killed, running around and making enough noise for bandits to hear ten miles away?"

"Relax, there's nobody here," said Joseph.

"That's the problem with you, Joey. You think you know it all. Those binoculars aren't foolproof. There could be an underground bunker here full of bandits that you didn't pick up. This isn't a game. Daddy can't swoop in to save you out here."

That last comment stung. Joseph wrenched himself away from Reuben's grip and stormed into the first building, regretting it even as he stepped across the threshold. His anger got the best of him, as it often did.

Reuben pulled out his stun gun and chased after him. Joseph hadn't been given a stun gun, and at the rate he was currently breaking protocols, he'd probably never get one. His heart raced, and right behind him he heard Reuben unleash a torrent of curses that were worthy of applause, but Joseph resisted the urge. Reuben might use the stun gun on him if he thought he was being snarky. He'd already pushed him to the brink.

Joseph focused his attention forward. You never knew what you might find in these places. The radioactive fallout had mutated the jackals and hyenas that had long prowled these parts. They roamed in packs and loved to hide in hovels like this. Just a year ago, Reuben had killed a jackal with two heads that had been leading a pack of more than a hundred of the blood-thirsty beasts. It now hung in the bunker as a constant reminder of the dangers of the outside world. Oh, how far they had fallen from the Garden of Eden, which according to Joseph's reading once resided in these parts. That was certainly hard to believe.

Joseph's eyes gradually adjusted to the dark, and Reuben put his hand on his shoulder again.

"Stop right there," he whispered. "I should pull you out right now and march you home, but I'm going to give you one last chance to prove that you're not a complete idiot."

With the stun gun hovering awfully close to his neck, Joseph decided to simply nod in agreement.

"Here's what we're going to do. You stay behind me, and we move together as a team. We're looking for old tech, tools, and canned goods. Anything of use that might have survived the nuclear fallout. Most of these little places have been picked over, but occasionally there's something good to be found," said Reuben.

Joseph nodded, and they moved quickly from building to building. In the rear of the town's abandoned medical clinic, Joseph pulled a first aid kit out from under a pile of wooden beams. Reuben gave a low whistle.

"How is it that someone so annoying can be so lucky?" he said, shaking his head.

"I'm just that good," replied Joseph.

"You need psychiatric help. Just open the case, and let's see what's inside."

Joseph unlatched the clasp on the metal kit with a satisfying pop and flipped open the lid. Inside was a full stash of medical supplies. It was a huge score. This little container of supplies was worth its weight in gold. Maybe more.

Reuben kneeled next to him and carefully looked through the contents before closing the kit back up. "It pains me to say this..."

"Please, do continue," said Joseph with a gloating grin plastered across his face.

"I almost can't get the words out. They just feel wrong."

"I'm waiting." Joseph was enjoying this far too much.

"Here goes, but if you tell the others I said these words I will categorically deny them. Well done. This is the biggest find we've had in a long time."

"I thought you were going to say how amazing I am, and that I clearly have a knack for this sort of work."

Reuben snorted. "Those words will never come out of my mouth. Your ego doesn't need any more feeding. Father does plenty of that already."

Joseph tried to let those words roll off his back, but it was easier said than done. Maybe this find would ease some of the tension over his jacket, and his brothers would see him as a good luck charm and invite him to come along on all their scouting parties. He began to play out all the scenarios in his head where he was the new family hero and completely forgot about the strange vision that had taken place on the sand dune.

CHAPTER 4

Welcome Home

The sun sank low in the sky even though it was only midafternoon. Ever since the apocalypse, the days had become shorter, which made going out more dangerous and made Abba more nervous. You didn't want to be caught out at night when temperatures plummeted and the jackals emerged. Joseph shuddered at the thought of a two-headed jackal appearing out of the darkness and tearing him to pieces. It would be a terrible way to die, ripped limb from limb and eaten alive by wild, mutated beasts.

They hurried home, Joseph soon lagging behind Reuben. It was everything he could do to keep moving. His legs were two sticks of lead from trudging through the sand, and the first aid kit he clutched to his chest felt like a massive weight, but he refused to let Reuben carry it. It was his find, and he wanted all the glory when they got home. There were no outward signs that they were close to the bunker. Even as they retraced their steps, everything looked different in the fading light. Finally, the cliff face that hid their humble abode came into view, and Joseph breathed a deep sigh of relief.

Reuben waited with his hands on his hips. "We need to put some muscles on that skinny frame of yours."

"Whatever," mumbled Joseph as he struggled up the incline to where his brother stood like a chiseled statue. Grandpa Laban's bunker came complete with a workout room, which was where the other brothers spent a good deal of their time. Joseph spent his time in the small library reading and learning about hydroponics and engineering with his father. It was just one more reason he didn't fit in with the Neanderthals.

Reuben pulled out the infrared binoculars and checked to make sure they hadn't been followed. He gave the all-clear sign and was about to duck behind a pile of rocks, but Joseph wasn't ready to go inside. He didn't want his first real adventure to end, so he tried to stall.

"Tell me what it was like when you first came to the bunker, Reuben."

"Come on, Joey. We don't have time for that."

"Please, nobody else will ever tell me. I want to know."

Reuben sighed, his stony demeanor cracking just a little. "I'll tell you, but you have to promise not to ask me a million questions along the way, like you always do."

"I promise. Scout's honor! That's a thing people used to say. I'm not entirely sure why though, to be honest..."

Reuben waved a hand and cut him off. "My memory's a little hazy, but we woke up to the sound of bombs falling. Father switched on the news, and immediately we knew it was bad. There was a huge explosion somewhere nearby, and then the power went out. We were all scared—even Father. More bombs went off, this time just a few houses down the street. Our house shook, and I swore the roof was going to fall on us. Outside, people were screaming, and the air was filled with thick smoke.

"That's when Father snapped into action. I'd never seen him move like that. He snatched all of us boys up and dragged us out the door at full speed. We didn't even have time to get our stuff, just the clothes on our back. We piled into the van and took off."

Questions buzzed around in Joseph's mind like hornets, but he managed to keep them in. He nodded his head for Reuben to continue.

"It was madness. Tons of people were trying to escape the city just like us. Roads were closed or blown to high heaven. Houses were exploding all around us. Mom told us to duck our heads and not look out the windows. The few times I snuck peeks out the back, I could hardly believe my eyes. I'd never seen a dead person before, but everywhere I looked there were corpses. I wanted to vomit. Somehow Father got us out. He drove like a madman. I could hear him in the front seat praying as loud as he could, shouting at God to make sure his voice was heard over the sirens and the explosions and cries for help from the wounded. God must have heard his prayer because we made it out alive."

Joseph could picture all of it so clearly in his mind. He could hear Abba praying at the top of his lungs. God had answered his prayers. Joseph believed that, believed that He still answered prayers. He swallowed a dozen more questions, not wanting Reuben to stop talking.

"We drove for hours until we came to Grandpa Laban's farm. When we arrived, all the structures on the property had been obliterated. There were a few stray goats in the paddock that had survived, but that was it. We rounded up the goats and started hiking. I thought Father had lost it, taking us into the wilderness, but then we made it to the bunker.

"While the world outside burned, we hid here. Sort of like an underground ark. Now it feels like home. Speaking of which, we better get inside before Father thinks I lost you or begins wondering if we were attacked by jackals. Come on." Reuben disappeared into the secret entrance to the bunker.

"Can I ask you one question?" asked Joseph as he followed right behind him, clutching the first aid kit.

"Not unless you're asking if you can do my chores tomorrow."

Joseph bit his lip and remained silent. He wanted to know if Reuben felt guilty for surviving when so many had died. The entrance to the bunker was a small, natural cave tunnel. There were loads of them in these parts, but after a while the stone walls turned to cement. The bunker was brilliantly hidden. Joseph had to tip his hat to Grandpa Laban for that.

He knew they were in what had once been the southern part of Israel, not far from the Egyptian border. If Egypt even still existed. Joseph had spent hours studying the old maps in the bunker. They fascinated him, covered with countries and cities. Back then, the world looked like a patchwork quilt. Humans had taken the globe, cut it up, and pieced it back together. The Great War had torn the garment to shreds and left humanity to fight over the scraps. If humanity survived, they'd someday make new countries with new names and new borders just as their ancestors had done. It was strange to think about. They were living in an in-between time. The old had gone, but the new had not yet come. Or perhaps that's how things always were?

Joseph was pulled from his thoughts when they arrived at the end of the tunnel and were greeted by the massive door that led into the main bunker. It was a rather impressive front door made of some sort of indestructible metal and a state-of-the-art password protection system.

Abba insisted they change the code every month. He was a cautious man who avoided taking risks as much as possible. His brothers said that he'd been different before the war, but much to Joseph's disappointment, that version of his father was long gone.

There was a soft hiss as the door released and swung open. Abba stood there with arms open wide and a look of relief on his wrinkled face. He took Joseph into his arms, all but ignoring Reuben, who squeezed by him and made his way into the common area.

"I was beginning to worry. How was your first venture out into the wilderness?"

Like a blind man seeing for the first time, thought Joseph, but he didn't want to make Abba feel guilty for making him wait so long. So, he flashed his warmest smile, knowing the effect it would have, and began to gush about the world outside. "It was wonderful, Abba. More than wonderful. To see the sky and the sand and..."

Abba nodded, his eyes gleaming. "I only wish you could see it the way it used to be. The Negev used to be such a captivating place. Rugged, sure, but also beautiful. Now it is only harsh, but don't let me spoil it for you."

"It's okay, Abba. Nothing could spoil this day. Also, I brought you back a present."

"What is this? On your birthday you should receive presents, not give them."

"Think of it as a present from God. It's for everyone to share." Joseph handed Abba the first aid kit. When Abba realized what it was, he cradled the first aid kit in his arms like a baby and looked towards the heavens.

"Blessed are you, our God, King of the Universe, the Good and the Doer of Good. Blessed are you, for you have not forgotten your servants even as we dwell in the valley of the shadow of death." Then he turned to Joseph. "We must show your brothers what the Lord has provided for us."

He wrapped his arm around Joseph, and together they entered the common room. The brothers were seated around the long metal dining table, laughing and talking, but at the sight of Joseph, the lightheartedness evaporated. Joseph felt their gazes shift back and forth between him and the first aid kit in his father's hands. Abba placed the kit on the middle of the table and opened it with a flourish for all to see and admire. It did not have the desired effect.

So much for being the new family hero, thought Joseph. Abba was painfully oblivious, his eyes fixed on Joseph, his beloved son. He turned to his other offspring, and pride dripped from his lips like honey. "Behold, your brother Joseph has brought home a great treasure. Tonight, he shall sit at my right hand in the seat of honor."

Joseph wanted to duck and cover from the death glares he received, but there was no use backing down now. Joseph stood tall and held his head high. The room grew heavy with grumbling. A storm was brewing. Abba was old and slowly going blind, but even he clearly sensed what was happening. He banged his fist on the table, making the precious medicine jump. Joseph's brothers fell silent, the calm before the storm.

Abba thrust Joseph forward, his hands resting squarely on his prized son's narrow shoulders. He fixed the rest of his offspring with a fierce gaze. "The hand of the Lord is upon Joseph. Do you not see? This is a sign of the Almighty's blessing. You should celebrate your brother, but instead you despise him. I am ashamed of all of you."

The brothers looked at one another, clearly searching for a spokesperson who would stand up to their father. Simeon slowly rose from his seat. He didn't meet his father's eye, but he did speak.

"I beg your pardon, Father. We didn't mean to offend you. I believe I speak for all of us when I say that we grow weary of Joey and his incessant boasting, his stupid dreams. It's enough to drive a man crazy. There's not enough space in the bunker for his ego. He acts like he's better than the rest of us, but Reuben just told us that today, on his very first trip into the wilderness, Joey passed out. If Reuben hadn't been there to wake him, he would surely have died."

Joseph's body tensed, and he found himself anxiously toying with the zipper on his precious new coat. He'd hoped Reuben would keep that little part of their outing to himself, but apparently not. Abba was clearly taken aback by this and turned to Reuben.

"Is this true?"

Now Reuben rose from his seat. "It is, Father. I did not wish to burden you with this since Joey seems to have made a full recovery, but he should be treated with caution. He may not be fit for such excursions."

Joseph's face flushed with anger at these words.

Abba's eyes were filled with concern as he addressed Joseph. "Is what they are saying true? Let me hear it from your own mouth. For you returned like a triumphant victor from battle, but now I hear this news."

Joseph looked around the room but found no compassion. He was a man standing trial, and the entire courthouse was against him. He refused to be rattled by his brother's jealousy. Trying to shake his nerves, he threw back his shoulders and addressed his father.

"I did not have a seizure or heat stroke, Abba. I am not sickly or weak as my brothers would have you believe." He hesitated just for a second before continuing. "Today I received a vision from God like the prophets of our people long ago."

A rumble of angry murmuring rolled through the room. This time Levi leapt to his feet, gesticulating angrily towards Joseph. "Please,

Father. Do you hear this? Little Joey claims to have had a vision from the Almighty himself. Who does he think he is? He should be punished for his nonsensical pride."

Abba's face grew stern, and he motioned for his sons to sit down. He turned to Joseph, and there was a dangerous fire in his eyes that Joseph wasn't used to seeing. He spoke in a measured voice. "It is no small thing to claim you have received a vision from the Almighty. Tell us what you saw."

Simeon interrupted. "Correction. What he *claims* to have seen."

"Hush, Simeon. You shame yourself. Tell us, Joseph, what did you see?"

Joseph cleared his throat. He must not be timid. They were looking for any sign of weakness they could find. So, he told them everything from the dream. When he finished, Judah slammed his cup on the table.

"If you think there's any world where you are going to rule over us and we'll bow down to you, then you've lost your mind. This is no vision from God; this is delusional. The mad ravings of a younger brother who does not know his place and thinks too highly of himself."

Abba raised his hand for silence. "Let us not be overly hasty to cast judgment. Joseph, if this is some sort of game you are playing to get attention, then you are playing with fire, for the Lord will not be mocked. We will not speak of this again. You will spend the next few days in the bunker to ensure that you are fully recovered."

Joseph's shoulders slumped. For once, Abba hadn't backed him up. Instead, he'd given a politician's response, noncommittal and safe. After his first taste of freedom, he was once again stuck inside the bunker. He had no choice but to join his brothers at the table for the world's most awkward family dinner. Joseph's metal plate was heaped with mashed beans. He didn't dare make eye contact with his brothers and tried hard not to imagine what terrible things they were plotting against him. He ate every last bean as quickly as possible and disappeared into the small library corner where he knew no one would bother him—until Reuben popped his head over the bookshelf he was hiding behind.

"Joey, I'm sorry for how that all went down. But you need to learn to keep your mouth shut. Claiming to have a vision from God?" He shook his head. "Would it be so bad for you to admit you passed out?"

Joseph prickled with indignation. "Yes, because that's not what happened."

Reuben sighed. "Joey, I was there. I saw you. There was nothing miraculous. You just passed out in the heat."

"That's not true. I can't explain it, but I know there was something more, and then finding the first aid kit. It was a sign. Proof."

"You're trying to make connections where there aren't any."

"If you're not going to believe me, then just leave me alone."

"I'm trying to help."

"You could have helped by not blabbing to everyone about what happened. You could have helped by letting me be the hero for one day by finding the first aid kit, but no!" Joseph felt his cheeks growing hot and a lump growing in his throat. He was teetering out of control, unable to keep his voice from rising.

"You don't know what it's like to be me in this miserable family. To be hated. You're the oldest. The one everyone else looks up to. Nobody looks up to me. They despise me, and no matter what I do, that will never change."

"I'm not your enemy, Joey. I'm just trying to help."

Joseph snapped his book closed as tears ran down his cheeks. "I know. I've just been looking forward to this day for so long, and..."

"And it all went to crap?" said Reuben with a hint of compassion.

"Yeah."

Reuben reached across the bookshelf and put his hand on Joseph's shoulder. "It's not all bad. Father's sending Levi, Simeon, and a couple of the others with the goats to Grandpa Laban's second property so they can graze there. I'm headed to Shechem with Judah to trade some of the medical supplies you found. They should fetch a high price, and hopefully we'll come back with some good stuff. I'll try and get you a chocolate bar as your part of the cut."

Joseph was grateful for Reuben's gesture of kindness, but he couldn't stop letting out a loud groan. "I can't believe it. You get to go to the trading post without me. Life is so unfair."

Reuben rolled his eyes and pulled his hand away. "Don't let the others hear you say that, or there might be a mutiny on our hands. You really riled them up. It's probably for the best that we'll be away for a few days to let things cool off. Just take care of Father while we're gone. We leave tomorrow after breakfast."

Joseph nodded his head begrudgingly and avoided making eye contact with Reuben. He knew he was too old to throw temper tantrums, but he didn't care. Being left behind while his older brothers went on an adventure was the icing on the cake of his truly terrible birthday.

Reuben left him to sulk in the corner and went to join the others getting ready for the trip. It was a rare occasion that they traveled to Shechem. It was the nearest trading post, but still a two-day journey. Joseph knew there were bigger trading stations farther away, but he'd never even been to Shechem, let alone one of the main hubs like Jerusalem or Tel Aviv. It could be a whole year before they took another trip like this, so missing this opportunity really sucked. Not even the thought of a chocolate bar made him feel better.

Joseph slouched his way to the communal bedroom and climbed up to his top bunk in the back corner. It was dark and cool, and he lay staring up at the cement ceiling for a long time, focusing on his breathing. He replayed the vision from earlier in the day over and over in his head. There was a sort of solidity to it, like it was burned into his brain. The others might not believe him, but he knew it was a sign. Deep in his bones, he knew it.

He could hear the excited voices of his brothers in the common room and the anxious pacing of his father as he oversaw the packing and preparations. He would be a nervous wreck while his sons were away.

Joseph finally fell into a fitful sleep, and in his dreams, he was floating far out in the galaxy surrounded by the sun and the moon and eleven glowing stars. There was a potency to the light they gave off that danced and swirled around him like the folds of a magnificent robe. Warmth radiated from the heavenly bodies, and the air crackled with energy.

Then, like in the first dream, all the objects drew near to Joseph and prostrated themselves before him. How long this continued, Joseph didn't know. But when he woke, he felt warm all over as if he was still wrapped in that mysterious heavenly light.

He knew immediately that the dreams were connected, but after yesterday, he wasn't about to say anything. He went down to the common room where his brothers were hurriedly scarfing down breakfast so they could be on their way. When he walked in with his long hair rumpled and his eyes still cloudy with sleep, Levi looked at him and laughed.

"Did you have any more dreams last night, Sleeping Beauty?"

Nothing like a large cup of mockery first thing in the morning. Joseph felt the warmth from the dream slip away, replaced by anger and shame. He had a split-second decision to make. Hold his tongue and live or speak up and get pummeled. The problem was, he had years of practice not holding his tongue. He glared at Levi, who was grinning from ear to ear. Suddenly, words started spilling out of him, and once he started, there was no stopping.

"As a matter of fact, you overgrown ape, I did!" he shouted. He knew Levi was self-conscious about being hairy, and the remark would cut right through him.

That got everyone's attention, and Joseph wasn't one to let a good captive audience go to waste. So, he plowed right ahead, telling his brothers about the second dream. He gave them all the juicy details—especially him hovering in the center of the universe with all the stars and even the sun drawn to his gravitational pull. The dream made him feel strong. He was so tired of being the pathetic little brother. His spirits soared as he related the dream, but when he finished, he saw Reuben shaking his head in disbelief. Joseph's heart sank. He knew that even Reuben, the family peacekeeper, wouldn't be able to save him this time.

Joseph didn't dare look at Levi, but he heard the cracking of knuckles. Then a voice from the other room overpowered the foreboding sound of prepped fists. It was Abba, and he didn't sound pleased.

"Joseph, come in here, now!" It wasn't often that Abba raised his voice toward Joseph. Some of the others were quite used to it, but not him.

"Coming, Abba." Joseph scooted back his chair and flashed a cheeky grin at Levi. "So sorry I have to leave." Then he darted out of the room.

"This isn't over yet," hissed Levi.

Abba sat in his chair, his eyebrows thick storm clouds hovering over angry eyes. Joseph gulped. "You called, Abba?"

"Yes, but I fear it may be too late. The damage is done. Why do you antagonize your brothers, Joseph?"

"They started it, Abba."

"Perhaps, but you must learn to hold your tongue, my dear son. To swallow your pride."

"I try, Abba, but..."

The old man held up his hand. "But what? I will not always be here to defend you. I fear I have spoiled you. Your mother, God rest her soul, would not approve. Now listen carefully, and swear to me that you will not speak to your brothers of what I am about to say.

Joseph nodded his head, curious what secret he was about to be told. "I swear, Abba."

"Good. It may be that these dreams are from God. Such things have happened before, and always in desperate times such as ours. Pray fervently, and trust that in time God will reveal to you the truth. Do not speak to them any more of your dreams."

"But—"

"I forbid it, Joseph! I am doing this for your own good. If these visions are from God, then nothing we say or do can stop them, but do not let them separate you from your brothers."

"Yes, Abba." Joseph burned with shame. Abba had never spoken to him like this before.

"Come near, my son. Give me your hands." Joseph drew near. "For the sake of peace, there must be consequences for your actions today. You will not like it, but you will do as you're told. Do you understand?"

Joseph nodded, and Abba patted his arm.

"Good. Now here is your punishment. You must keep an eye on Benjamin while you clean the entire bunker. Scrub every centimeter until it shines. Most importantly, stay out of the way of your older brothers as they prepare to leave. You are to begin at once."

Joseph's head hung in dismay, but he didn't dare complain as he made his way to the small grow room. Inside the sliding glass doors, the room was hot and humid. The bright fluorescent lights made Joseph squint as his eyes adjusted. He could barely squeeze between the rows of plastic tubes and hoses that housed and watered their small crop of tomatoes and lettuce and beans. Joseph loved the way this room smelled. Being in here always calmed him. It's why, since he could barely walk, he'd followed Abba around learning everything he could about how to keep these precious plants alive, stealing little nibbles whenever he could. Someday the garden would be his to tend. He lingered as long as he dared before starting his other chores. Before the brothers left, Levi poked his head into the cramped laundry room where Joseph was hunkered down amidst the large tubs of water and dirty clothes.

"Make sure you wash my underwear nice and good. Oh, and don't think I'm going to forget about this morning." His words dangled in the air as he and the others headed out.

The bunker grew strangely quiet, and Joseph was left with only his thoughts for company as he cleaned and scrubbed. After five long days of solitude and suds, the bunker was spick and span, even Levi's undies. Abba had locked himself in his room and could be heard pacing and praying away the hours.

Meanwhile, Joseph grew unbearably bored. He didn't do well alone. He'd spent his whole life in the tiny bunker, surrounded by people. The bunker felt eerily still and silent. Suddenly, the hushed prayers from Abba's study stopped, and the door opened a crack.

"Joseph, I must speak with you."

Joseph leapt up and scurried into the study. Abba was seated in a chair and looked even more haggard than Levi's undies. Joseph stood at attention, waiting for him to speak. He hadn't forgotten their last conversation in this space.

"Come closer, my son. Don't be afraid."

Joseph felt his whole body relax. He'd been worried he was in trouble.

His father coughed, his chest rattling like a cup of dice. He gathered himself and then continued to speak. "I am glad to see you have done your penance without complaint. I know you were angry about being left behind, but still you worked diligently."

"Thank you, Abba. I am glad to have made you proud."

"You have indeed, but now I fear that you may very well get your wish to leave. Your brothers were supposed to be back two days ago, but still there is no sign of them. I am worried that something has happened."

Joseph's heart began to pound. Was he about to be sent on a rescue mission?

"You must hurry to your Grandpa Laban's old grazing ground. It lies but a few miles from here. There are markers along the way. Do you think you can make it there on your own?"

A wave of excitement washed over Joseph. This was really happening. "Of course, Abba. I've studied the maps. I could walk there blindfolded."

"I know that you are eager to go, but do not be prideful. Remember that pride cometh before the fall."

"Yes, Abba. I remember," replied Joseph, but his mind was elsewhere. He couldn't believe he was really being sent out all by himself. How quickly things had changed in just a couple of days. This was a chance to prove himself to Abba, and maybe to his brothers. He began to play out different scenarios in his mind. Perhaps his brothers had been captured by bandits. He'd sneak down and rescue them in the dead of night. They would be forever in his debt. He'd be a hero. He could see it all unfolding, like the stories in his beloved books.

Ready to save the day, he squared his shoulders and looked Abba in the eyes. His eagerness was dampened by the worry lines engulfing his father's forehead. They told the true story—sending Joseph out was an act of desperation, not an act of trust in his capabilities.

"Please be careful," Abba pleaded. "I cannot bear to lose you. My heart is weary already. Return to me by evening."

Joseph wanted to ask why it was safe for his brothers but not for him to spend the night topside, but now wasn't the time. He leaned in for a quick hug and bolted out the door.

CHAPTER 5

To The Rescue

Soon he was out in the open. The world splayed out before him as if he was its master. Joseph was drunk with the prospects of such freedom and power and maybe playing the hero. That would teach his brothers. They'd kneel and kiss his feet with gratitude when he saved their lives, just like in his dreams.

His visions of glory faltered at the sight of the rocky road winding downward into a gray, barren landscape. Before him was a shadow land. The hills were an immense carcass picked clean by the wind and sand that scoured everything in its path. A thick silence hung over everything, disrupted only by his footsteps that echoed into oblivion. He was a stranger in this land. He was no hero. He was a trespasser.

His well-stocked imagination got the better of him. He began to play out new scenarios, but this time it was him being caught by bandits and cornered by starving jackals. Fear trickled in around the edges of his thoughts. The whole "being a hero" thing felt suddenly beyond him. The sense of inevitable doom that permeated the landscape seized him.

If his older and much more capable brothers had gone missing, something truly awful must have happened. What was little old Joey going to do about it? He couldn't even grow a mustache, let alone take on a pack of scoundrels or bone-crunching beasts. Panic and adrenaline screamed at him to turn around and run back to the safety of the bunker, but that would just prove he really was the weakling his brothers thought he was.

As he trudged forward, it seemed everywhere he looked there were hiding places. The jagged landscape left him vulnerable to attack from all sides. He picked up the pace until he was nearly running. Stumbling over the uneven ground, Joseph tried to keep his head on a swivel for danger. The wind moaned through the boulders like a giant whistling through broken teeth. The sound made his hackles rise, and somewhere in the distance he heard the call of a wild animal.

Letting go of all dignity, he broke into a full sprint, cursing himself for not having brought at least a knife to defend himself. Woefully out of shape, his lungs heaved while trying to suck in as much oxygen as they could. Air seemed to be elusive, and what little he managed to intake had a sickliness to it. As if in response to his pathetic huffing and puffing, the wind whipping around him stirred up dust devils of sand and ash until Joseph became gray like the land itself.

As he raced along, he could see the signs that his brothers and their flock had been this way. Their footprints gave him a smidgen of hope that kept him moving, but then he heard the call of that wild animal again. It was much closer now; far too close for comfort. The first call was joined by others, and Joseph's stomach plummeted. It was a hunting pack, and he was the prey.

Sweat dripping into his eyes and hair flying every which way, Joseph could barely see where he was going. He had to be close to his family. That's when he saw them. Ten stocky figures standing in the distance. Relief flooded through him. He'd found them. He was safe. He screeched to a halt, then covered the remaining distance at a leisurely pace, trying to look relaxed.

When he got close, he gave his brothers a big smile. "Hi guys, fancy meeting you here."

No one laughed.

Tough crowd, Joseph thought.

"You're supposed to be back in the bunker. Why are you here?" demanded Levi.

Joseph smiled awkwardly to try and break the tension. "Funny you should ask. I know time flies when you're having fun, but you were supposed to be home like two days ago. Abba's a nervous wreck and sent me to come find you."

"Of course he did," muttered Levi. "Daddy's favorite little errand boy. Well, we're not going back, and neither are you."

Joseph was startled. *What did he mean?* Before he could respond, Levi grabbed Joseph in his powerful grip. Simeon was by his side in an instant. They tore Joseph's new jacket off him and threw him to the ground.

They acted so fast, Joseph couldn't wrap his head around what was happening. Down on his hands and knees, he looked up at his brothers in surprise, which turned to terror when he saw the violence in their eyes.

"You're not so big and tough without Father around, are you, Dreamer Boy?" scoffed Judah. "Looks like you're the one bowing to us now."

Joseph glanced at Reuben for help, but he looked away and stepped back. The betrayal stung, but there was no time to dwell on it as the other brothers circled Joseph like jackals around a wounded animal. Legs and fists slammed into Joseph's ribs and head. He curled up in a ball to protect himself and begged his brothers to stop. Blood flowed from his nose like a faucet. His body screamed in agony, but there was nothing he could do to stop the onslaught.

His brothers had whipped each other into a frenzy. They were going to kill him, Joseph was certain of it. Mustering what little strength he had left, he cried out, "Please, please. Have mercy on me. I'll do anything you ask."

The last thing he saw before he blacked out was Simeon's leering face.

CHAPTER 6

Visitors in the night

Their blood still running high, Levi and Simeon dragged Joseph's limp body to a nearby dry well and tossed him in. Levi snickered as Joey's head banged off the wall with a thud. He was going to wake up with a terrible headache.

Judah held Joey's precious jacket aloft, and the brothers cheered. "To the victor goes the spoils," Judah shouted. He pulled out a knife and sliced through the jacket. Once the first cut was made, they tore at it until it was nothing but shreds.

At the back of the angry throng, Reuben was overcome with shame. As the oldest, he was the one in charge. He should have stopped them, but he was too afraid. He was too cowardly to stand up for what he knew was right and protect his brother. Sure, Joey was a pompous, self-absorbed brat, but he didn't deserve this. They'd gone too far. Unable to watch, he turned and retreated into the hills, disgusted with himself. He could still make this right. When everyone was asleep, he'd rescue Joey from the well and take him back to the bunker.

The brothers decided to celebrate their "courageous" overpowering of their younger brother and satiate their bloodlust by killing a goat for dinner. It had been a long time since they'd tasted fresh meat, but Reuben was too ashamed to eat a single bite. All he wanted to do was sneak away and pull Joey out of the well, but he was too much of a coward. Instead, he sat in pained silence as his brothers told stories around the fire, salivating as the juices dripped into the fire sputtering, hissing, and filling the night with the delicious smell of roasting mutton.

Eventually, the embers of the brother's fire burned low, and out of the darkness stepped a Bedouin man, his almond hands extended to show he was unarmed. "Do not be alarmed. I mean you no harm. My men and I come asking only to share your fire."

The brothers relaxed. They knew from their few dealings with the Bedouin at the nearby trading posts that they could be trusted. They welcomed them to sit, and after a few minutes Simeon said, "Tell us what news you have of the outside world."

The Bedouin leaned forward and scratched his thick black beard before responding. "I am afraid I have little good news to share. Everywhere we go, we find destruction. All that remains is rubble. The earth itself is ruined beyond repair. We live at the end of days in the world foretold by the prophets of old."

The brothers nodded sadly. From their few interactions with others, this was always the news.

But then the Bedouin continued. "Let me share a small spark of hope. There are rumors of a city rising out of the ashes on the banks of the Nile."

"Is that where you are headed?" asked Simeon excitedly.

"Indeed. To Avaris we go, to see if the whispers are true."

"Heeeeeelp!" Joseph's raspy voice cried out and shattered their fragile musings about the world beyond. Reuben cringed at the sound.

The Bedouin looked at Simeon, his eyebrows raised. "Have you a prisoner?"

"We do," replied Simeon, deciding against getting into the full backstory. "A sixteen-year-old boy."

The Bedouin reached into his pocket and produced a small pouch. "Would you consider selling him? You would be well compensated."

Simeon looked at his brothers. All but Reuben nodded.

"How much would you pay?"

"Twenty pieces of silver. Good at any trading post."

Simeon weighed the offer. If they took the deal, then Joey's blood wouldn't be on their hands. He took a deep breath and made up his mind.

"We have a deal. The boy is in the pit at the base of the hill. Be warned, he has a tongue on him."

"He will learn."

The man's tone made Simeon shiver. They shook hands to seal the agreement.

"I thank you for your fire and for the pleasure of doing business," the Bedouin said. "I will see to my newly acquired property and be on my way. May our paths meet again some day."

Before Simeon could respond, the Bedouin melted back into the shadows and was gone. The brothers sat in stiff silence around the fire. The bag of silver suddenly weighed heavy in Simeon's hand.

CHAPTER 7

I am your master

Down in the bone-dry well, Joseph groaned. He felt his body, trying to assess the damage his brothers had done, and realized with a pang of grief that his beautiful coat was gone. He was half naked and covered in bruises. He lay in the grit and grime like the ancient prophets covered in sackcloth and ashes. Beneath the ground, like a corpse in waiting, he prayed to the Almighty for help. His hope of rescue had faded with the light, and he wondered if he would live to see another day.

Then the orange light of a burning torch flickered at the mouth of the well, and a face hovered into view high above him. Even with his left eye nearly swollen shut, he could see that it was not one of his brothers. The man's face was weathered, and he had a beard like a bristly broom. The stranger stared down at him intently, greedy eyes taking his measure. The man gave a soft grunt, and his face disappeared back into the darkness.

Other faces came into view, a rope was lowered, and Joseph was hoisted out of the pit. His heart was filled with relief as he stood on wobbly legs before his rescuers. "Thank you. My name is Joseph, and I was—"

"Silence," said the man with eyes like chips of ebony. "You are now my property. You will speak when spoken to. You will eat what you are given. You will march when I give the order. I am your master now. My name is Ishmael. Do you understand?"

Ishmael's words struck Joseph with such force that his legs buckled. He looked up from the ground, and for the second time that day, he pleaded for his life. "Please, sir. There must be some mistake."

A powerful hand cuffed him and then wrenched him to his feet. "There has been no mistake. You belong to me now. If you cannot answer a simple question, I will have to train you like a dog."

Ishmael tied a stiff piece of cloth across Joseph's mouth to gag him and bound his hands with the very rope he'd used to rescue him from the pit. Ishmael held the end of the rope and gave it a tug. "This way, my boy. We have a long way to go. We are headed for the city of Avaris."

Joseph followed obediently—muzzled and leashed.

CHAPTER 8

The Road to Avaris

Joseph stumbled and plowed face first into the scorching sand. His hands were bound tightly in front of him, and he was tied to a long rope dragging behind a scrawny camel. Exhausted, he lay and waited for the inevitable bite of Ishmael's whip. The harsh leather sank into his back, tearing at the skin and sending a wave of excruciating pain washing over him. He knew from experience that two more lashes were coming. He clenched his jaw and waited. Ishmael was painfully consistent.

Joseph held back the cry that threatened to escape his parched lips. He would not be weak. Joey was weak, but Joey was dead. Joey died in that godforsaken well. He was Joseph now. A survivor. A slave. The thought of revenge was the only thing that kept him going as he rose from the sand and staggered along behind the plodding camel.

Ishmael was the leader of the small band of Bedouin, and Joseph had the pleasure of being attached to his beast. There were five camels in all. Each was loaded with gear, and three of them trailed prisoners in their wake. One prisoner was a young woman covered from head to toe in some sort of flowing garment. She carried herself with grace, seemingly unfazed by the rocky ground or the jerking of the camel. Joseph had never seen a woman before, other than in books, and of course the one time he managed to sneak one of Simeon's infamous magazines.

Something about the way she moved stirred his heart, but he didn't have time to reflect on this. He had to focus on surviving.

The other prisoner was an elderly dark-skinned man clearly plucked from somewhere on the African continent.

Well, the continent formerly known as Africa. Who knew what it was called anymore, thought Joseph.

The man had a patchy gray beard and thick-lidded eyes weighed down with perpetual sadness. He and Joseph exchanged occasional sorrowful glances, but the woman never looked up from the steaming sand. She strode along in silence like a captured queen from ancient times. He had yet to catch a glimpse of her face, but her dark brown hair flowed behind her like a cascading waterfall, an oasis in the desert. She was a beautiful mystery.

Joseph lost all sense of time and direction as his Bedouin captors wove through the wilderness. The air was thick and warm, and Joseph swore that every inch of him was covered in sand. His feet ached. His skin stung. His unprotected eyes were bloodshot. He wished God would have mercy on him and strike him dead, but then he would never get his revenge. He ground sand between his teeth and pictured his brothers' faces. He had to survive.

They made camp as the pale orb of the sun disappeared. For a moment, there was peace before the desert was swallowed in darkness and the temperature plummeted. Ishmael came over to where Joseph and the African sat, tied together to ensure they couldn't escape. As if they had the energy. Ishmael was a mountain of a man clothed in a long gray cloak that blended into the ashy wilderness. Tangles of black hair peeked out from beneath his head cloth, but nothing could hide the ferocity in his dark eyes.

It's no wonder this man has survived, thought Joseph as Ishmael loomed over them, his fingers never far from his whip.

Ishmael stared down at them for a while with eyes that seemed to see too much. Then he tossed a canteen at their feet along with a small bag of food.

"Here's food and water. If you are foolish enough to try and run in the night, there will be no more food after I catch you. And I *will* catch you. Do you understand me?"

Joseph nodded, his eyes darting back and forth between Ishmael and the rations.

"Very good. Continue to obey, and you will survive. Tomorrow, if you behave, I will provide you both with a blanket." He retreated to the small camel-dung fire where the other Bedouins huddled. The smell of burning offal seeped into the night, and in the distance, the jackals filled the air with spine-tingling howls.

Joseph shivered. His body was crusted with salty sweat that had dried like an extra layer of skin. Every bit of him ached from the day's long march. The sounds of the jackals seemed to be getting nearer, and Joseph looked around nervously. Leaning closer, the African man spoke in a low voice that was half whisper, half rumble.

"There is no need to be afraid of the jackals, young man. They won't come close to the fire. My name is Emmanuel. What is yours?"

"I'm Joseph." He looked over to see if the Bedouin had noticed them talking.

Emmanuel followed his gaze. "They will not bother us so long as we are quiet. It is a pleasure to meet you, Joseph. Yours is a good name. A strong name. How did you end up here?"

Joseph sighed. "It's a long story."

"It always is," Emmanuel said. "Let us eat first. Then you can tell me the whole thing."

Hands bound, they awkwardly opened the canteen and divided up the meager food rations. Emmanuel bowed his head and closed his eyes. Joseph knew this posture well. He must be a man of prayer. Joseph could not bring himself to join him in giving thanks for the food. How could he be thankful? God had abandoned him. He would not thank Him for sandy scraps.

Emmanuel opened his eyes, his mumbled prayer now complete. They began to eat—strangers brought together by fate and misfortune.

After the final crumbs had been scooped up, Joseph told his story. He didn't remember being tossed into the well, but his brothers had obviously pitched him in and then sold him to Ishmael. While he spoke, Emmanuel never moved, never said a word, and never took his eyes off Joseph. When the tale of woe was spun, Emmanuel shifted his weight and looked up at where the moon should have been and then back at Joseph.

"I am sorry for your suffering, especially for one so young as yourself. The world is filled with great evil for men to bomb one another and brothers to sell brothers into bondage. Do not give in to the darkness, Joseph. Your name means 'to increase,' in the old Hebrew. Before you lies the choice to increase the darkness or to increase the light. May you choose the light, though it is the more difficult path."

Joseph knew these words were true. He sensed the darkness inside of him, the powerful desire for revenge slowly consuming him. But he wasn't ready to let it go. The pain and betrayal were too fresh. The darkness gave him strength. If he let go, there would be nothing left. No reason to keep going. Until he found another reason to live, he would cling to the darkness.

He looked at Emmanuel. The old man sat cross-legged with his gangly arms folded gently in his lap. He seemed to understand Joseph's struggle but said nothing. Somehow, he was a man at peace.

Joseph envied him. "Your turn. How did you get here?" he asked.

Emmanuel's eyes seemed to glow, coals revealing an inner fire. "It is a long tale, but I will try to keep it brief. I was born in Nairobi, Kenya. As a boy I wanted to be a priest, but my family wanted me to become a doctor and make money."

Joseph studied Emmanuel. "So what did you do?"

"I honored my parent's wishes and became a doctor. From there I joined the Red Cross and took up a post in war-torn Palestine. If I could not be a priest, then at least I could help heal those in need."

"Were you ever married?" asked Joseph.

"Yes. She was the love of my life, and God gave us five beautiful children."

Emmanuel's voice trailed off. Joseph watched the fire drain from his eyes, replaced by pools of sadness. The man before him with his gently folded hands and soft raspy voice was a man well acquainted with sorrow.

At last Emmanuel found his words again. "The next part of my story is difficult to tell. I was back in Kenya visiting family when the Great War began. Thousands of bombs dropped on Nairobi. The Four Horsemen of the Apocalypse bathing the earth in blood."

"From what my father told me, it was the same in Israel," said Joseph, fascinated to hear the story of the Great War from another perspective.

"It was the same in all the world's major cities. Foolishly, I went into the city to find my relatives, but Nairobi had become hell on Earth. They were nowhere to be found."

Joseph leaned forward. "What did you do then?"

"I tried briefly to care for the wounded, but fighting broke out and I fled the city."

"Where did you go?" asked Joseph.

"To Palestine, in search of my wife and children."

Joseph couldn't hold his tongue. "Did you find them?"

Emmanuel's eyes welled up with tears. "No. They were all dead too. Their loss was more than I could bear, and I fell to the ground. I cursed God, and I cursed my name."

"God with us," Joseph whispered.

Emmanuel closed his eyes as if basking in the warmth of the sun. "Yes, but God had not forgotten me."

"What do you mean?"

"You will see. I lay in the dirt, I suddenly found myself surrounded by a gang of armed men. I was sure I was going to die, but that's when I heard God's voice."

This surprised Joseph. "Really? What did God say?"

"I am with you, do not be afraid."

"How did you know it was God?" asked Joseph skeptically.

Emmanuel smiled. "That is always the question, isn't it? All I can tell you is that I knew in my bones."

Joseph nodded as he pondered his own story. Perhaps it was God who had spoken to him in his dreams. Maybe there was still a chance to see them come true.

Emmanuel cleared his throat. "The rest is simple. The armed men sold me to Ishmael, and now here I am."

"I am sorry for all that you have lost," said Joseph.

"I receive your kindness. It is an ember of light in the darkness."

After that, they fell asleep until Ishmael woke them well before dawn. "Get up. We march in five minutes. There is no time to waste."

As soon as Joseph moved, every muscle begged for mercy, but he knew there would be none. He willed himself to sit up. Tears dribbled out of the corners of his eyes. Getting to his feet felt like an insurmountable task. Emmanuel bent over him.

"I know that look. Let me help you."

Joseph took Emmanuel's outstretched hands, and the old man gently pulled him up from the sand. He teetered for a second before gaining his footing. Emmanuel showed him how to stretch his aching muscles. By the time Ishamel shouted again for them to move, the pain had dulled.

The camels expressed their distaste at being forced to rise at such an ungodly hour with loud grunts, but they were quickly silenced. Neither man nor beast stood up to Ishmael and his whip. Joseph had no illusions of escape. He walked in silence as rugged hills and drifting dunes emerged out of the darkness under the silvery disk of the rising sun.

Joseph's mind was filled with another sun. His old dream had returned where he was the sun and his brothers were small stars bowing before him. The echoes of that dream still filled him with warmth like a lingering promise. A prophecy. Hope carrying him across the desert even as his muscles threatened to cramp and his parched throat made it hard to swallow. If the dream was true, then he didn't need to be afraid. He began to mumble one of Abba's ancient prayers.

"El Shaddai, El Beracah. God of the mountains, God of the valleys, hear my prayer. Watch over me and guide my path. El Shaddai, El Beracah, hear my prayer."

There was power in those words. Power in believing he was not alone, not forgotten. Joseph looked up and saw the towering figure of Ishmael, and he seemed somehow smaller than the day before.

CHAPTER 9

Over the mountains

Mid-morning, they took a break in the shade of a large overhang. Flat cakes of bread were passed around, and Joseph ate his like a starved jackal. He looked up, hoping for more, but it was wishful thinking. They weren't fattening him up to eat him. They just wanted him to keep walking.

The female slave sat nearby. This was the closest he'd been to her, and Joseph thought she must be roughly around his age. Her curves left no doubt that she was a woman, but she was still young. He couldn't help staring at her. She must have sensed Joseph's gaze, because she turned and looked at him. Their eyes met for the faintest second before Joseph looked down at the desert floor. Her eyes... They were filled with the very rays of the sun.

Surely, she must be an angel, to carry within her such brilliant light, thought Joseph.

A few minutes later, Ishmael gave the signal to march, and Joseph's steps felt a little bit lighter, for he was traveling with angels.

This game of stolen glances continued for days, weeks maybe, but Joseph lost track of time. The world was an endless swirl of gray and black skies, plodding feet and the occasional break for food. Every day when they stopped to rest, he looked over at the nameless beauty until she returned his gaze. Their eyes would meet only for a second, but it was enough. Enough light to push back the darkness. The impression of those moments lingered with him throughout the day like a warm, glowing lantern.

Some nights he and Emmanuel would talk, but usually they were too tired. Ever so slowly, the mountains in the distance began to grow. When they finally made it to the base of the mountains, Joseph stared in awe. He felt as small as a grain of sand. He'd seen mountains in his books and understood how the coming together of the earth's plates pushed them upward, but seeing them with his own eyes provided a different kind of knowing that had previously eluded him.

Ishmael strolled over, his face in its perpetual grimace. "Your first time seeing mountains?" Joseph nodded. "Well get ready. They're pretty to look at, but don't be fooled. They're treacherous to cross."

"Have you ever crossed them?" asked Joseph.

Ishmael turned his gaze to the mountains, and his face tensed. "Only once. It was an ill-fated journey. If Allah wills, we will cross safely this time. We rest for an hour, and then we summit while it is still light."

An hour later the camels were settled down. No match for the mountains, they were being left behind with two of the Bedouins. Joseph and the others were given packs to carry and then tied together with lengths of stiff rope.

They waited anxiously for instructions. Ishmael shouldered his pack and turned to them. His face was a storm cloud. "Avaris lies on the other side of those mountains. If you wish to see it, do not stray from the path. These mountains are hungry for human blood. Do not be their next sacrifice."

Joseph fixed his eyes on the mountains and muttered, "El Shaddai, keep me safe."

Ishmael set a rapid pace. They were soon following a narrow trail that cut back and forth up the mountain. They passed giant slabs of stone teetering precariously, and Joseph feared that the slightest touch would send them tumbling into the valley below.

As they climbed higher, Joseph felt as if his lungs would explode. He'd read about such things—the rapid change in altitude and its effects on the body. In front of him, Emmanuel was gasping for breath. The pace was too much for him. Joseph put his arm around the old man's waist to steady him. "Come on. God's not done with you yet. Remember?"

Emmanuel smiled through the sweat dripping down his forehead. "This is true, but what a way to go, to perish at the top of the world."

"Don't say that. Lean on me and keep walking."

Emmanuel obliged, and they pressed onward, staggering like men who'd had too much to drink. Joseph focused only his taking his next step. The rest of the world faded away.

Ishamel was somewhere up ahead with the female prisoner tethered to him. A piercing whistle drifted down the mountain, and Joseph looked up. Ishmael was standing on an enormous rock bigger than Grandpa Laban's bunker. Slowly, he and Emmanuel half climbed, half crawled to where Ishmael stood. When they reached him, they collapsed at his feet.

Joseph looked down into the valley, amazed at how far they had come. He couldn't even see the men and camels hidden in the shadow of the mountain far below. The desert stretched on and on, a gray cloak with no end. Somewhere out there was his bunker. What would it be like to sprout wings and fly home for dinner?

Emmanuel groaned and pulled himself into a sitting position. "Just look at it. I told you this would be a good way to go. A running jump off the rock, and then the long fall into eternity. Straight into the arms of God."

Joseph looked at him with concern. "I can understand the attraction, but I'm not giving up yet. Eternity is forever, right?"

"Yes. Infinite bliss. The shadows of beauty in this world finally come to life."

"I have plenty of time to get there and enjoy all those things. Right now, I have to make it to Avaris. *We* have to make it to Avaris," said Joseph.

Emmanuel's head nodded with exhaustion. "You're right. It was my weakness speaking. Forgive me and my old, tired bones."

Joseph reached out and put his arm around Emmanuel's drooping shoulders. "I forgive you. We are in this together, friend."

"Indeed we are."

A flash of color caught Joseph's attention, and he looked over to see the female prisoner racing for the edge of the lookout rock. Horrified, Joseph watched as each stride carried her closer to the drop off. Her legs bent to launch. The wind whipped at her clothing, trying to pull her off the face of the mountain.

She leapt, feet pushing off stone, arms flailing; a bird taking flight. Ishmael saw her jump and dived toward her, grabbing her and landing on her with a horrible thud. She gasped, Ishmael's weight likely forcing the air from her lungs.

Spitting with rage, Ishmael dragged her back from the edge, away from freedom. She beat at him with her tiny birdlike arms but soon gave up and broke down in a ragged mess of trembling tears. There was no use resisting Ishmael.

"You are a coward," he spat. "Even for a woman. Only a coward would try and take her own life. Now get up."

"Get up," Joseph whispered. He willed her to rise, but she didn't move. She looked up, and her vivid brown eyes had lost their shine, the light was gone.

Joseph's heart sank. Ishmael reached for his whip. Joseph had never seen him whip her. She was too delicate. Before he realized what he was doing, he ran and kneeled over her quaking body. He laid his hand gently on her shoulder. "Get up," he whispered. "Get up, or you will—" the whip lanced into his back.

He felt her flinch as he cried out in agony. "Please," he whimpered. "This is no place to die." Above him, he sensed Ishmael pulling back his arm for another lash.

"Stop." The woman's voice was half choked with tears, but it was the first word Joseph had heard her utter.

"She speaks," declared Ishmael. "At long last."

"What use have I for words that fall upon deaf ears?" she spat. "Neither my words nor my life matter to you."

"That's where you're wrong," sneered Ishmael. "They are worth a great deal to the right buyer. There are but a few true desert flowers that remain, and you, my beauty, are one of them. I will ask you only once more. Get up."

She did as commanded and rose to her feet. Joseph's hand fell away from hers, but the warmth of her remained on his fingertips. She did not grovel before Ishmael as Joseph had. She had an invisible strength.

Ishmael grunted and tied the rope back around her. "You will remain bound until we reach Avaris. Now for you, boy." He struck like a viper. The whip bit into Joseph's side, knocking Joseph to the ground and leaving a long red gash that oozed blood. "Do not interfere with me again." With that, Ishmael turned to march.

Joseph felt a soft hand on his shoulder and looked up into the woman's perfect face. She smiled at him. "Thank you," she whispered. Her smile was worth a thousand lashings. The rope pulled her away, but not before Joseph saw the light return to her eyes, like the sun coming out from behind a cloud.

CHAPTER 10

On to Avaris

Daylight was rapidly fading when the weary travelers reached the summit. Wind whipped all around them, and this high up Joseph could taste the ash in the air. The wound from Ishmael's whip continued to burn like smoldering fire. He looked down below and saw the outline of a town clinging to the base of the mountains. He squinted to get a better look. If this was Avaris, it was much smaller than he'd imagined.

Emmanuel seemed to read his mind. "No need to be disappointed," the old man said. "That's not Avaris."

Joseph groaned. "So that means more walking?"

"I am afraid it does."

"I'm beginning to think we'll never get there."

"If my memory of African geography serves me right, then we should only have a few more days."

"You'll have to forgive my skepticism," replied Joseph. Before Emmanuel could reply, Ishmael stood before them, seemingly unfazed by the climb.

"We must move quickly. Thieves crawl all over this mountain after dark. Take a swig of water, and then we fly."

Darkness followed them as they scrambled down the mountain. Slipping and sliding, as they went. Ishmael refused to make them visible to bandits by lighting a torch, so they made their way blindly in the dark. Joseph and Emmanuel latched on to one another for support. Up ahead, Joseph could hear the muffled cries of the female slave as she struggled along.

He ground his teeth in frustration. Everything in him wanted to help her. To be near her. To see her smile again. He had a million questions he wanted to ask. How did she end up here? How old was she? Did she grow up in a bunker? As they got closer to Avaris, he knew he was running out of time.

Ishmael refused to let up the pace, and little by little, the incline became less steep.

They had nearly completed the descent when the air was suddenly filled with the sound of barking and howling.

Joseph's blood ran cold. They were doomed.

"Jackals!" shouted Ishmael from up ahead. "Follow me." Joseph and Emmanuel raced for their lives as the maniacal jackal calls bounded after them.

They caught up with Ishmael who was frantically untying the female slave. "The buildings are up ahead. Find shelter, and I will hold them off," he shouted.

Ishmael had the look of a madman. This was clearly not a heroic act of kindness. It was the desperate act of a man trying to protect his investments. The three slaves did as they were commanded and ran together until they came to a small building. They tumbled inside and barred the door. Behind them they could make out the sounds of battle. Ishmael roared, jackals yelped, and the whip cracked. The jackals had met their match.

Inside, Joseph and Emmanuel were still tied together. The female slave sat nearby. Joseph's heart was pounding more from being this close to her than from having just nearly been eaten by wild animals. He desperately wanted to start a conversation, but he was tongue-tied, which never happened to him. He'd read about such things in his books, about how the brain would seemingly shut down when a boy was attracted to a girl. Some powerful release of chemicals called hormones caused the brain circuitry to go haywire and palms to start sweating and so forth. He'd always imagined these descriptions were fabrications, but his racing heart and profuse sweating could attest to their validity. He felt completely incapable of stringing together words, as if he'd tapped into the caveman portion of his brain. He wiped his hands on his grimy trousers and managed to produce sound.

"My name is Joseph. What is your name?"

The young woman turned her head slowly and looked at him, taking him in and weighing him from the safety of the shadows. He felt naked and afraid, like Adam and Even in the garden.

"Mariam," she said quietly.

Never has there been a more beautiful name, thought Joseph.

"Thank you for helping me earlier," she said.

Joseph felt as if his heart might explode. "My pleasure. I've always wanted to save a damsel in distress." He winced at his own words and sensed Emmanuel rolling his eyes next to him.

Mariam gave him a long look. "It would seem to me that we are far from the 'happily ever after' of the old fairy tales."

She was right, of course. In the storybooks, the knight in shining armor and the princess rode off into the sunset, but this was no sunset. It was quite the opposite—a dark shack on the far side of a mountain surrounded by mutant creatures in the night.

Joseph sighed. "I guess this is where I should tell you that I'm not really a knight in shining armor."

Mariam laughed. "I imagine that was painful to admit. Young men love to think of themselves as heroes."

Joseph was glad that she could not see him blush, because, of course, she was right.

"The good news for you is that I am not a damsel waiting to be rescued."

Joseph cringed. This wasn't going well. "Ah, yes. I didn't mean to infer that you are weak or unable to take care of yourself."

"I receive your previous comment in its best possible light," she said, soothing his anxiety. "With all that has happened since the Great War, what hope there was for feminism and equality has been obliterated."

"Indeed," replied Joseph, trying to sound knowledgeable about things like feminism. Not surprisingly, there had been no books on the subject in Laban's bunker. All he knew was that the strong preyed upon the weak. This he knew too well from personal experience.

"I am sorry that we find ourselves in this predicament, but I am just glad to finally know your name."

"And I yours."

Suddenly the door exploded into pieces from a mighty kick. All three slaves dived for cover. Ishmael stood in the doorframe with his whip dangling from his hand. "There you are. You were wise not to try and run. I chased the jackals off for now, but they will be back. The beasts are hungry. There is a better house nearby to spend the night. Come."

Begrudgingly the three slaves followed Ishmael and soon fell asleep on the dirt floor of their safehouse. All night the jackals howled, but Joseph was so tired he never heard them. He woke to small rivulets of light sneaking in through the cracks in the boarded-up windows. Ishmael leaned against the door, his piercing eyes wide. Joseph wondered if he'd slept at all.

Nearby, Emmanuel and Mariam stirred. "On your feet," barked Ishmael. "I plan to reach Avaris by sundown."

Outside, the land ran out before them flat and sandy as far as the eye could see. Old cell phone towers and cars dotted the landscape like bits of rusted shrapnel. Ash drizzled down from the low-hanging clouds as they marched.

Moldy manna falling from Heaven. Where is God's provision now?

They came to a highway that once connected cities and carried tourists from around the world to the ancient sites of Egypt. Laban's library had been well stocked with such books, and Joseph knew all about the Sphinx, sarcophaguses, and the pyramids. He wondered if any of them still existed, especially the pyramids. He really wanted to see the pyramids. He scanned the horizon hoping to see them, but the masterpieces of ancient civilization had been destroyed during the Great War. Yet somehow, this thin strip of road had survived. It wound its way through the desert, leading them to Avaris, the last hope of human civilization.

As the late afternoon sun began to dip, they came to a military checkpoint. A man wearing desert camo pointed a large gun at them from behind a barricade of sandbags and commanded them to halt.

Ishmael put up his hands as if in surrender. "I come in peace. I am but a humble Bedouin come to sell slaves to aid in the building of Avaris."

The soldier stood at attention, gun raised and eyes scanning for danger. "How did you hear of Avaris?"

Ishmael smiled and knelt before the man in a sign of humility that Joseph imagined must have pained him, for he was not prone to groveling. "I have traveled far and wide and have heard of Avaris in whispered conversations, a name drifting on the wind. I have come to do my part in bringing workers and to see if the rumors are true."

"Do you carry any weapons?"

"I have but my whip. I ask that you do not seize it, for I use it to ensure my slaves behave." He held up the whip for the man to see.

The soldier lowered his weapon. "You and your slaves may pass. The Bedouin are always welcome, and your slaves will certainly fetch good money. Especially the woman."

Ishmael missed the rage that flashed in Mariam's eyes, but Joseph didn't. She clearly knew why men would pay good money for her. Joseph wished he could save her, but he could not even save himself. He was far from the knights in shining armor in the old stories or the Marvel superheroes from grandpa Laban's DVD collection.

The guard handed Ishmael a small, round piece of red cloth. On it was stamped the sign of the pyramid with an eye looking out. "Show this at the next checkpoint. It will grant you access to Avaris. If you hurry, you may arrive before dark."

Ishmael thanked him and pushed the prisoners as fast as they could go by threatening them with his whip. After another kilometer, the city came into view, wrapped in the grayish light of dusk. It was a strange mixture of mud and metal buildings. The town was ringed with a wall made of scrap metal, old cars, and an abundance of tires. Barbed wire ran along the top of the wall, and machine gun nests stood every hundred meters or so. It looked like a garbage heap gone feral. Joseph shivered as a spike of icy fear lanced through him.

Avaris was not a happily-ever-after destination. It was the end of the road. He was a slave, and this city rising out of the desert was his last stop. The oppressive reality of his situation began to sink in.

The traveling party made its way to the large gates of Avaris where they showed their cloth pass and were given an armed guard to guide them. Inside the walls of the city there was plenty to see. Shops, smiths, and soldiers on patrol. Some houses even had power run by solar panels and generators much like the one back at the bunker. Strings of wires and cables ran helter-skelter. Lights shone in windows, and there was the faint hum of generators and the oily smell of petrol in the air. Inside, Avaris felt much less threatening. This gave him a small glimmer of hope.

Their guide led them through the maze of buildings and back alleys until they arrived at a building that looked like an elongated shipping container. The guide knocked on the door and spoke to someone inside. There was the sound of bolts sliding, and then the metal door swung wide open.

A single bulb shone inside. The man in the doorway was short and squat with a thick black beard. He wore Arabic robes topped with a Kevlar vest and a handgun tucked conspicuously into his belt. He looked them over greedily before speaking.

"Welcome to Avaris. You have traveled far. I am Abasi, a humble servant of Pharaoh, ruler of Avaris and hope of the nations. You will stay here for the night, and tomorrow we will talk business. Come in."

Ishmael bowed his head ever so slightly. "I receive your hospitality and offer of rest. For this we are most grateful."

Joseph and Emmanuel were tossed into a cramped room that reeked of urine. Abasi pulled out his large ring of keys and locked them in. "Sweet dreams. Tomorrow the nightmare begins." He laughed to himself as he walked away.

Joseph shuddered. He wondered where Mariam was being kept. Was she alone? What would tomorrow bring for her? He didn't dare to answer his own questions. Instead, he closed his eyes and prayed for sleep. His dreams were filled with the old visions—stars and planets swirling about and his brothers bowing before him. A steady voice whispered underneath it all, "Have faith."

He woke to the sound of keys jiggling in the door. The grandeur of his visions was reduced to the small cell. Ishmael peered in at them.

"All right now, you've had your beauty sleep. I need you looking your best. Today is the big day." He stepped inside and tied the two men together and then double checked that the knots were tight.

"Where are we going?" asked Joseph.

Ishmael yanked on the rope and pulled them to their feet. "The slave market. Today you meet your new masters. Pray to your God that you might find a favorable home. If such a thing exists in Avaris."

Joseph wanted to ask about Mariam, but he didn't dare. He'd read about the ancient slave auctions where innocent men and women were transported from Africa across the Atlantic and sold in the Americas. He wondered how much he'd sell for.

They stopped at a room down the hall. Ishmael went inside and dragged Mariam out. Joseph was greatly relieved to see her in one piece, but he didn't dare speak to her as Ishmael tied her behind him, and they shuffled awkwardly down the hall, past the dangling light, and outside where Abasi was waiting. He stood beside a large basin filled with water and had a tattered towel draped over his shoulder.

He looked the three of them up and down. "A clean slave is a valuable slave," he cackled. Then he began furiously scrubbing Joseph, bringing tears to his eyes when he touched the sensitive area where he'd been whipped. Layers of dirt and sand and ash came away until Joseph's olive skin was once again revealed. The same was done to Emmanuel until he glistened like polished ebony. Then Abasi turned to Mariam. "Now for you, my lovely."

She raised her head proudly. "I will not be washed by the likes of you. Give me the towel, and I will do it myself."

"That will not do. I've been looking forward to this." Abasi stepped forward and reached out to touch her, but Mariam spat in his face like a cobra. Her saliva ran down his cheek and into his scraggly beard. The smug grin disappeared from Abasi's face. His eyes bulged out of his head as he wiped away the spittle. "You'll pay for that, you harlot."

His hand flew towards her face but stopped mid swing. Ishmael towered over Abasi, gripping his wrist as if the full-grown man were nothing more than a child.

"I wouldn't do that if I were you. A clean slave is a valuable slave, but so is a slave without bruises across her face. You will let the girl wash herself, or I will snap your wrist. The choice is up to you."

Abasi grunted, and Ishmael released his hand. Joseph watched as Mariam washed away the grime. Her skin underneath was luminescent. She was beautiful beyond words. His heart began to pound so loudly he feared she'd be able to hear it. When she finished washing, she threw the towel at Abasi's feet. He spat on it and refused to pick it up.

"Now that the Queen of Sheba is ready, we will go. Don't think I will forget this disgrace," growled Abasi. Though he likely wouldn't forget Ishmael's threat anytime soon either.

Joseph glanced around as they marched through Avaris and was amazed by what he saw. The buildings that had survived the Great War stood battered and bruised. They leaned dangerously in all directions. At their base was a host of new construction. Mud huts made of sunbaked bricks seemed to have sprung up everywhere. It was a rat's nest of debris somehow repurposed so life could flourish. Everything was grungy, including the people.

Abasi wove his way through the tangled mess of streets and buildings. Finally, they emerged from a narrow alley, and Emmanuel let out a long whistle.

"That, my boy, is the Nile River."

Joseph could barely believe how massive it was. A few boats drifted across the surface with men casting nets. On the steep banks, people made bricks with all sorts of hand-made tools. Water was being funneled away from the main river into narrow channels that ran to fields of green plants. The sight of them made Joseph want to cry. These were real, living things. He hadn't thought it possible. People were building things, fishing, and growing food. Life was rising out of the ashes. It was nothing short of a miracle. A miracle far removed from his safe, secluded life in the bunker. He couldn't help but wonder if Abba had known about Avaris and kept it from them.

Ishmael shoved him in the back. "Quit your gawking. You don't want to be late to your own party, do you?"

They walked along the bank of the Nile until they came to an old fort. The walls were made of cement and topped with broken glass. At the sight of Abasi, the gates were opened, and they were quickly ushered inside by two armed guards.

A group of men sat around a simple fire, but there was something different about them, a sort of heightened alertness in the way they sat and a readiness to attack that made Joseph shiver. The men slowly sipped tea and talked in hushed tones while their hands never strayed far from their visible handguns.

Joseph whispered to Emmanuel, "What sort of men are those?"

"Military men. Trained to kill, from the looks of things. Before the Great War, men made a career of killing."

Joseph gulped. His brothers could be cruel, and they loved to tell stories of their exploits killing jackals, but they were nothing like this. These men were different. They were the top of the food chain, and Joseph was all the way at the bottom.

One of the men stood. He was tall and muscular with wisps of silver in his hair and beard. Abasi stepped forward and bowed until his forehead touched the ground at the man's feet. He spoke reverently, his lips brushing the dirt. "I have brought the slaves you requested, oh Potiphar. I pray they will please you."

"Save your prayers, Abasi. I will see for myself. The last ones you brought were half starved and barely human. Rise."

"Thank you, Your Honor."

Potiphar circled the slaves like a shark. He grabbed Joseph by the jaw. "Open your mouth, boy."

Joseph did as commanded. Potiphar grunted, then released his face.

"What is your name and where are you from?"

"I am Joseph, son of Jacob, from the country of Israel."

"How did you survive the Great War?"

"Living in a bunker."

"What skills do you possess?"

"I can read and write, sir. My father was a well-educated man, and he taught me a great deal."

Potiphar's eyebrows raised. "This is indeed a pleasant surprise. Such knowledge is hard to come by these days. Most of the bookworms died a long time ago."

He turned to Emmanuel. "How about you, old man? Why should I have interest in you? Are you fit enough to make bricks?"

Emmanuel bowed before Potiphar. "If it pleases you, sir, I am a doctor."

Potiphar's eyes grew wide. "A doctor! Abasi, you have brought me a learned young man and a doctor. You have done well."

Then he turned to Mariam. He walked around her, looking her up and down in a way that made Joseph's skin crawl. Mariam stood tall and stared unflinchingly at the man as he ogled her. Potiphar chuckled. "She has spirit, this one. Like a thoroughbred mare, she will need to be tamed, but it can be done."

Now, at last, he turned to Ishmael, who had been standing silently to the side. "Come, let us sit by the fire, drink tea, and discuss a fair price for your merchandise."

An hour later Ishmael and Potiphar rose and exchanged payment. Then without so much as a word, Ishmael disappeared like a character in a bad dream. In his place stood a new master.

"I am Potiphar, captain of the Pharaoh's guard and leader of the troops who protect Avaris. Your lives belong to me. Should you try to escape, I will take one of your feet as payment. Should you try to steal from me, I will take a hand. Should you be disrespectful, I will take your tongue."

Uh oh, thought Joseph. He wasn't one to run away or steal, but talking back and being disrespectful to authority was definitely his thing. He would have to be very careful.

"You will serve in my house and do as I command. Do you understand?" asked Potiphar. The three slaves nodded. "Let us be off then. My wife awaits."

On their way back through Avaris, Joseph noted how people quickly moved out of the way of Potiphar and his men. He was clearly a man of importance and not one to be trifled with. All this Joseph filed away as he tried to get a handle on his new situation.

They came to the outskirts of town, and there, sitting on the bank of the Nile, was a lavish estate. While the old buildings in Avaris were wounded survivors of the Great War, this facility was seemingly untouched.

Potiphar called a halt. "Behold, the palace of Rameses. A reminder of what was and a promise of what will one day be again. In the days of despair, Rameses united those of us who survived. He is a light in the darkness. His will is not to be questioned, and his name is to be honored at all times. Do I make myself clear?"

Joseph understood. Pharaoh was not like other men. He was a god amongst mortals. A man to be feared even more than Potiphar. They came to a compound with high walls that backed up to Rameses' palace. The metal gate opened to reveal a large stone house with an expansive porch and metal roof. The house was set in the middle of a garden of flowers and fruit trees. Joseph felt as if he was entering Eden itself.

Reclining in the garden was the woman of the house. She had long black hair that hung to her waist. Her eyes were done up with colors in a way that Joseph had never seen before, and her mouth curled at the edges in a dangerous smile. With a simple wave of her hand, she beckoned them into her presence and rose to meet Potiphar. She was slender standing next to him, but the power that emanated from her matched his in every way. Potiphar kissed her hand. "These are the new slaves you requested, my love. I have brought a young woman to attend to you and a new errand boy. The old man is a doctor." Potiphar looked at her, clearly waiting for a response, which struck Joseph as strange. Why did Potiphar kowtow to her like this?

"You have done well, Husband." She patted Potiphar's hand and leaned in for a swift kiss. "As always, you care for my every need. I know you are a busy man. Please do not linger for my sake. I will see that the new slaves are well cared for." Joseph felt her eyes slide over him, lingering too long for his comfort.

Joseph could see the relief that flashed across Potiphar's face. "I am glad you are pleased. I will leave them to you. Pharaoh has summoned me, and I fear there are more raiders about." Then he turned to the slaves. "This is my wife, Zuleika. You will listen to her every word. When she speaks, it is as if I am speaking. You now exist to serve her."

Potiphar looked at them with a ruthless intensity, and Joseph could see the muscles in his arms rippling. They had been warned. Without another word, Potiphar turned and marched away. Once Potiphar and his men were out of earshot, Zuleika spoke.

"You mustn't mind my husband. He can be a little overprotective. Come now, tell me your names. Starting with you, young man."

Joseph stared at the ground, nervous about making eye contact. "I am Joseph."

"How old are you, boy?"

"Sixteen, Mistress."

"Excellent." She reached out and stroked his beardless face. "Still entering the prime of your youth." Joseph tried not to flinch at her touch. The woman made him uneasy. She smiled, and her eyes twinkled playfully. "My husband always had good taste."

Then she turned to Mariam and pursed her lips in distaste. "What is your name, girl?"

"Mariam."

"Do you have any skills, or are you just a pretty face?"

Mariam's eyes flashed, and Joseph knew her blood must be boiling. He hoped she'd be able to keep her emotions under control. Zuleika was watching her like a hawk. Mariam met Zuleika's gaze unflinchingly as she replied, "I am able to read and write."

Storm clouds rolled across Zuleika's face—lightning waiting to strike. "My, my, you are a haughty little thing. I have long prided myself on my ability to read people, and it's clear you have not spent enough time doing real work. Do not fear though. You will have plenty of opportunities to work until you develop the proper demeanor for a slave. Whatever you were in a former life doesn't matter anymore. You are a slave now and nothing more. Remember that. Have I made myself clear?"

"Yes."

Anger flashed across Zuleika's face, and there was a new edge to her voice. "Yes, Mistress. You will refer to me as 'Mistress,' slave. Now, try again."

Mariam's face twisted painfully into submission. "Yes, Mistress,"

"Better. You're already learning. Now for the doctor." Emmanuel's interrogation was short and sweet. It was clear that Zuleika was not nearly as interested in him.

With the introductions out of the way, Zuleika led them into the house. It was a fascinating mishmash of old-world grandeur and post-apocalyptic jerry rigging. Joseph could see where items had been strategically placed to cover flaws, but even the newish paint couldn't hide all the wear and tear. But the overall effect was spacious and tasteful—a far cry from his family's colorless metal bunker.

The best part of the house was that a gentle breeze blew in carrying the scent of the citrus trees in the garden. Much better than the smell of Simeon's cooking and body odor that permeated the bunker. Those were the smells of survival; this was the smell of life.

Mariam was quickly ushered into the kitchen and put to work. Zuleika watched with open pleasure before leading Joseph and Emmanuel on a tour of the house and grounds. The property was surrounded by a high cement wall topped with broken glass, letting everyone know the residents inside were important. The tour ended in a small room at the back of the house. This was to be their living quarters. Zuleika then left to check on Mariam.

Joseph looked at Emmanuel. "It's not much to look at, but it could be worse. What do you think?"

Emmanuel looked to the heavens with gratitude. "I think that God has had mercy upon us, but I fear that woman is dangerous. Watch your step around her."

"Me? What about poor Mariam?"

Emmanuel shook his head. "Don't get caught in the middle of those two. Just keep your head down and work hard."

"I will do my best, but it'll be easier said than done."

"I know." A smile twitched at the corners of Emmanuel's mouth. "I've seen the way you look at Mariam."

Joseph felt an anxious knot form in the pit of his stomach and his cheeks flush ever so slightly.

"Is it that obvious?"

Emmanuel patted his back. "I may be old, but I still remember what it was like to be your age."

"I thought I was being subtle."

Emmanuel laughed out loud. "I would say there's little that's subtle about you. Some might see it as a character flaw, but I like it. What you see is what you get with you. There's something very refreshing about that."

"Hopefully Mariam sees it that way," said Joseph with a smile.

"If not, you'll know soon enough. Now if you don't mind, I will take my pick of the two sleeping mats that have been graciously provided to us."

"As you should. Age before beauty."

Emmanuel ignored him and sat down on his new mat. Then he began to pray. "Blessed are You, our God, Ruler of the Universe, who is good and causes good. Bless the work of our hands here in this place." He invited Joseph to join him, which he did, but only because listening to Emmanuel pray reminded him of his Abba.

The rest of the day passed quickly as Joseph began to learn the ins and outs of the property and his new responsibilities. Potiphar's house was much larger and nicer than the bunker, but the idea of being a slave didn't sit well with him. He chafed at the idea of being at Zuleika's beck and call. He missed the freedom of his previous life, but the necessary efficiency of life in the bunker had taught him a great deal. Coupled with his constant reading and lessons from Abba, he was well prepared for the situation he now found himself in. Out in the fields there were opportunities for improved irrigation, hydroponics and more. He took careful mental notes to relay to Potiphar when the opportunity arose. If he was going to be stuck here, he might as well improve his lot by showing Potiphar that he could be an asset.

That evening, he caught a glimpse of Mariam as she made her way to her sleeping quarters. She was assigned a room the size of a cupboard, just down the hall. Joseph couldn't help but notice when he'd peeked in that there was no sleeping mat in her space. All she had was a hard brick floor, not even a window. This couldn't be a simple oversight by Zuleika. The mistress struck him as more calculated than that.

Joseph waited until Emmanuel was asleep before he stole down the hall to Mariam's room. He knocked quietly on the door. There was a faint rustling noise inside.

"Who is it?" asked Mariam, her voice muffled through the wood.

"Joseph."

The door opened a crack, "You do know how late it is, don't you?"

"I couldn't sleep."

"So, you thought you'd come and wake me up?"

"In hindsight that might not have been a good choice."

"You can say that again."

This was not going according to plan. Unsure what else to do, Joseph held out his rolled-up floor mat. "I brought you a gift."

The door opened a bit wider, and Mariam peeked her head out and looked at him with sad eyes. "That is very kind of you, but I can't accept it."

"I insist. With what Zuleika has in store for you, you're going to need some sleep. Please take it."

Mariam rolled her eyes. "Fine, but you had better go. If anyone catches you here, we're both going to be in big trouble with my new evil mistress."

"Come on. Can't I just stay a little longer?" asked Joseph.

Mariam's face twitched. I think that might be a bad idea."

Sort of like me waking you up in the middle of the night after you were stuck washing dishes all day?" asked Joseph.

"Exactly."

"Then I will bid you goodnight before you decide never to see me again."

Joseph turned to go, but Mariam asked him to wait.

Thank you God, mouthed Joseph. He turned around, unable to contain his smile. His new situation wasn't without its bright spots.

Mariam met his smile with one of her own. "Thank you for the sleeping mat. It's very kind of you."

"My pleasure, and"—he hesitated—"sweet dreams." Joseph darted down the hall before he managed to ruin the moment. Even the hard bricks felt soft that night as he slept the sleep of a man falling in love.

CHAPTER 11

Time to Shine

The next few days slipped by with no sign of Potiphar. Joseph didn't see his friends much either. Mariam was stashed away in the kitchens, and Emmanuel was busy taking inventory of medical supplies. Meanwhile, Joseph found himself caught up in Zuleika's gravitational pull. She was the sun, and he was forced to orbit around her, tending to her every need. Eventually he got up the courage to request a small notepad to jot down his ideas for improving the compound.

When Potiphar finally returned a week later, he looked weary. Emmanuel was called to tend to a nasty-looking gash on his arm that had begun to turn unnatural colors. Zuleika waited for her husband in the house, dressed in a fine gown of purple silk.

"A little something to cheer him up. What do you think?" she asked Joseph as she spun in a circle.

Joseph blushed and looked down. "Ummm—very lovely, Mistress. He will certainly be pleased." He bowed and darted out the front door to avoid any further awkward conversation.

Once outside, he took a deep breath to steady himself. Potiphar was coming up the front steps, and Joseph greeted him. "Good afternoon, Master. I pray you are not seriously wounded."

Potiphar merely grunted. "I was fighting in wars long before you were born. This is but a scratch. While I'm sitting here doing nothing, give me a report of your first few days."

"Things have been going well, sir. I have nothing to report at this time." Joseph hesitated, unsure whether to say more.

Potiphar grunted again. "Out with it. I appreciate a man who speaks his mind, and it's clear you have more you'd like to say."

"I don't want to overstep my bounds, but I believe that I could improve the efficiency of your property, sir."

Potiphar raised an eyebrow. "You do, do you? I'm listening."

"Thank you, sir. If you'll permit me, I've taken down some notes." He pulled out his notepad and handed it to Potiphar. "My father was an engineer and hydroponics specialist. He taught me a great deal, and I believe I could use some of these same techniques to assist you. With your proximity to the Nile, there's a lot of possibilities. Take a look."

Potiphar looked over the notebook carefully. After a minute, he put the pad down and stared curiously at Joseph, who was standing as stiff as a board, hardly daring to breath. "This is most intriguing. Had that slaver known you were capable of such things, he would have sold you for ten times the price he did."

Joseph finally released the tension in his body. "Thank you, sir,"

"You've been here little more than a week and already you have put together a comprehensive plan for renovating the property. I am thoroughly impressed. I like a man with an entrepreneurial spirit. Killing is more my specialty than farming, but I'm a fair and honest man. If you make my life easier, then I will see you are rewarded. Can you actually accomplish the things written here?" Potiphar stared at Joseph with the intensity of a predator, but Joseph didn't let himself shrink.

"I believe I can, sir. With some hard work and God's help, anything is possible."

"You are young, but there is something about you that I like. I will give you a chance to prove yourself rather than seeing your forwardness as an insult to the way that I run my household."

"Thank you, sir."

"My wife loves her garden. If you can complete the watering system for the garden as outlined in your notes, she will be very pleased, which means I, too, will be greatly pleased. Do you understand what I'm getting at?"

He certainly did. Being on Potiphar's good side would make being a slave a lot easier.

Joseph nodded. "Thank you, sir. I am grateful for the opportunity to prove my worth."

"Good. You start in the morning." Potiphar shooed him away.

Joseph knew this was his chance to get on Potiphar's good side, and he didn't plan on messing it up. He floated through the rest of the day making mental plans and lists for what he would need. Once everyone was asleep, he stole over to Mariam's room and knocked softly on the door.

"I'm here for Cinderella," he said. Something thudded against the inside of the door. A shoe, perhaps?

"Go away."

"But I have a glass slipper for you to try on." There was an audible groan from inside followed by the sound of footsteps. Finally, the door cracked open and Mariam looked out at him with a hint of annoyance.

"I don't have any idea what you are talking about. Who is Cinderella? And why does she have a glass slipper? Sounds like complete nonsense. Anyway, the only thing I'd do with a glass slipper is use it to stab Zuleika. That woman drives me mad."

Joseph had assumed that everyone would know fairy tales. There was so much he didn't know about Mariam. He tried to explain. "Cinderella is a character from an old story. My comment was supposed to be funny."

Mariam studied Joseph hard for a moment, as if she were trying to decide whether to open up to him. "The only stories I grew up with were from the sacred texts. Not a lot of comedy there."

Joseph lit up. "I know what you mean. My father was...er...*is* a religious man. We did devotions every day."

Mariam scoffed. "Try three services a day your whole life with your dad being the priest."

Joseph laughed. "Try growing up with ten brothers who never sit still and your father keeps yelling at them because they won't pay attention to the readings. Oh, and did I mention that they all hated me." His face fell for a second, but he didn't want to get into that whole story just now.

Mariam's expression softened. "Tell me about this Cinderella. I could use a fun story."

Joseph took the bait, happy to change subjects. "Not sure I'd call it fun, but I'll let you decide. And, while I do love standing awkwardly with you peeking out from behind a half-closed door, maybe we could sit in the hall for the story?"

"I guess that would be better." Mariam stepped out from behind the door, and they sat in the hall. Not too close; Joseph didn't want to make her uncomfortable. Storytelling was one of his true loves, and he came to life as he spun the tale. All the while, Mariam sat silently, eyes closed, taking in every rich detail that Joseph shared. When at last he was finished, she opened her eyes.

"That is a good story. Not really fun, but good. You told it well."

Joseph sat up a little straighter. "Thank you. It's nice to have an appreciative audience for once."

"Well, my father wouldn't have liked it. He would have said it was secular. Nothing worse than something secular in his opinion, but I think it contains a good deal of truth. Like one of the parables."

"Agreed," said Joseph, "but I think I like your version where Cinderella, tired of being mistreated, finally stands up for herself and takes matters into her own hands. Beware Cinderella and her deadly glass slipper."

"I'm pretty sure that version doesn't end happily ever after."

"You're probably right, but in your case it's nice to pretend."

Mariam nodded. "Are there other stories like Cinderella?"

Joseph grinned. "So many of them! They were all written by two brothers who traveled the world, collecting stories."

Mariam's eyes grew wistful. "Imagine traveling the world."

"We were born in the wrong time," said Joseph.

"Yes. People used to say it was hard being a kid during the social media age. Try being a kid during the apocalypse."

"Exactly," laughed Joseph.

"You will have to tell me more of these stories," said Mariam. She gave Joseph a small smile that filled him with hope and a sudden rush of endorphins.

"It would be my pleasure. I'll come back tomorrow night."

"That would be nice." Mariam paused. "I have to confess that you are growing on me, even though you keep showing up in the middle of the night."

Joseph grinned as wide as the ocean.

"Don't let it go to your head."

"I most certainly will. It's not every day I receive such good news. Speaking of good news, I have something else to tell you."

She lifted an eyebrow.

"I have managed to get the attention of our esteemed master."

"Ha, and his wife as well. That one has her eye on you."

Joseph felt his face flush beet red. "Don't ruin this moment for me."

Now Mariam was the one grinning. Joseph cleared his throat. "As I was saying, Potiphar has set me in charge of a significant project to upgrade the grounds. If this goes well, I could be on the up and up."

Mariam gave him a small round of applause. "Maybe you will be the male version of Cinderella. A lowly slave rising through the ranks."

"Maybe something like that, but I don't need a fairy godmother to help me. I have years of working on the irrigation system in the bunker to rely on. It should be rather easy, all things considered." Joseph leaned back, feeling quite good about himself.

"I hope so, for your sake. Otherwise, you'll be out in the fields—or worse—in no time. Potiphar strikes me as the type of man you don't want to disappoint."

"I don't plan to," said Joseph with all the confidence he could muster.

"That's good. Now I need to get my beauty sleep before Zuleika calls for me at the crack of dawn to massage her feet."

Joseph stood and gave her a grand bow. "Until tomorrow night then, and sleep well."

He lay for a long time on the hard floor of his room, staring at the ceiling and praying with all his might until he fell asleep. The morning came with a heavy mist that smelled strongly of sulfur. Joseph dressed and kneeled on the ground in prayer as he had seen his father do many times.

"Lord, bless the work of my hands. May today be a day of favor." He looked up and saw Emmanuel smiling. "What?"

"I'm just giving thanks," Emmanuel said. "You are not the same young man I met on that first night. You have changed."

"How so?"

"You are more humble."

Joseph stood. "Maybe you're wearing off on me."

Emmanuel shrugged. "Perhaps. Who am I to question the methods of the Creator? Let me bless you before you go and show Potiphar what you can do."

"How could I refuse such an offer?"

Emmanuel placed his hands on Joseph's head. "You cannot. We have been through much together, and you are like my son. Only a fool refuses the blessing of his father. Now, May God bless you and keep you and cause His face to shine upon you, both this day and forever more."

Tears dripped onto Joseph's curly hair, a divine anointing. Joseph hugged Emmanuel. "Thank you for your blessing and for believing in me."

Then he turned and headed towards the garden. He walked by Mariam's door, but she was already gone. She'd see soon enough what he could do.

The day flew by. For the first time in a long time, he felt a fragment of control as he oversaw the water project for the garden. Things were humming along nicely until Zuleika strolled over to check on the progress.

As she drew near, she fixed her eyes on Joseph, making him feel strangely vulnerable. He wanted to run and hide in the garden, and Emmanuel's words about Zuleika being a snake echoed in the back of his mind. Joseph waited for her forked tongue to emerge, but she stared at him silently, apparently waiting for him to make a move. Mariam trailed behind her, and Joseph sensed her watching him carefully as well. Flustered and uncertain, he knelt at Zuleika's feet.

"Welcome, Mistress. I apologize for the inconvenience of my work here. Your husband made it abundantly clear how much you love this garden."

He felt her hovering over him, weighing him, and then she sighed. "Such formality for one so young. Rise. I do not intend to stare at the top of your head while we speak."

He stood but tried not to make eye contact.

Zuleika seemed to enjoy his discomfort. "Look at me, boy." Joseph slowly lifted his head and looked her in the eye. A small smile tugged at the corners of her lips. "Much better. Now I can take a good look at you. You are a scrawny little thing, but you have a kind face. I hope my husband will not turn it to stone like his. The world needs gentle things. Beautiful things. Once it was full of such things, but they are long gone. All that remains is stone and ash."

She cocked her head. "What do you think of that, boy?"

Joseph paused, choosing his words carefully. "Sadly, I never knew the world you speak of, but I have read of it in books."

She clapped her hands. "Kind and educated. A rare combination. Most excellent. You will have to recount the stories you have read so that I might escape from this harsh reality, even if it is just for a few brief moments."

He'd much rather tell stories to Mariam, but he kept that piece of information to himself.

"As you wish, Mistress, but first I would ask to complete my task for your husband."

"Of course. I can see that you are eager to please. That is good. We will have plenty of time for stories once you have brought my garden to life." Her voice oozed seduction.

Joseph looked back down at the ground, blood rushing to his face. "I am no miracle worker, but I do pray that when my work here is done, this garden will be more beautiful than ever."

"Are you religious?" Her voice rang with surprise, and Joseph looked back up and shuffled his feet nervously.

"Yes, Mistress, but I hope I did not offend you if you are a non-believer."

"I have been many things, and seen many things, and believed many things. You may pray to your God all you like. If God listens, all the better. But I give you fair warning, not all feel as I do. Most think God has abandoned us. I would be careful about revealing your religion to others."

"Thank you, Mistress. My words reveal my ignorance."

Zuleika reached out and gently touched his shoulder. "Indeed, but do not fret. I may be cooped up here day and night, but there is much I can teach you about the ways of the world."

Joseph was stunned by Zuleika's action and stumbled over his words. "Um, thank you, Mistress. You are... I mean... I am most grateful."

She smiled at him wickedly. "As you should be. Now return to your work. I am curious to see your vision come to life."

She turned to Mariam, and her smile evaporated. "Go and fetch me some water, you lazy girl." Joseph ached for Mariam as she darted back into the house. There was no love lost between the two women. In fact, it seemed there was a storm brewing, but he didn't dare get involved. Instead, he hurried away trying to make sense of what had just occurred with Zuleika.

He spent the rest of the day working on the new watering system. Then the next and the next, working from sunup to sundown until he lost track of the days. He'd never worked so hard in all his life. Abba would have been proud. He tried not to think of him. It was too painful.

Joseph poured over every inch of the project until it was finished to his liking. Then he went to find Potiphar.

"Master, I come with good news."

Potiphar looked up from the bone he was picking at with a knife. "What might that be, slave?"

"I have finished the watering project for the garden."

Potiphar wiped the blade on a napkin. "I am glad to hear it. I have been waiting to see how this contraption works."

"I would be happy to explain, Master."

Potiphar shook the now spotless knife in his direction. "No need. Seeing it in action will be enough for me. I am not interested in a science lesson."

"As you wish, Master."

Potiphar twirled the knife back into his belt and rose from his chair. "Let us go."

Joseph followed nervously behind Potiphar, not speaking unless asked a direct question. Potiphar carefully examined every inch of Joseph's work. They'd covered most of the garden when Zuleika appeared with Mariam in tow.

"My dearest husband, what do you think of our young slave's work?" She placed her hand gently on Potiphar's muscular arm.

"He has done well. Surprisingly well, in fact. He is a clever one."

Joseph felt a jolt of pride at Potiphar's praise.

"Indeed," cooed Zuleika, and she winked at Joseph.

Horrified, Joseph looked back down at the ground, praying Potiphar had not noticed.

"Does that mean you'll let me keep him around then?" Zuleika's long fingers caressed Potiphar's skin. Even a man like Potiphar was no match for her powers of sensual persuasion. Potiphar stood tall, clearly attempting to regain some semblance of control.

"The boy will stay here as long as it pleases you. In fact, I have a mind to put him in charge of the grounds. Is that to your liking, my love?"

"It most certainly is."

"Then it is done."

Potiphar turned to his manservant. "Go and fetch me my red cloak at once."

The man bowed and ran off as fast as he could.

Then Potiphar addressed Joseph. " Come here, boy."

Joseph took a hesitant step forward. He was grateful for the promotion but mortified to be under Zuleika's close watch.

"Look me in the eye like a man," Potiphar said. When Joseph did, he continued. "From this day forward, I place you in charge of the compound grounds. You will train my field workers how to build watering systems, and you will undertake the other projects laid out in your notes. Now kneel."

Joseph did as he was told, catching sight of the manservant running towards him out of the corner of his eye. Potiphar took the cloak from the servant's outstretched arms and spoke. "Rise, Joseph. This garment is a symbol of your new status as the head groundskeeper." Potiphar placed the robe on Joseph. It fit him well.

Joseph felt stunned by how fast all of this was happening. "Thank you, Master. I will not let you down. God as my witness."

Potiphar cocked his head. "Do you not know that God is dead?"

Zuleika slithered her way into the conversation "The boy will learn, honey. He has lived in a bunker his whole life. He still believes in fairy tales. It is not his fault."

Potiphar looked condescendingly at poor, backwards Joseph, who decided this was a good time to say something.

"I serve at your request, Master, but I tell you truthfully that it is God who guided me across the desert and brought me safely to you. I cannot turn from Him after all He has done."

"I will not begrudge you your archaic beliefs, but we will see whether it was God who brought you here or fate."

"Thank you, Master. That is all I can ask. May the God of my ancestors bless this home, and may those who live here know only prosperity and peace."

"Either by God's hand or by yours, may it be so. Now leave us. You have much work to do."

Only when he was back in his room did Joseph dare to breathe. He'd done it. He'd passed Potiphar's test. He sat there, stunned. He'd come a long way from being left naked to die in the bottom of the well. What would his brothers say if they could see him now? He grinned and ran a hand over the red coat. It was nice. Not as nice as his birthday jacket, but it was a step in the right direction.

A rap came at the door. Joseph looked up, and there stood Mariam, her eyes aglow and the beginnings of a smile on her lips. She was so beautiful. Joseph felt the urge to tell her that, but he was afraid she'd pull back. He couldn't bear that.

"I still can't decide if you're brave or a fool," she said.

Joseph grinned. "Let's go with brave. At least for today."

"Just for today. Congratulations on your promotion and your new wardrobe. Red is a good color on you."

"Thank you," said Joseph, trying not to blush. "Do you want to take a seat?" He gestured to the floor space beside him.

A look of indecision passed over Mariam's face as she leaned against the doorway. "If my father saw me sitting alone with a young man, he'd give me a lecture."

"Luckily your father isn't here, and I promise to be a true gentleman."

Mariam stepped gracefully into the room. "You had better, otherwise I'll cut you with my knife... Just kidding."

Joseph had a sneaking suspicion that she wasn't though. She was truly something else. "What should we talk about?" he asked.

Mariam shrugged as a dejected look crossed her face. "Doesn't matter too much. I'm sure Zuleika will be calling me soon anyway."

"It would be so nice for both our sakes if she just forgot you were alive for a couple of hours," said Joseph.

Mariam sat down a little way from him, and Joseph got the hint. This was not an intimate moment. "Sadly, I don't think that is going to happen. Zuleika is like a hawk waiting to attack."

Joseph held back a shudder. He felt *exactly* like prey when Zuleika ogled him. "Oh, I know. I've seen the way she looks at you. If looks were talons, you'd be torn to shreds."

"She does plenty of that with her words. I'm just a pet that she intends to break in."

"Don't let her," whispered Joseph.

Mariam looked up at him. "I said 'intends.' She doesn't know who she's dealing with. I didn't survive—oh, never mind."

Joseph edged closer to her. "You can tell me."

She sighed. "It's complicated. I grew up as part of this crazy religious cult. My father was the leader, and we moved to the Qumran caves a little before the Great War began. Everyone thought he was a prophet, and they were always watching me and then my mother..."

Now his curiosity was *really* piqued, and Joseph didn't want her to stop talking. "You can tell me. You don't have to carry all of it alone."

She gave him a long stare, then lowered her gaze. "Maybe someday."

Someday. He wanted to take her hand, but he knew better. Someday would come. He only hoped it was sooner rather than later.

He heard swiftly moving feet, and then one of the servants appeared in the doorway. The mistress wants you, Mariam. Come quickly."

Mariam rolled her eyes. "I'm sure she does. Run along and let her know I'm on my way."

The other slave shifted uncomfortably. "I was told to bring you myself."

"Of course you were. The woman has so little faith in me." She turned to Joseph. "Until next time, and congratulations again."

Joseph watched her go, hanging on to her promise of "some day."

CHAPTER 12

The Forbidden Fruit

A year went by, and Joseph and Mariam continued their late-night meetings. Little by little she came out of her shell. With each new story, Joseph loved her more, but he was too afraid to tell her, and so they remained only friends.

At work, though, everything Joseph touched flourished, and Potiphar eventually put him in charge of the entire estate—behind Zuleika, of course. But hidden beneath Joseph's success was the festering thorn of bitterness towards his brothers. He couldn't forgive them for what they'd done to him.

As rumors of raiders and bands of beggars reached his ears, Joseph noticed a stark increase in Potiphar being away for days at a time. But life carried on, and Joseph didn't worry too much.

A second year went by so fast that Joseph could barely believe it. So much had happened and changed, including him. At eighteen years old, he was no longer wispy like when he'd arrived. He'd grown tall. The makings of a beard now sprouted on his once baby-smooth face. His voice was deep, and his muscles bulged from hours of hard work. People treated him with respect. He was a man now.

One early morning, Joseph was sitting in the garden, as was his habit. All was quiet. The city of Avaris had yet to wake. He closed his eyes and prayed the words Abba had taught him as a boy. Words they'd recited a thousand times together. "I thank You for the rest You have given me through the night and for the breath that renews my body and spirit."

Joseph opened his eyes, and saw Zuleika standing in front of him. She wore only a silk nightgown that left little to the imagination. Her hair hung loose about her shoulders, and her long legs were freshly shaved. She was the picture of temptation.

"I thought I'd find you here," she whispered while her eyes took him in. "Come to bed with me. My husband is gone, and the rest of the house is asleep."

The air whooshed out of Joseph's lungs. Zuleika had flirted with him from the beginning, but he'd thought it was all just a game to her. Clearly, he'd been wrong. Zuleika's words were like those of the serpent in Eden. They sang in his ears, tempting him. Like the fruit in the garden, Zuleika was pleasing to look at, there was no denying that. He was so close he could reach out and touch her. She was a beautiful woman, and she wanted him. He could smell her perfume, sweet like flowers. She dripped with secrets waiting to be discovered. "No one will know," she promised.

As if being pulled from a trance, Joseph came to his senses and thought of Mariam. She was the one he wanted to hold and kiss. She was the one he loved. He thought about the way she listened to his stories and asked deep questions and noticed the tiny, beautiful things in the midst of the mundane. He could see her eyes full of light and her face aglow with laughter. He shuddered that he had even been tempted by Zuleika. Words came tumbling out all jumbled as he took a step backwards from her.

"I...I cannot, Mistress. My master has put everything he owns under my care. All, that is, except for you. How could I do such a wicked thing against him? And not just him, but against God?"

Disappointment flashed across Zuleika's face before she plastered the cloying smile on her face again. "You and your devotion to your unseen God. If there is a God, He does not care what we do. He has left us to our own ends. God has abandoned us. You are right to fear my husband though. I will make sure he never finds out. Now come with me." She stepped forward and reached for his hand.

Joseph rose to his full height and looked down on Zuleika. His legs trembled. "I can't. Now please excuse me, there is work to be done." He escaped to his room and woke Emmanuel at once. He choked on his words, afraid to share what had just happened.

"Out with it now," Emmanuel said, rubbing the sleep from his eyes. "It can't be that bad."

Joseph told him what had happened, and Emmanuel shook his head.

"I knew that woman was a snake. There's no love lost between her and her husband. He's put her up here in a nice fancy cage, but it seems you've flown into the cage and caught her eye."

"I thought I was just making it up in my head before. Her lingering glances, innuendos, the occasional wink. It's why I never said anything, but now— Lord help me. What am I to do?"

"First of all, you haven't done anything wrong. None of this is your fault. It's that evil woman. I fear she will have it out for you now that you've denied her. Have you mentioned this to Mariam?"

Joseph's face burned. "Absolutely not. What would I say?"

"I just needed to know. The fewer people we tell, the better. The last thing we need are rumors swirling around and reaching Potiphar."

"He'd kill me in a heartbeat," Joseph said, his heart sinking.

"Most likely. You should start carrying a concealed knife. I'm not an advocate of violence, but self-defense is another thing."

"I don't think I could kill a man," said Joseph, thoroughly mortified at the thought of it.

"You might surprise yourself. We are capable of more than we imagine, both for good and for evil. You can decide about the knife, but you need to stay far away from Zuleika. Never be with her by yourself."

"Easier said than done. She's in charge of me."

"True. She is not one to give up until she gets what she wants. I am sorry, Joseph."

"Me too. I wish she had a thing for older men, then you'd have to be on the lookout."

A smile twitched on Emmanuel's face, then vanished. "If I could take this cup from you, I would. Promise me you will constantly be on your guard."

"I promise."

"Good. Then all we can do now is pray," said Emmanuel.

Joseph slipped away to the fields where he was sure not to run into Zuleika. It was long after dark before he snuck back to his room. The following morning, he didn't dare pray in the garden. He rose early and went back out into the fields. He kept this up for the better part of the week and only caught fleeting glances of Zuleika from a distance. Much to Joseph's relief, Potiphar returned from a brief excursion defending the outskirts of the city from raiders. Surely, Zuleika wouldn't dare do anything with him nearby.

That afternoon a messenger summoned him to the house for a meeting with Potiphar. He hurried back not wanting to keep his master waiting. He knocked on the door to Potiphar's office and stood at attention waiting to be called in. The door to the office opened slowly, and out slid Zuleika. Her makeup and hair were all done up, and her lips were a deep shade of red. She smiled at the surprised look on Joseph's face.

"Not who you were expecting?" she teased.

"No, Mistress. I am sorry. You surprised me, that's all."

"Oh yes, I can be full of surprises." She took a step towards him. A lump rose in Joseph's throat, and he suddenly realized that there was no one else around. "You have been avoiding me." Her lips formed a sad pouting expression.

Sweat broke out along Joseph's hairline. "N-n-no, Mistress. I've just been very busy."

She took another step towards him. "We both know that's not true."

Joseph could smell her rich perfume and was finding it hard to breathe again. "I'm sorry, Mistress. Perhaps I should return when Potiphar is present."

"You naïve boy. It wasn't my boring husband who summoned you. It was me." She placed her hand on his shoulder and ran it along his back, encircling him like a snake. Joseph shivered as Zuleika leaned in and whispered gently in his ear, "Why don't we try this again? Come to bed with me."

Joseph was hypnotized. Her smell, her warmth, her breath against his cheek. How easy it would be to slip into her dark lair. Time stood still, and two paths twisted ahead, awaiting his decision. Joseph pulled away, refusing to partake in her forbidden fruit. He turned to flee. As he did, he felt her grasp at his cloak and pull it from his shoulders, but he didn't stop. He ran down the hall and out into the garden. There in the cool of the trees he leaned over, feeling the urge to vomit. What should he do?

From inside the house came a horrible scream and then Zuleika shouting, "Help! Joseph has tried to attack me!"

Footsteps thundered as every servant and guard within earshot came to her aid. Hiding behind the bushes, Joseph began to tremble with fear.

Zuleika's voice reached a fevered pitch. "Look! I have his red cloak. My husband gave it to him. This is how he has repaid our trust. Search the grounds and find him before he tries to escape."

Against all his instincts, Joseph decided not to run. Fleeing would only make him look more guilty, and the house guards might shoot him on the spot. He knew it was a long shot, but maybe Potiphar would hear his side of the story. He sat on the ground in the shade of the garden and prayed. This is how Mariam found him and threw her arms around him.

"It can't be true. Tell me it isn't true."

Joseph hugged her back and wept. "Of course it isn't. How could I so much as look at another woman when I only have eyes for you?" He'd been aching to tell her for so long, but he'd been too afraid of losing her. What if she didn't feel the same way? But now he had nothing to lose.

Mariam burst into tears. "You have the worst timing, you know?"

"I'm sorry." Joseph held her in his arms, wishing this moment could last forever, but already he could hear people combing the grounds nearby.

"This isn't how things were supposed to end between us, Mariam, but I can't let them find you here with me. Zuleika will have your hide. I'm going to give myself up."

"Please don't." She clung to him. "At least try to escape."

"I can't. My only hope is the truth." He leaned in and kissed her gently on the cheek, savoring the sweet softness of her skin on his lips. "I've been wanting to do that for a long time." He stood and walked out into the main courtyard with his hands up. "Please don't shoot. I'm turning myself in."

The guards pointed their guns at him and advanced with military precision. Joseph kneeled with his hands behind his head. Looming over him at the front door was Zuleika. She held his cloak in a death grip, his life in her hands. Rough arms grabbed Joseph and dragged him to a small holding cell near the guard house. Zuleika sent a messenger to bring Potiphar home, and Joseph was left to wait.

All Joseph could think about was how he should have told Mariam that he loved her. Now, he'd likely never get the chance. Those unspoken words were worse than whatever pain awaited him. It was long past dark when he heard a small commotion outside the front gate. The bolts were unlocked, and a series of men holding torches came into view. Potiphar's face was like that of a terrible beast. He stormed over to the cell and thrust his torch against the metal bars. Joseph flinched but didn't retreat. He must not be a coward.

One of the guards fumbled at the lock, and Potiphar kicked at him. "Hurry up, you bumbling oaf." At last, the door swung open, and Potiphar leapt inside and grabbed Joseph by the scruff of his neck. "Come with me, boy. If half of what I heard is true, then not even your God can save you."

Joseph said nothing as Potiphar dragged him into the house and waved off the guards. "I will handle him myself."

Inside, they found Zuleika sitting stoically at the dining room table. The house was silent as a tomb, and shadows danced on the walls like spirits. Zuleika's face was streaked from crying, and Joseph's robe lay across her lap. At the sight of her husband, she burst into another round of tears.

Chest heaving, she rose from her chair and pointed her finger at Joseph. "This slave slipped into our house and tried to overpower me while you were away, my dear husband. He put his hands on me and dragged me toward our very bedroom, but I screamed for help. He tried to escape, but I grabbed hold of his cloak. I have it here as proof of his attack. This boy is a monster in disguise. I can barely stand to look at him." She fell back into the chair as if on the verge of fainting.

Potiphar bellowed with rage and pounded the table. Then he drew a long, serrated knife from his belt and held it to Joseph's throat. "I should kill you right now. Do you deny what she said?"

Joseph felt the tip of the blade tickle his Adam's apple, and fear coursed through his body. He looked past Potiphar and saw the satisfaction on Zuleika's face. She was enjoying this. It was now or never.

"I beg your pardon, Master, but I deny her statement. I have been unfairly accused. I would not slander the good name of your wife, but I swear by my God whom I serve that I am innocent. I have served you faithfully all this time, and I beg that you would spare my life. Do as you must, but know that I am innocent."

Potiphar withdrew his blade slowly. "So, it is your word against hers. Show me your arms. Are you scratched or bruised?"

Joseph held them out. "No, sir, because there was no attack, no struggle. I never laid a finger on your wife."

"Were there any witnesses to what happened?"

"The house was empty except for the two of us."

"Why were you in the house?"

"I received a message saying I was to come and see you at once."

Potiphar's eyebrows raised. "Do you have this letter?"

"I do, sir. It is in the pocket of the red cloak."

Zuleika leapt to her feet, but this time she was spitting with rage. "The boy is a liar! You must have him killed. If you love me, this boy will not see another sunrise. Will you not defend my honor?"

"I will, but first I will see the cloak."

Zuleika's face was pale as she handed it over. Joseph held his breath, praying the note was still in the pocket. It was his only hope. Potiphar reached in, fished around, and finally pulled out a small slip of paper. After reading its contents, he looked up at Joseph.

"It would seem that I have been put in an impossible position. It gives me no pleasure to do this, but I will grant both you and my wife your wishes. You will live, and her honor will be maintained. Joseph, as captain of the guard, I hereby sentence you to a lifetime in prison."

Potiphar stepped towards the large candle on the table and lit the note on fire. As he watched the proof of his innocence turn to ash, Joseph crumpled to his knees.

"Please sir, no. I'm innocent."

"The world cares not about innocence or goodness, right or wrong. All that matters is survival, and I am giving you a chance to survive. May your God have mercy on you, because no one else will."

Then Potiphar turned to Zuleika. "I hope you are satisfied."

She smiled innocently. "Of course, my sweet husband. Thank you for your protection. Now if you will, I would like to freshen up after today's most unfortunate events."

"Unfortunate indeed," remarked Potiphar as he watched her go. Her hips swayed as she sauntered off into the darkness.

"On your feet, boy. Do not make this harder than it needs to be. I will take you in myself to ensure you arrive at the prison in one piece."

Joseph's legs were heavy, and his heart was filled with dread as he rose slowly from the floor. He wanted to believe this was all some terrible nightmare, but he knew the truth. Part of him wished that Potiphar would just kill him and put an end to his misery.

As they walked out of the dining room, Joseph spotted Emmanuel. The old man stepped forward and bowed to Potiphar. "Master, please pardon my interruption. I have come to speak on behalf of Joseph."

"Save your words, Doctor. A decision has already been reached. I will permit you a minute to say farewell, but that is all."

"Thank you, sir."

Emmanuel embraced Joseph. "Do not lose heart. God will see you through. Where it seems there is no way, He will make a way. He has done it before, and He will do it again. I will pray for your deliverance and that we will see each other again."

Joseph wished he had the strength to believe Emmanuel's words. He tried to smile to reassure his old friend that all would be well, but it was a half-hearted effort. "I hope you are right. Thank you for everything," he said through tears.

Potiphar pulled them apart. "Time to go. The night is getting late." He marched Joseph into the courtyard where he was instantly surrounded by Potiphar's personal bodyguards. They tied his hands behind his back. Joseph took one last look around the compound, and his eyes fell on Mariam, peering out from behind a pillar. She waved to him, and tears glistened in her eyes like stars. A guard shoved Joseph, and he stumbled. When he looked back over his shoulder to catch a final glimpse of Mariam, she was gone.

As they made their way through Avaris, the farther away they got from the river, the more rundown things became. Shelters and shacks were built on top of each other, reminding Joseph of the old pictures of slums. The area reeked of garbage and human waste. Fires burned and curious faces stared at him from behind flickering shadows.

They emerged from a particularly seedy section of houses and approached the edge of a large walled compound topped with razor wire. Armed guards stood at the entrance, and surveillance platforms rose above the compound housing more guards. The guards snapped to attention when they saw Potiphar and immediately opened the gate.

The gate creaked open on giant, rusty hinges. The prison guards grabbed Joseph and marched him inside under the watchful eye of Potiphar. Joseph found himself in a courtyard lit only by a small central fire. Apparently, the prison's budget didn't include a generator to run lights. Even in the semi-darkness he could see how rundown the place was. It was a miracle the walls didn't cave in.

Softly muttered curses emerged from a small room nearby, and an older-looking man stumbled out. Unlike the others, he was not in uniform and had clearly just woken up, but he stood at attention before Potiphar.

Potiphar looked at the bedraggled man as if he were a stray dog. "Good evening, Warden."

"Good evening, Captain. I apologize for my lack of preparation. I was not alerted that you would be coming this evening."

"Indeed, this evening's visit was a surprise to us all. I have a new prisoner for you."

"Yes, Captain. May I ask why he is being brought in at this hour?"

"You may not."

"Very well then. Let's get the paperwork over with."

Joseph and Potiphar followed the warden to an office where the old man began to fill out some intake paperwork.

"Is there anything I should know about the prisoner?" the warden asked.

Potiphar looked at Joseph and then back at the warden. "He is highly educated and might be of help to you in the running of this fine establishment."

The warden clearly missed the sarcasm, but Joseph didn't. He also didn't miss the fact that Potiphar was throwing him a bone.

The warden's face registered surprise. "An educated prisoner? I beg your pardon, sir, but that is truly unusual. Perhaps his presence will be an unexpected gift. As you know, we are always understaffed."

"I am aware of your regular requests for increased assistance."

"I am glad to hear that, sir. I was beginning to wonder due to the lack of response."

Potiphar narrowed his eyes. "You should do less wondering and more filling out of the prisoner's paperwork. Quickly now."

"Of course, Captain. As you wish." The warden scribbled in a few more things then handed the document to Potiphar to sign. One final flourish of the pen, and Joseph was officially a prisoner of Avaris.

The large gate closed behind Potiphar, and the warden grinned at Joseph, revealing a set of twisted, yellow teeth. "Welcome home. Let me show you to your room."

Joseph followed the odd warden while flanked by two prison guards. The warden produced a large set of keys and jingled them merrily before inserting them into an oversized padlock on a stout wooden door. All the while he hummed to himself and tapped his foot to the tune. At last there was a loud click, and the rusty lock popped open. The warden unbolted the door and swung it open with gusto.

"Home sweet home. In you go."

The guards tossed Joseph into the cell, and the door banged shut behind him. The warden's face appeared in the small, barred window in the door. "Sleep tight, don't let the bedbugs bite." He laughed as if he'd told the world's funniest joke. Then he whistled and clinked his way back down the hallway, leaving Joseph completely alone.

Joseph's eyes slowly adjusted to the dark, and he took in his surroundings : a metal chair, a ratty mattress, a small bucket for doing his business, four cinder block walls. This was his life now. He slumped on the mattress, and the coiled springs stuck into his back; at least it was better than the floor. Joseph hung his head and wept bitterly.

How could this happen again? Just when things were looking up, he was back in the pit. Back in the darkness. Better he had died in the first pit than go through all of this. He heard Emmanuel's words. "Keep the faith. God will make a way."

Joseph looked up at the ceiling. Eyes wet, heart weary, and fists clenched, he spoke softly into the silence. "God if you're listening, I don't know how I'm going to make it through this. Help me, please." He didn't know what else to pray, so he rolled over and tried to sleep.

CHAPTER 13

The Prison

"Rise and shine, sleepyhead," cackled the warden as he knocked on Joseph's cell door. "Don't want you to be late for breakfast. Your new family can't wait to meet you."

Joseph shuddered. He thought he'd left awkward family meals behind him. But no use delaying the inevitable. When he walked into the small courtyard, the prisoners milling about turned and stared at him. Joseph knew exactly what was happening: they were sizing him up.

A broad-shouldered man with a sneer stamped on his ugly mug stepped toward Joseph. A scar peeked out from his thick beard, and his few remaining teeth looked like black pebbles.

"Look what the cat dragged in. What's your name, pretty boy?"

Something about this guy reminded Joseph too much of his brother Simeon, all brawn and no brain. Irritation prickled up Joseph's spine.

"I'm Joseph. It's a real pleasure to meet you. To whom do I have the joy of speaking to this fine morning?"

"Are you being smart with me, boy?"

"I tried not to use my advanced vocabulary, but perhaps it was still too advanced for you."

The man grabbed Joseph's shirt and pulled him in real close. "Now you listen here, you little twit. I'm Cain, and when the warden's not around, I run this place. I don't take kindly to people insulting me."

The all brawn no brain type rarely do, thought Joseph, but he'd already said too much. Best to try and get out of this without a black eye.

"My humblest of apologies. I won't let it happen again."

"You'd better not, or I'll shut that mouth of yours and feed you some of your own teeth. How'd you like that?"

"Not very much."

"I didn't think so," said Cain, clearly pleased with himself. "Now that we got that out of the way, let's talk about my protection fee. You give me one of your meals each week when I ask for it, no questions asked. Got it?"

A classic bully move. Simeon used to do the same thing to prove his dominance back in the bunker when Abba wasn't watching. Well, Joseph would play along for now, but not forever. He replied in his calmest voice.

"I understand."

"Good." Cain patted Joseph on the head like a child and released his grip on his shirt. "You're learning quickly. I'm feeling especially hungry this morning, so I think I'll take my protection fee now."

Joseph noticed all the other prisoners watching to see what he'd do. Half of them were probably hoping for a fight. In this case, it would be more of a pummeling. Joseph didn't plan to give them a show. "No problem," he replied.

Cain flashed his ugly smile for the whole prison to see. "I didn't think so. Now go wait in line for food and bring it to me. Then I'll introduce you to the rest of the crew."

Just then the warden popped into the courtyard. "Looks like you're already making friends, Joseph. That's good."

"Thank you, Warden." Joseph put on his best smile for the man. The warden seemed pleased and hopped up on a small stool he somehow procured out of thin air.

"Attention please. After breakfast we're going to the fields to work. Oh, silly me, I nearly forgot. A special welcome to Joseph. I trust you all will show him the ropes. Play nicely with others, all those sorts of good things. Now let's eat."

The prisoners all lined up to receive a bowl of watery gruel. There were no chairs, so they sat on the ground to drink the lukewarm liquid. Joseph had the honor of sitting next to Cain who promptly snatched his bowl and poured it into his own. "Mmmm... It always tastes better when someone fetches it for me."

Joseph tried to distract himself from Cain's loud slurping by looking around. All the prisoners were men, and all but Cain looked malnourished. They had shaggy beards, wore threadbare clothing, and hunched over their meager fare like vultures. Growing up with ten brothers meant that Joseph was used to some ripe smells, but the stench that emanated from the group was a whole other level. Bathing was definitely not a regular part of life here in prison. This was quite the family he was joining.

On the other side of the courtyard, the warden sat alone at a table. Joseph watched in awe as the man tucked a cloth napkin into his shirt and picked up a sparkling set of silverware to eat his special breakfast. He carefully cut into the hard-boiled egg on his plate and sliced it into thin sections, seemingly unaware of the filth and grime all around him as he sat on his island of decorum and gently dabbed at the corners of his mouth with his napkin.

Cain finished with a belch and then turned to Joseph. "How long are you in for?"

Joseph shrugged. "Nobody's told me anything yet."

"Lucky for you, I can help you out. Tell me what you did, and I'll give you an idea of how long you'll be here."

"I'd rather not talk about it."

"I'd rather you did," growled Cain. "In fact, I think you should tell the whole group. No secrets here amongst family. I'll go first. I'm in for murdering a man. He had it coming to him, though, so I don't feel bad about it."

Joseph was shocked by how nonchalantly he spoke of killing a man, but then he realized it was a power play to remind the rest of the inmates what he was capable of. Maybe Cain wasn't as dumb as he seemed. He had that old-fashioned neanderthal intelligence. He and Simeon would be buddies. Cain tossed his empty bowl at Joseph to put away.

"See, that's not so hard. Your turn."

The circle of prisoners stared at him, waiting for him to spill the beans. He had no choice. "Sexual assault."

Cain whistled. "Look at you, using fancy words again." He spoke to the group. "Let me translate for you lot. Our new friend here had his way with a woman against her will." He turned back to Joseph. I guess you're not as much of a gentleman as you look."

Shame flooded Joseph's body. There was no point trying to defend his name; these men would never believe him. His only solace was that Mariam knew the truth.

"I just hope it was worth it," said Cain. "I hope she was a real beauty because you're going to be in here for a long time. Looks like we'll get to be good friends."

Joseph was suddenly thankful he hadn't eaten breakfast, or he might have vomited. The warden saved him from having to reply by ringing a small silver bell.

"I do hate to be the bearer of bad news, but breakfast is over. Time for work." The men grumbled as they got to their feet and placed their bowls in an old metal tub.

"Joseph, I'll have a few words with you in my office. The rest of you can head out," said the warden as he carefully folded his cloth napkin.

"Yes, Warden," replied Joseph.

"Yes, Warden," mimicked Cain. "Don't take too long or it might seem that you aren't pulling your weight. Not a good look on your first day."

Joseph escaped to the other side of the courtyard and followed the warden into his office as the rest of the prisoners filed out under the watchful gaze of their armed guards.

The warden motioned for Joseph to sit. The office was so small it could barely hold the desk and chairs where they sat. A faded picture of flowers in a vase hung on the wall, covered in layers of dust. Van Gogh, was it? Joseph couldn't quite remember. Boxes were stacked to the ceiling, and they were partially covered by a rat-chewed tarp. The warden's desk housed a strange collection of glass items: colored marbles, a cracked green vase, shot glasses, and a set of feline salt and pepper shakers. The warden petted the salt and pepper shakers absent-mindedly as he began to speak. "This is a classic good news-bad news conversation, so which do you want first?"

Joseph tried not to let the petting of the glass figurines distract him. "I'll take the bad news first, Warden."

"Good man, get the hard part over with first. Let me say for the record that it brings me no joy to fulfill this part of my job. Do you understand?"

"Yes, Warden."

"Excellent." He cleared his throat and picked up the top sheet of paper from the overflowing pile on his desk. Holding it at arm's length, the warden squinted at the paper and began to read. "By the command of Potiphar, captain of the guard, blah, blah blah—let's get to the important part. Here it is! Joseph is hereby sentenced to twenty years hard labor for the assault of Potiphar's wife. Upon completion of his assigned sentence, the prisoner is to be banished from Avaris."

The warden continued scanning the page for a few seconds then dropped it and let it drift lazily back onto the table. "That's the bad news. You're stuck here for the next twenty years. Of course, that's if you survive."

Joseph felt all hope drain from his body. Twenty years. It might as well be a life sentence. He sighed. "Could you tell me the good news please, Warden?"

"Most certainly. Better not to let the bad news sink in too deep. Here's the good news. I am searching for a new assistant, and Potiphar thinks you might be a good fit. Not sure why. After you tried to put your hands on his wife and all, it's a miracle you're even alive. That man is terrifying. I hear he's single-handedly killed more than a hundred men." The warden shuddered, picked up one of the glass marbles, and started rubbing it with his thumb and forefinger.

After a minute he snapped back to attention. "Terrifying man, most terrifying. Anyhow, here's how the job will work. You'll work part time in the fields and part time here in the prison with me. You'll have a three-month trial, and if I'm pleased with your work, then the job is yours permanently. What do you say to that?"

A small flicker of hope reignited within Joseph.

"When do I start?" Joseph knew that Cain wouldn't be happy, but making himself indispensable to the warden might provide him some protection. It was a risk he had to take.

"Splendid. You'll start tomorrow morning. Now wash up the dishes from breakfast. When you're done, you'll be escorted to the fields to join the rest of the prisoners."

With that, the conversation was over. Joseph made his way to the stack of dishes and began to work. He didn't mind it so much—it actually reminded him a little of home. When the last dish was scrubbed and dried, he stood up and stretched.

The warden appeared out of nowhere, scaring him half to death. "You work fast. Most of the inmates take twice that long."

"Thank you, Warden. I've had a lot of practice. I had ten older brothers back at home."

"Ten brothers," sputtered the warden. "I didn't even know such a thing was possible in today's world. How did you manage to feed all those mouths?"

Joseph smiled, sensing an opportunity. "Technology. I bet I could do it here, too, and double or triple your output on the prison farm."

The warden drummed his fingers on his chin. "You've got—what's the word, wait, it'll come to me—chutzpah! Yes, chutzpah, I like that. Perhaps Potiphar was right about you. You might be of use after all. Triple the farm output, and I'd be a rich man, not to mention the apple of Pharaoh's eye."

"I would see that you got all the credit," declared Joseph.

"Of course I would," scoffed the warden. "You don't think I'd let a slave receive the glory. Oh no, that wouldn't do. They'd take you from me, and where would I be? Best if people forget you even exist. Now go and see the farm and give me a full report when you return."

The warden was wringing his hands with glee and spending money he did not yet have as Joseph was escorted away by the guards. That was a good sign for Joseph. Now all he had to do was make good on his word to the warden.

CHAPTER 14

The Farm

For all the time he'd lived in Avaris, Joseph knew very little about the city. He hadn't been allowed to travel outside Potiphar's property, which he realized was a different world from the poor part of town he now called home. The prison was on the outskirts of Avaris. No surprise, the wealthy didn't want to see or be near the dregs of society.

Joseph couldn't help but admire the ingenuity of the poor as they scraped out a living for themselves. These people were survivors. This city with its houses crammed on top of one another would have been called a slum before the apocalypse. Now, Avaris was the wealthiest and greatest city in the world, the crown jewel of humanity. These ash-covered citizens were the luckiest people alive.

The few people Joseph saw as his guard led him to the fence that ringed the city paid him little attention. They were used to seeing prisoners. He was just another low life. Just inside the fence, Joseph and his guard stopped at a checkpoint manned by three heavily armed soldiers dressed in mismatched camouflage uniforms.

"State your business," demanded the oldest-looking of the three soldiers. Joseph could tell by his demeanor that he was in charge. The prison guard took a step forward and stood at attention.

"I have a prisoner to bring to the fields for labor, Sergeant."

The sergeant rose from the chair where he'd been sitting with his feet propped up on a pile of sandbags. "He's a little late for work, isn't he?"

"Yes, Sergeant. He's new. Just came in last night, and the warden had to get him settled."

"I see. Let me get a good look at you boy." Joseph stood still while the man approached him, leaning in so close Joseph could smell the rankness of his breath. The sergeant stepped back after a few seconds. "What's your name prisoner?"

"Joseph, sir."

The sergeant smiled. "This one has manners. That's a good start. Well, Joseph, let me tell you a few things that will make your life much easier. First, I never forget a face. So, if you try to escape, I will find you and I will kill you. If you don't believe me, ask the other prisoners who have been here more than a year. That's about when I killed my last runaway."

Joseph nodded attentively.

"Second, my men patrol the perimeter of the fence. If there's any funny business involving prisoners, they have been advised to shoot first and ask questions later. Third, before you leave the fence, you will always wear leg irons. This will allow you to do your work but will stop you from being able to run away. You will pick up your leg irons here each day before work. Do you understand?"

"Yes, sir."

"Excellent. That'll be all." The sergeant returned to his seat, and Joseph was fitted with leg irons. They clapped around his ankles sending a chill up Joseph's spine. Walking with the irons was tricky, but by the time he got to the farm he'd mostly gotten the hang of it. Already though, he could feel blisters forming where the cold metal chafed against his exposed skin.

Up ahead, the other prisoners were at work in a dry field. The soil was mostly ash, and only a few scraggly wheat plants had managed to push through the ground. The prisoners dug haphazardly, like children in a giant sandbox. There was no rhyme or reason to their efforts. The guards formed a perimeter around the field, watching the prisoners work, but they were clearly much more interested in playing cards and chatting. This was all a form of glorified babysitting.

Joseph turned to the guard escorting him. "What happens to the food the prisoners produce?"

"Some goes to the prison, and the rest goes to Pharaoh. And the warden takes a small cut."

"Who's in charge of the farm?"

"That would be the warden, but he rarely comes out to supervise."

Joseph continued to pepper the guard with questions, and it didn't take long before his hunch was confirmed that the farming was more of an excuse to keep the prisoners busy than anything else. There were almost no expectations that the prisoners would produce a good crop because the land was so bad. It was all a joke.

The guard finally growled at him. "Stop trying to get out of work. Go and find Cain. He runs things for the most part."

Joseph could see that. It annoyed him to no end to be under Cain's command. Not far away, Cain was leaning on a makeshift shovel, giving orders. When he spotted Joseph, he smiled that hellish smile of his. "Well, well, well, look who decided to finally show up. I've been saving the best job of all for you."

Joseph's hackles rose. This was not going to be good.

There were a couple of chuckles from the surrounding prisoners, and Joseph grimaced. He knew the drill—make fun of the new guy and force him to submit. Cain was the alpha. Joseph would have to deal with Cain, but all in good time. For now, he needed to play along and not be a threat to the hierarchy.

"And what might that be?" asked Joseph.

"It's real simple. See that bucket over there?"

Joseph nodded.

Cain rubbed his hands wickedly. "That's for carrying human waste. It's how we make the soil all nice so we can grow this precious grain to make bread for the Great Pharaoh."

Joseph wanted to make a snarky comment about how pathetic the crop was, but for once he held his tongue. He could see where this job was headed, and it was not a pleasant trajectory.

Cain continued, "Lucky for you we got a nice big pit of the stuff for you to use. A giant hole just filled with—"

"I get it," Joseph said. "Is this solo duty, or do I have a partner to work with?"

"I think for today we'll make it a solo job, but you'll need someone to show you where to go on your first trip." Cain looked at the prisoners who were all suddenly hard at work, save for one.

"Sticks, you can be his tour guide."

The man nodded to Cain and walked over to Joseph. He seemed to move in slow motion. His leg irons clinked, and his body teetered like a man walking on stilts. Joseph had a sense that this man couldn't rush even if he tried. When Sticks got close, he spoke in a gentle, lilting voice. "Come on now. I'll show you where to go."

Joseph picked up the bucket. It buzzed with flies and stank to high heaven. Why couldn't flies have died out in the apocalypse? He did his best to not act bothered by the bucket or the flies, and he felt Cain's eyes on him as he and Sticks walked back across the field and inside the fence. All of this was a test.

Joseph could smell their destination long before they arrived at the cesspool of human feces. At some point in Avaris's development, a massive pit had been dug and slowly filled with excrement. A crude wooden walkway jutted out over the pit like a bridge that had only been half built. It was about three meters high so the locals could toss their waste into the pit without getting splashed.

At the end of the walkway was a small pulley system. Sticks pointed to it. "That contraption is for lowering your bucket into the pit. Then you carry it back and dump it wherever Cain tells you. Nice and simple."

Joseph just barely managed to control his gag reflex. "Thank you. Not sure what is worse, having to carry this mess or having to do whatever Cain tells me to do."

"You got that right," laughed Sticks. "Just between you and me, don't cross Cain. If you shut up and do what you're told, he'll forget about you soon enough. Sort of like dealing with a wild animal. No sudden movements. Move nice and slow, be quiet, and you'll be all right."

Joseph groaned. "People have been telling me to shut up my whole life. Turns out I'm just no good at it."

Sticks gave a long, low whistle. "Then you are in for a whole heap of trouble, but I'll be here if you need something. The first few weeks can be real tough."

"Thank you. Can I ask why they call you Sticks?"

Sticks leaned down and pulled up his pant legs. "On account of my legs being long and skinny, like two sticks. Not much of a story really."

He wasn't lying. Sticks was a good head taller than any of the other prisoners and probably weighed less than most. He reminded Joseph of a stork bird he'd seen pictures of in one of his old books.

Joseph tried to keep the conversation going. "Let me guess, Cain gave you that nickname?"

Sticks smiled. "Good guess. He'll give you one in time too. When he does, don't fight it."

"I won't. Anything else I should know?"

"Make sure the bucket is good and full, otherwise Cain will get upset. You don't want that. You seem like a good kid. Try and stay out of trouble, and if you need anything, you come find me."

Sticks turned and strolled away as if the foul stench of the pit wasn't even there. Joseph watched the man's long, skinny legs carrying him away. He was as cool as a cucumber. Joseph wondered what nickname he would get. Only time would tell, but at least something good had come of today. He liked Sticks.

Joseph spent the rest of the day carrying buckets of waste back and forth to the field. He lost count of the number of trips he made, but each time he got back to the field, Cain was there leaning on his shovel with a twinkle in his eye as he ordered Joseph around. When the guards finally called a halt, Joseph wanted to collapse. His arms and shoulders ached. His legs burned, and he was covered in a layer of slimy excrement.

From a safe distance away, Cain called out to him. "Hey, smelly, I think with a few more days of practice you'll manage to get more crap in the bucket than on your clothes." Cain snorted at his own joke, and the other prisoners laughed politely. Joseph had a feeling this wasn't the first time they'd heard this particular zinger.

With Cain in the lead, the group filed back to prison. Joseph waited until the end of the line and made sure there was some distance between himself and Sticks, who happened to be the last prisoner. Sticks looked at Joseph with pity, then spoke in a low voice.

"I can't make too big of a show of helping you because of Cain. He has a thing about enjoying the suffering of others. Can't change that, but when we get back to the prison, I'll get you a bucket of river water so you can rinse off. Just wait outside the main gate."

"Thank you," Joseph whispered back. Sticks' genuine act of human kindness warmed his heart. Sticks was true to his word and even brought Joseph a second bucket after the first became thoroughly contaminated. Joseph said a prayer of thanks as he did his best to wash off the remnants of his day's disgusting work. He only had one pair of clothes, so he stripped down and washed them. Being wet and clean was the better of his two options.

When Joseph was finally clean, he walked into the courtyard. Most of the prisoners were huddled around Cain, who was busy telling a story. The rest were begrudgingly helping with dinner.

Joseph didn't particularly want to be around Cain, and he assumed the prisoners wouldn't want him contaminating the food, so he sat in a corner by himself to observe. There were seventeen prisoners and ten guards. The courtyard was small with walls made of thick concrete. He could see where it had been patched and repaired numerous times. Broken glass bottles were stuck into the top of the wall along with a healthy dose of barbed wire to deter prisoners escaping. The ground was dirt, packed hard by the wear of many feet. Next to him was a small doorway that led to the cells, most of which housed two prisoners. Across the courtyard, just off the main gate, was the warden's office.

He had the only furniture in the whole place. There was no color, no comfort, no culture— just survival.

When dinner was called, Joseph took his place at the back of the line. The faint smell of food made his stomach growl, and he wolfed down the small bowl of soup without even tasting it. Shortly after, one of the guards approached him.

"The warden will see you now."

Joseph nodded. It was time for his report.

He sat in the spindly chair opposite the warden and tried not to stare enviously at the bit of flat bread that remained on the warden's plate from his dinner. The warden leaned back and stroked his beard, which emerged from his chin like a billy goat. Joseph waited for him to speak.

"Unless my nose deceives me, you were given the honor of bucket duty today."

"Your nose is correct, Warden."

The warden nodded his head and scooted his chair away from Joseph ever so slightly.

"A bit of a rite of passage as I understand it."

"Just a little welcome to the neighborhood. I have no complaints," said Joseph as he inched his own chair backwards towards the door. He didn't want to overwhelm the warden with his stench.

"Glad to hear you're taking it in stride. I don't much appreciate complainers, but what I would appreciate is your assessment of the farm."

"Sir, I don't mean to delay, but I would ask that you give me two weeks so I have time to make a full report to you. I would hate to jump to any hasty conclusions."

The warden studied Joseph. "My father used to say, 'slow and steady wins the race.'"

"My father had a similar saying: the slow tree bears much fruit."

"An odd saying, but, oh, what I wouldn't give for a sweet pomegranate," the warden pined. "Alas, we must settle for lesser things." He glanced at the remnants of his dinner and pushed the plate away. "The smell of you has curdled my appetite. Report back in two weeks' time. You are dismissed."

Joseph apologized for his stink and hurried out of the cramped office.

CHAPTER 15

A New Sheriff in Town

When Joseph rose the next day, he was pretty sure every muscle in his body was on fire. He rolled off the sorry excuse for a mattress and stretched like Emmanuel had taught him.

After a few minutes the warden began his rounds, and Joseph joined the rest of the prisoners in the courtyard. The faint glow of the sun was just creeping over the horizon, and Joseph shivered in the chilly morning air.

Cain was already seated on the large rock that served as his courtyard throne. Joseph tried to avoid eye contact, but Cain waved him over. Cain leaned back against the wall and looked like he'd slept like a baby. Joseph's body twinged with every step he took. Being sore would have been bad enough, but he'd barely slept as he shivered his way through the night in his wet clothes. After a few steps, Cain called for him to stop.

"That's close enough. Can't have the smell of you ruining my breakfast."

Joseph froze. The last thing he wanted was more trouble, but he guessed it was coming his way no matter what he did. Cain's piggy eyes squinted at him.

"Tell me what the warden wanted with you last night. He doesn't normally have meetings with prisoners, certainly not ones that smell like you."

Joseph shrugged. "Just new prisoner stuff. The meeting didn't last long when he got a good whiff of me." He tried to keep things light, and Cain took the bait and chuckled.

"Can't blame him, but you listen here. If you think you're going to weasel your way onto the warden's good side to get special treatment, you have another think coming. He may do the books, but I run this prison." He said the last part loud enough for the prisoners nearby to hear. They all nodded. "Have I made myself clear?" asked Cain.

"Loud and clear," replied Joseph.

"Good. A few more days of bucket duty will help make sure the message sticks. Now get out of here."

Joseph retreated to the corner until breakfast was served and then took his place at the back of the line. Sticks was in front of him and turned around to talk.

"A little word of advice for your second day. Just do half buckets. Easier to carry, less messy, and Cain already made his point with you. Just imagine you're somewhere else, and the time will fly by. That's what I do."

Sticks' words brought Joseph immediate relief. He could have hugged him, but he didn't want to rub his stink off on the poor man.

"Thanks for the tip. How long do you think Cain will have me on bucket duty?"

"That all depends on how long it takes for him to break you. Show him you're not a threat, and it'll just be a few days. You do something or say something stupid, it'll be longer."

"So, insulting his intelligence in front of the rest of the prisoners would be a bad idea?"

Sticks snorted. "Oh boy, you really do have a death wish. Cain tends to be a little sensitive when it comes to comment about his smarts, or lack thereof."

"I would, too, if I was dumb as a rock and walked around like a caveman."

"Better not say that too loudly. He's got spies. I'm not one of them, but be careful. There are worse things than carrying crap all day."

"Yeah, like being ruled by a maniacal tyrant in a dirty prison in a post-apocalyptic wasteland? How's that sound?"

"Sounds like my life the past three years. You'll get used to it."

I don't think so, thought Joseph. He'd play along for now, but in a few weeks they'd all see who was really in charge of the prison, the warden or Cain. Joseph sure hoped he was tossing his lot in with the right one.

After three more days of bucket duty and more self-control than Joseph had thought possible, Cain called the prisoners to circle around Joseph after dinner. Once everyone was in place, he launched into a little speech.

"Listen up! As the leader of this little gang, I declare that Joseph has done his time on bucket duty and is ready to be promoted. With his promotion comes a new name. From now on he will be called 'Mouse.'" He leaned in and said to Joseph, so only he could hear, "That's because you are small and insignificant. Don't ever forget it."

This was not a joyful rite of passage ceremony. It was the creation of a power-hungry egomaniac. Joseph looked Cain in the eye. "I receive my name." Then, playing to the crowd of prisoners, he declared, "From now on call me Mouse. Joseph is dead."

There was a smattering of fake applause, and afterwards some of the prisoners clapped him on the back and shook his hand. The last was Sticks.

"Congratulations, Mouse. Now you're one of us."

"Thank you. I appreciate your help, and I will find a way to pay you back."

"The best payment is friendship. A man can't have too many friends in this place. Plus, I like your spirit."

"That sounds like a deal to me. Friends." Joseph stuck his hand out, and Sticks took it.

"Friends," replied Sticks.

Joseph was one of them now, a prisoner of Avaris. That night, he lay in bed and thought about his new nickname. He couldn't help but laugh, because what Cain had meant as an insult, he took as a compliment. Mice were survivors. One of the few creatures to make it through the apocalypse. They were careful and quick and hard to kill. Cain would learn soon enough that all these things were also true of Joseph.

The next day, "Mouse" was promoted to digging. There wasn't much clarity as to what he was supposed to be digging, only that he should always look busy. The next two weeks dragged on for what felt like an eternity, the days blending together. At night Joseph lay on his mattress and thought of Mariam. Did she miss him? How was Zuleika treating her? Was there a way that he could communicate with her? He wished he could just walk down the hall to visit her, to smell her, to hear her laughter and be lost in her eyes. He vowed to find a way to get back to her.

At last, the two weeks had passed, and it was time for Joseph to meet with the warden. Joseph was summoned after dinner and could sense Cain's gaze as he walked across the courtyard. The man would want some answers.

Joseph's heart hammered as he sat down in the warden's office. The warden was busy caressing his glass cats and staring off into space. He didn't seem to notice Joseph's presence for the longest time. When he finally did, he jumped so hard that he nearly fell out of his chair.

"I say, I beg your pardon. I was having one of my daydreams," he said as he regained his composure. "It's a sad thing to be pulled into the present, but nonetheless we must make do with what we have."

He went back to stroking his cats and looked up at Joseph inquisitively. Joseph tried to smile and act as if nothing unusual had just happened. He took a deep breath to calm himself. This was the moment of truth.

"Sir, after observing the farm for the past two weeks I would say you have two major issues. The first is access to water."

The warden rolled his eyes. "It doesn't take a genius to figure that out. Our plot is too far removed from the river. There's no irrigation out here."

Joseph nodded. "I assumed that was the case. I have some ideas to improve the water situation. That will be the easy part."

The warden leaned forward, suddenly more engaged. He looked pleased and twirled his ring finger in his pointy beard. "That is what I like to hear. Even fools can see problems, but a wise man can see solutions. Now tell me the second problem."

Joseph hesitated for a moment. "Sir, your biggest problem is not the water. It's management. It's clear that Cain doesn't know what he's doing. Most of the men's time is being wasted. With a competently managed crew of seventeen men, we could run a proper farm."

The warden frowned. "What you are really saying is that if *you* were in charge, things would improve."

Joseph nodded. "That is precisely what I'm saying, but I'll need protection. Cain's not going to like me being put in charge instead of him, not one little bit."

The warden nodded. "The man is a menace. Reminds me a bit of the old rugby chums back in the day. It seems we find ourselves in a delicate situation, then. What would you propose?"

This was the opening Joseph had been hoping for, and he didn't hold back. He spent the next thirty minutes relating his plan to the warden and emerged from the office feeling confident. But as soon as stepped back into the courtyard, a powerful hand grabbed his shirt and yanked him off his feet. He found himself staring straight into Cain's glowering eyes.

"If you know what's good for you, you're going to tell me exactly what your little meeting was all about."

The courtyard fell silent, all eyes and ears focused on the two of them.

"Put me down. I don't answer to you," Joseph said calmly.

"Like hell you don't. Everyone here answers to me," shouted Cain. He tossed Joseph to the ground like a rag doll and brought his foot down on his chest with such force Joseph was sure his ribs were broken.

Fists balled, Cain snarled at Joseph. "Give me an answer if you like your teeth the way they are now, pipsqueak."

"Take your foot off my chest, and I'll tell you everything," Joseph wheezed as he struggled to breathe.

"That's more like it. No need to do things the hard way." Cain took his foot off Joseph's chest, but not before he gave him one last rib-cracking squeeze. Feeling a little wobbly, Joseph gingerly got back on his feet, clutching his ribs. Maybe they weren't broken, but they were certainly bruised. He wished Emmanuel were here to check him out. He ran his tongue over his teeth, hoping he'd get to keep them all. It was time to lie his way out of this.

"You win, Cain. The warden learned that I can read and write, and he wants me to help him with some record-keeping. That's all."

Cain cocked his head. "What's in it for you? Because if there's something in it for you, then there better be something in it for me."

"There will be. The warden offered me one small loaf of bread a week, which I planned to split with you. It's a win-win."

Cain grunted. "You bring me the loaf, and I'll do the splitting." He shoved Joseph back down onto the ground. "I don't like you, Mouse. A little bread won't change that." He stormed off. Joseph took a second to catch his breath and thank God that he was still alive and mostly in one piece. Tomorrow would be the day of reckoning.

The next day Joseph woke early, stretched, and took a few moments to pray. Today might very well require some divine intervention. After breakfast, the prisoners lined up with Cain in the front and Joseph in the back. *The first shall be last and the last shall be first,* thought Joseph as the warden stepped out of his office to address the prisoners, much to the surprise of everyone except Joseph.

The warden was flanked by two guards with guns ready, and there was an unsettled murmuring amongst the prisoners. Naturally, the warden was oblivious. He clapped his hands theatrically and began to speak. "Today is a very special day. I have some extraordinarily important news to share. Some good and"—he paused for emphasis—"some bad. Let me start with the bad news."

The prisoners shifted nervously, and the warden raised his hands to calm them. "No need to be alarmed. Unless, of course, you are guilty."

Joseph felt the anxiety rising among the prisoners. The warden needed to get on with it before things got out of control, but the warden was not a man to be rushed. The old buffoon began to pace as he spoke.

"It has come to my attention that we have someone in our midst who believes himself to be the true prison warden; moreover, someone who has attempted to usurp my authority. There is, as they used to say, a snake in the grass." He held out the last syllable and stared at the men with his wild, shifty eyes.

Joseph shot a glance at Cain. The big man stood rigid with fists clenched and face smoldering. The warden clapped his hands again, and two guards stepped forward. The warden unveiled a toothy grin. "Gentlemen, please subdue the snake."

Before anyone could react, the guards grabbed Cain. He tried to squirm away until the barrel of a gun pressed against his neck. The guards dragged Cain through the dirt and deposited him at the warden's feet, who calmly placed his foot on Cain's head. "He comes to me on his belly, just like a snake. Do you have anything to say for yourself, you conniving serpent?"

Cain spoke quietly, his spittle dripping into the dirt. "I was only trying to help keep things orderly, Warden. I swear on my mother's grave."

The warden looked appalled. "Let us leave your poor mother out of this. I am sure she would be rolling over in her grave if she could see you now. Cain, I am hereby relieving you of your self-appointed duty to keep order. I am a lenient man, so I will let you live. It is more than you deserve. Have I made myself clear?"

"Yes," Cain mumbled.

"A little louder so everyone can hear."

"Yes," said Cain with a rage that caused the guards to tighten their grips on their guns.

"Stupendous. Now for the good news. I would like to formally appoint a new leader. Joseph, would you please step forward?"

Another murmur ran through the prisoners. Joseph glanced nervously at Cain and then stepped forward and cleared his throat. "Warden, I am ready to serve as you best see fit."

"Music to my ears. I hereby place Joseph in charge of running the prison farm. You will listen to him and do as he says. Should anyone so much as lay a finger on him, they will answer with their life. Do you understand?"

There was a chorus of "yeses" from the prisoners, even Cain. A wave of anticipation rippled through Joseph. This was his moment to take charge. He turned toward the men.

"I do not take my new position lightly. I promise to serve you as best as I can. I will not lead with violence or threats, but with fairness. It is in all our best interests to work together. The more food we grow, the more we get to eat. My father trained me to grow plants from the time I was a child, and I plan to use that knowledge to benefit each one of you. If you listen and do as I say, we can succeed. Are you with me?"

The men cheered at the promise of more food. As Joseph walked over to Cain it was difficult not to gloat. "Cain, you answer to me now. I need you to affirm that for the men to hear."

"I answer to you," he spat.

A smug smile crept across Joseph's face. "Good, now that we are clear on the new chain of command, my first official order is to assign you to bucket duty for the next month. If you behave well during that time, then you will be promoted to digging. If not, you will continue as long as necessary until you are thoroughly reformed."

Joseph could see the smiles on the faces of the men as Cain got a taste of his own medicine. He just hoped this whole plan would work. Time would tell, but for the moment things were going according to plan. He was on his way up again.

And he sure wished that Mariam could see him.

CHAPTER 16

Unexpected Visitors

In the month since Joseph assumed leadership, he'd divided the men into three work teams and assigned each team a different job. As a symbol of his new position as foreman, Joseph no longer had to wear leg irons. This allowed him to move back and forth between the groups of workers with ease. Gone were the days of standing around pretending to shovel dirt. The farm hummed with a sense of purpose under Joseph's watchful eye. All the while, Cain made trips back and forth to the sewage pit, muttering threats under his breath.

Darkness was falling, and one of the guards gave the command to halt work. Joseph watched the prisoners line up to tromp back to the prison. His gaze drifted to the small plot of land they'd been busily transforming into a real farm. It was a thing of beauty. Abba would be proud. Beyond their farm, the land was flat and barren as far as the eye could see. Somewhere out of sight were towering mountains, and beyond them was the bunker.

He felt a pang of homesickness. Was Abba still alive? Were his brothers? Did they regret what they'd done to him?

As he stared at the horizon, he noticed something strange. Shapes moved stealthily in the dusky shadows, darting from one rocky outcrop to another. Joseph looked more carefully, and, sure enough, the shapes moved in unison, and they were headed toward him. He would swear that the shapes were human.

Joseph turned to one of the guards nearby and motioned subtly to him. The guard walked over. "What is it? You're not in charge of me," said the man gruffly.

Joseph spoke in a hushed voice. "I'm sorry, but I think there are people out there. If you look carefully—"

An explosion rent the air, and the guard staggered and cursed as a bullet ripped through his shoulder. In an instant, the air was alive with bullets. Tiny balls of fire whizzed all around Joseph.

Chaos broke out as the prisoners ran for cover, tripping over their leg irons. The guards abandoned their posts and ran for cover as well. Time seemed to slow as bullets zipped by and men screamed and fought one another to get to the gate. Bodies fell to the ground and writhed in pain.

Joseph looked over his shoulder and saw men with painted faces dressed in camouflage, demons emerging from the desert. Adrenaline pumping, Joseph ran toward the gate, but someone grabbed him and wrestled him to the ground. Lying on his back, he stared into Cain's face.

Cain's eyes burned with hatred. He seemed oblivious to the pandemonium around them as he pinned Joseph's arms to the ground with his knees and snarled like a wild animal. "We're all going to die, Mouse, but I won't let these bandits have the satisfaction of taking your life. I'll do it myself."

Cain raised a large stone to strike. Joseph closed his eyes and whispered, "Adonai, have mercy on me, a sinner." He waited for the blow to come but instead felt Cain's body tense and then slump to the side. Joseph opened his eyes and saw his enemy lying beside him. Cain's shirt was slowly growing scarlet, and his eyes were wild, even in death.

The soldiers at the gate regained some measure of order and began to retaliate, which was bad news for Joseph because he was now caught in the crossfire. He lay motionless, pretending to be dead as he listened to the cries of the wounded all around him. He'd read about skirmishes and firefights in the tales about the Great War, but nothing could have prepared him for this, the true horror of war.

He stayed flat on the ground for what felt like an eternity. Gunfire, shouting, moaning, smoke drifting over him like a sulfuric shroud. He waited for the enemy to find him. He heard them moving nearby but stayed still as a corpse. His ears throbbed from the gunshots, and it took everything in him not to cover them. Eventually he realized that the gunfire had ceased. He waited to be sure. Slowly, Joseph rolled over and found himself staring into Cain's unblinking brown eyes. The man would have happily killed him in cold blood, but he was still a person. Joseph reached over and closed Cain's eyes.

"I forgive you. May Adonai bless you and keep you and cause His face to shine upon you and give you peace." He felt like he should say more, but he began to sob, because in the face of Cain, he had seen the faces of his brothers. It was all too much. Too much hurt. Too much sorrow, and underneath it all was the call to forgive. To rise out of the blood-stained dirt and keep living.

Joseph felt a hand on his shoulder, then someone pulled him to his feet. It was dark, and his vision was blurred by tears. He couldn't see who his rescuer was, but then the man spoke.

"Joseph?"

Embarrassed, Joseph hurriedly tried to wipe away his tears. Before him stood none other than Potiphar. There was an awkward moment as neither man knew exactly what to say. Joseph broke the tension. "Thank you for fighting off the raiders, sir. It would seem that once again I owe you my life.

"It would seem that once again you have given me a reason to believe there might very well be a God looking out for you."

"It would certainly seem that way, sir."

"Are you hurt?"

"No, sir. Just a few scrapes and cuts."

Potiphar shook his head in wonder. "That's a minor miracle. I'll have the doctor look at you, just in case. Can't have the new overseer of the prison farm out of commission."

Joseph's eyes grew wide with surprise. "How did you know that, sir?"

"I make it my job to know. Plus, I'm curious to see what happens to you. Call it intuition, but I think our paths will cross again."

"Thank you, sir. I hope your intuition is correct."

"It usually is. Go back to the gate and wait for the doctor." With that, he turned and darted off.

Still reeling, Joseph made his way to the gate where he found the other surviving prisoners. Most of them were in rough shape. A handful rocked back and forth in shock while others tried to stop the blood flowing from their cuts and bullet wounds. Joseph watched as Potiphar and his soldiers disappeared into the darkness in pursuit of the attackers, then he turned back to the injured men.

Joseph had always been squeamish around blood. One of his many traits that his brothers had mocked, but he knew he needed to do something. Grimacing, he kneeled by the nearest prisoner and gently touched his arm. The man flinched.

"I'm here to help," said Joseph. "Let's get that bleeding stopped." Joseph took off his shirt and tore it into strips. He began to wrap the man's shoulder, and it took everything in him not to vomit as the sight of so much raw flesh. Once the shoulder was wrapped tightly, he moved on.

He was halfway through the group of injured men when he heard his name. Joseph would have known that voice anywhere, and it filled him with joy.

Emmanuel. The doctor. Of course.

Joseph leapt up and ran to his friend, engulfing him in a massive hug. "I can't believe it. I never thought I'd see you again," he cried.

Emmanuel wasn't bothered by Joseph's blood-covered hands wrapped around his torso and hugged him right back. The old man's eyes were filled with tears as he choked out words.

"Joseph, oh how it does my heart good to see you. There will be time to talk later. First off, are you hurt badly?"

Joseph shook his head.

"Okay then, let's tend to the injured."

Side by side, they cared for the men. Emmanuel moved swiftly, making the most of the few items in his medical kit. The last man they came to was Sticks. Joseph gasped when Emmanuel lifted Sticks' shirt to reveal an ugly bullet wound just above his hip. Sticks' eyes had a glazed look, and he'd clearly lost a lot of blood. Emmanuel gently assessed the wound while Joseph tried his best to hold Sticks still.

"The bullet is still inside," said Emmanuel. "I need to get it out immediately. In the old days we would have taken this man in for surgery, but I don't think there's anything we can do for him here."

Emmanuel's words made Joseph feel sick to his stomach. "Please, you have to try. He's a good man, a friend, his name is Sticks."

"I will do my best, but I can't make any promises," said Emmanuel hesitantly.

Emmanuel calmly explained to Sticks that what he was about to do was going to be excruciatingly painful, and there would be no pain medicine. Avaris did not allow such things to be used on prisoners. "So, would you like us to still try and extract the bullet?"

Sticks couldn't even get up the strength to speak. Instead, he gave a feeble nod of his head. Joseph wadded up the remains of his shirt for Sticks to use as a pillow, and Emmanuel pulled out a set of long, sharp tweezers. It was so dark that Joseph wondered how Emmanuel would be able to find the bullet, but there appeared to be no time to waste.

Joseph clamped down on Sticks' shoulders, and Emmanuel inserted the tweezers. Sticks gasped and went rigid.

"Try and stay still. Focus on your breathing," whispered Joseph, as Emmanuel dug around, searching for the bullet lodged somewhere deep inside. Drops of sweat beaded on Emmanuel's forehead as he worked without success. Sticks writhed in pain, and Joseph did his best to hold him down, marveling that Sticks could endure such pain without passing out. At long last Emmanuel let out a "Hallelujah!" and Joseph joined him in his jubilation.

Emmanuel cleaned off the small chunk of metal and handed it to Sticks. "You're a brave man. Keep this as a reminder of the day God gave you a miracle. You're not out of the woods yet, but at least now you have a fighting chance."

"Thank you," mouthed Sticks as he took the bullet and held it to his chest.

"What do we do next?" asked Joseph.

Emmanuel looked down at Sticks with compassion. "First, I need to bandage him up. Then we get these men back to the prison, and we pray for the best."

Two guards stood at the front gate of the prison with torches and guns when they finally returned. *Cowards*, thought Joseph. *These were the same men who ran away at the first sight of danger.*

Inside, the warden anxiously paced the courtyard, mumbling to himself as the prisoners limped in. Only eleven returned. Joseph and Emmanuel had taken up the rear position to keep the stragglers moving. Together they'd half-carried, half-dragged Sticks back. He was in the worst shape of the survivors.

The warden rounded on Joseph. "I need to know what in God's name happened out there. Come to my office."

Joseph soon found himself recounting the events in private while the warden vigorously petted his glass cats while shaking his head disapprovingly.

When Joseph finished his story, the warden leapt up and began to walk in circles around his chair. He spoke out loud but seemed to be talking to himself rather than to Joseph.

"I say, I knew this would happen. I knew that word of a thriving city like Avaris would get out, and we'd all be in trouble. This is just the beginning." Then the warden froze. He turned toward Joseph as if surprised to see him there. "Joseph—yes, of course, we were talking. The hour is late, so I will release you."

"Thank you, Warden, but if you don't mind, I'd like to ask you a question first."

"Just one, and then off you go."

Joseph nodded. "Sir, when you say this is 'just the beginning,' what exactly do you mean?"

The warden massaged his brow. "You're too young to remember the way things were. The way humans fought and squabbled over everything. There was no end to their greed and destruction. It's what led to the Great War, that horrible culmination of human evil. And now even as Avaris rises from the ashes, the greedy and the jealous are circling like buzzards. Today was just a test. A test of our strength and our readiness. If what you said is true, war is coming, Joseph. Mark my words."

The warden's ominous words chilled Joseph to the bone.

Having given his soapbox speech, the warden flopped back into his chair with a sigh. "You should go," he said.

"Thank you. You have given me much to think about."

The warden didn't reply. His attention had already drifted away, like a leaf on a river.

The prisoners had been herded back into their rooms for the night by the time Joseph emerged. Only Emmanuel remained. His gentle eyes were illuminated by the ambient light from the torches. They were the only two stars shining on this dark night. Joseph sat beside him in silence. Only then did the adrenaline begin to wear off, and Joseph realized how exhausted he was. He looked at Emmanuel. "I take it you will be staying the night?"

"Yes."

"Then it will be like old times."

"Indeed, it will be."

A few minutes later, Emmanuel was snoring softly in Joseph's small cell. There was something wonderfully comforting about having his old friend nearby. Maybe it was from years of sleeping with a slew of brothers in the bunker, but hearing the breathing of another human calmed him. At least for one night, he was not alone in this place.

As tired as he was, Joseph couldn't sleep. Seeing Emmanuel had reminded him of Mariam. He wanted to sneak out of the room and knock on her door. He wanted to listen to her laugh and see her smile. He wished he'd had the courage to reach out and take her hand in his and kiss her perfect lips when he had the chance. But he was too late. She'd slipped through his fingers, and like everything else, she was gone.

When sleep finally came, he dreamed of Mariam, of what might have been. He was pulled from the sound of her sweet laughter by someone pounding on the main gate of the prison. Then a heavy rap on Joseph's cell door made him jump. This was followed by an assortment of savory curses as one of the guards fumbled with his keys and struggled with the lock. There was a click, and the door swung open. The prison guard looked like he'd been dragged out of bed and was not very happy about it.

"This way. The warden wants you," he said, stifling a yawn.

Joseph looked at Emmanuel. He'd rolled over during the commotion but was somehow still asleep. Let the old man rest. Let him dream of happier times. Joseph slipped on his shoes and followed the guard. Out in the courtyard things were a jumbled mess. A platoon of soldiers stood guard around two well-dressed men in chains. The warden stood sulkily off to the side and motioned Joseph to come over.

"Good morning, Warden," said Joseph.

The warden harrumphed. "It most certainly is not. I don't know who these soldiers think they are waking me up at this God-forsaken hour."

"I am very sorry, sir." said Joseph, trying not to laugh at the warden's disheveled state.

"That makes two of us! I will most assuredly be reporting this to Potiphar himself. This is unacceptable behavior."

"You won't have to wait long," said someone from the back of the platoon.

"I should hope not," retorted the warden. "Not a good look for him to be sleeping while we're all here."

"I can assure you, he's not sleeping," said Potiphar as he stepped to the front of his men.

The warden gave a little yelp. "My apologies, sir. I didn't see you there."

Potiphar approached the frail warden. "All is forgiven. I have an urgent message for you from our most esteemed leader."

The warden's eyes nearly bulged out of his head. "From Pharaoh himself? For me?"

"Yes, and he advised that the message be delivered without delay."

"Of course." The warden suddenly lit up. "Come this way, Potiphar, and do remember to put in a good word for me with Pharaoh. I'd rather not stay in this hellhole forever." The warden bowed and scraped his way to his office, yammering like a fool. Potiphar stopped at the door and turned to Joseph. "Join us."

Joseph was surprised but did as he was told. He squeezed into the office and stood behind the chair where Potiphar sat. Once the door was closed, Potiphar fixed a stern gaze on the warden. "Here are your instructions from Pharaoh. They pertain to the two prisoners I have brought you. These men are both under investigation for high treason against Avaris. The first is Pharaoh's personal assistant, and the second is the head cook in the palace. Both are thought to have ties to the insurgents who attacked Avaris yesterday."

The warden's woolly eyebrows shot up so violently Joseph thought they might pop off his face. "I knew it. So it *was* an inside job!"

Potiphar took a deep breath. "We don't know that yet, but we have our suspicions. These are top priority prisoners and are to be carefully monitored at all times."

The warden snapped to attention and saluted. "Loud and clear, sir. The prisoners will not go missing on my watch."

"Good," Potiphar said and turned to Joseph. "When the new prisoners are outside the prison, they are to be chained to another prisoner for extra security. Under no circumstances are they to be left alone."

Joseph was pleased that Potiphar trusted him with this important task. "Yes, sir. I will see to their care personally."

Joseph could tell that Potiphar had little trust in the doddering excuse for a warden. After avoiding the warden's invitations for tea and breakfast, Potiphar and his men left the prison. The gate shut behind them with a heavy thud. They were free to go, but Joseph was not. He was and would forever remain a prisoner. The thought made his heart shrivel.

He turned to the two new prisoners sitting uncomfortably in a pile of rusty chains. One of them was tall and skeletal with lips that puckered as if he'd just tasted something sour. He had a manicured beard that tapered to a sharp point. The other man looked like the embodiment of a pastry, and his big eyes were red and puffy from crying. It was hard for Joseph to imagine that either of these men were criminal masterminds, but then he'd never imagined that his brothers would sell him as a slave either. Humans were capable of nearly anything when pushed to the edge.

He wasn't going to let these men out of his sight for a second. If he played his cards right, things might improve for him. He marched over, trying to look as confident as possible.

"My name is Joseph, and I'm the head prisoner here. You will both report directly to me. No funny business. No trying to escape. I don't care if you are guilty or innocent. If you cause problems for me, you will shovel feces for a week. Do you understand?" The two men nodded. "Very good. Now, tell me your names."

The chubby one spoke first, his voice quavering. "I am Ahmed, and I cook for Pharaoh. Please, I don't know why I am here. This is all some terrible mistake." He threw himself at Joseph's feet and sobbed.

Joseph shook him off. "Enough of that, Ahmed. Pull yourself together. The other prisoners will be out soon enough, and if the first thing they see is you crying like a baby, things will not go well for you."

The skinny man sneered at his companion. "He is weak. Too many years stuffing himself with Pharaoh's food while the rest of us suffered and fought to survive. I am Salim, long-time personal assistant to Pharaoh and a servant who has been unfairly judged." He bowed his head, steepled his hands, and said no more.

The two men could not have been more different, and yet here they were, both accused of conspiring against Pharaoh and the people of Avaris. It was very curious. Joseph would watch and listen, and eventually one of them would let something slip. Growing up in close quarters with older brothers who never willingly confessed to wrongdoing had trained Joseph well. Guilt was a difficult thing to keep secret forever. It had a way of coming out, and when it did, he'd be ready.

"The two of you will room together," Joseph said. "I am afraid the accommodations will be significantly less comfortable than what you are used to in the palace, but you'll get used to it."

The prison guards hauled Ahmed and Salim off to their cell. Oh, how the mighty had fallen.

CHAPTER 17

Blessings and Dreams

The morning light sifted through the overcast skies, revealing a courtyard filled with hungry, wounded men. Emmanuel was busy tending to bloody bandages. Some of the men were worse for wear after the long night. The color had seeped from their skin, and they looked like ghosts. Emmanuel moved with a sense of solemnity, and Joseph guessed that some of these men were not long for this world. Without proper medical supplies, there was little hope other than to try to ease their suffering.

In the far corner of the courtyard sat the two new prisoners. Ahmed had managed to pull himself together, but his puffy eyes betrayed his blubbering from the night before. Salim was stoic, a statue in the early morning light. *There's something unnatural about him,* thought Joseph, as he made his way over to them.

"How was your first night?"

Ahmed groaned. "Worst sleep of my life. There's not even a mattress."

"Poor sleep is the curse of the guilty," mused Salim. "I slept well."

Joseph raised his hands. "I am not your judge, merely the one tasked with keeping you from escaping, so don't try your mind games on me. Now, seeing that the two of you are in good health, you will be put to work. Ahmed, go help with food. Salim, you will assist the doctor."

Ahmed looked like he might cry again when he saw what was being prepared for breakfast, and Salim proved rather handy as an assistant. When breakfast was ready, those who could lined up to get a bowl of gruel. Thanks to Ahmed, the gruel had more flavor than usual. Joseph sat down beside Emmanuel. The old man studied him.

"Are you going to ask?" he said.

"About what?"

"Not about 'what.' About whom?"

Joseph blushed. "How is Mariam?"

Emmanuel leaned back. "She is as lovely as ever, a flower in the desert. I can't decide who has it worse, though, her or you."

The thought of Mariam suffering broke Joseph's heart. He needed to communicate with her.

"Would you take a letter to her for me?"

"Smuggling things out of prison is a dangerous game, and then if Zuleika was to find out! Heaven help me, she would fly into a rage. It would end especially badly for Mariam. Zuleika beats her when she is not pleased, which is often. Mariam comes to me on occasion for ointment to soothe her bruises. What she has had to endure this past year, since you left, is wrong."

Joseph felt a surge of anger, but it was quickly overwhelmed by a sense of powerlessness. He could do nothing to help Mariam. His breakfast suddenly tasted like ashes.

Emmanuel studied him. "I will carry a note to Mariam. It will do her good to hear from you. A letter will be better medicine than any of the ointment I've provided."

"Thank you, Emmanuel. I know it is a risk. I will write the note as soon as possible. Now, how long do you think you'll be staying?"

"Not long, I'm afraid. Potiphar will have other places to send me. Sometimes he forgets I am an old man, the way he has me running about the city."

"Have there been other attacks?"

Emmanuel looked around, and Joseph could tell he was checking to make sure the guards weren't listening. "I am sworn to secrecy, but there are no secrets amongst family. There have been a series of attacks over the last month. Each in a different part of the city. I fear the worst is yet to come."

Anxiety roiled Joseph's stomach. "That's what the warden said too."

"Indeed. Don't underestimate the wisdom of age. What will be, will be."

The warden announced no one was to go to the farm today, so Joseph and Emmanuel spent the day together, talking and doing the rounds amongst the men. It was almost like going back in time. They were only apart when Joseph went to write a note to Mariam on the back of a used bandage wrapper. He ran out of space long before he'd said all the things he wanted to say, but it would have to be enough.

As expected, an armed escort collected Emmanuel shortly after dinner. Joseph hugged his old friend. Emmanuel's frail arms wrapped around him, then Joseph felt a warm hand rest on his head. "A blessing for you, Joseph. May God bless you and keep you and cause His face to shine upon you."

"Amen," whispered Joseph. Then he watched Emmanuel walk out into the darkness, wondering if he'd ever see his friend again.

The following morning came with the kiss of death. Two prisoners had passed in the night. Joseph and the guards took the bodies outside to be buried as the wind whipped around them, howling, and blowing ash everywhere. Usually, the warden accompanied any deceased and said a few words at their burial, but he was barricaded in his office and refused to come out. When the shallow graves were dug and the bodies placed in the ground, all the men stood around awkwardly. No one seemed quite sure what to do next.

Joseph took it upon himself to speak. He looked down at the graves and the poor men lying inside them. How easily it could have been him they were burying. He didn't know quite what to say, so he quoted King Solomon. "From dust we came, and to dust we will return. May God have mercy upon their souls." Joseph was sure there were much more eloquent words and prayers, but these would have to do. The men seemed to agree as shovels of dirt were tossed upon the open graves.

Soon the corpses were covered, and the small band returned silently to the prison.

The mood was solemn as they took their breakfast and huddled around the edges of the courtyard. The wind clawed at their faces and moaned eerily around the courtyard. It was like the souls of the dead prisoners were fighting their retreat to the afterlife. Joseph shivered and looked over at Ahmed and Salim, who were both awfully pale.

"You okay? First time seeing a dead body?" asked Joseph.

Ahmed shook his head.

"What, then?"

"I had a dream."

"We both had dreams," interjected Salim.

Joseph's ears perked up. "What sort of dreams?"

"The sort that stick with you and feel so real you can't shake them," Salim said.

Ahmed's hands trembled so hard that he nearly dropped his bowl. "I know they mean something."

Salim nodded. "Me too. In the old days I knew a man who could interpret such dreams."

Joseph's heart beat faster, and before he knew what he was saying, words flew out of his mouth. "I can interpret them. Well...not me, but God. He is the giver of dreams. I've had a few in my day. Tell me your dreams, and I'll ask God for an interpretation."

Salim spoke first. His voice was hesitant. "In my dream I went back in time to before the Great War. I was walking beside a river, and along its bank was a sprawling vineyard, but there were no grapes. As I strolled along, a giant vine suddenly sprouted out of the earth. It rose above all the other plants, and from it sprang three new branches. These were covered in grape buds that blossomed and produced the most magnificent grape clusters. I reached for the clusters and plucked one from the vine. As soon as I did, I was transported to Pharaoh's palace. The grapes were heavy in my hand, and I squeezed them into Pharaoh's cup. When it overflowed, I offered him a drink. He took the cup, and then I woke up. Even now I can still smell the sweet fragrance of the grapes. It's the strangest thing."

Joseph considered the words he'd heard. It was certainly an unusual dream, but what mysteries did it contain? He'd never really done this before, but if he believed God spoke to him in his dreams, then why not other people?

He prayed quietly, "God, grant me wisdom to interpret these dreams. Not for my own glory, but for yours." As he prayed, he felt a powerful sense that he was standing on holy ground and the wind whipping around the courtyard was the very Spirit of God. Suddenly, he knew in his spirit what the dream meant. Filled with gratitude, he shared what God had revealed.

"In three days, you will be restored to your position in the palace. You will once again serve Pharaoh as his personal assistant. I ask that when all goes well with you, please remember me and how I have treated you. I am an innocent man and have been unfairly thrown into prison here."

Before Salim could respond, Ahmed butted in. "Please, interpret my dream as well. I, too, was walking by a flowing river, and on my head were three baskets of freshly baked bread. As I walked, giant crows swooped down and began to devour the bread. I tried to shoo them away, but they continued to swarm. I ran, but they followed me, calling more crows down from the skies until I was surrounded by a swirling cloud of crows. Everywhere I looked there were black wings and beaks and beady eyes. I woke in a terrible sweat and swear I heard the sound of flapping wings disappearing off into the distance. What does it mean? Give me good news as well. Please."

Again Joseph prayed. First there was nothing, and then, just like before, he received the interpretation. He immediately felt sick with dread at what had been foreshadowed. He hesitated, but he knew he had to speak the truth. "You won't like this, but you must hear it anyway. The three baskets represent three days. At that time, your head will be severed from your body and placed on a pole outside of Avaris. It will warn everyone who sees it what happens to traitors."

Ahmed gasped and started to speak, but Joseph cut him off. "I'm not done. The birds and the jackals will feast on your flesh, and no one will mourn your death."

The cook's entire body shook, and tears ran down his wobbly cheeks. He was a man destined to die.

Joseph reached out to comfort him, but then thought better of it. Instead, he turned and walked away with a heavy heart.

CHAPTER 18

On the Third Day

Two days passed, and on the third came a knock on the prison gate. Joseph looked up from his breakfast and saw Potiphar at the entrance, flanked by his regular entourage. His voice thundered across the courtyard.

"Salim and Ahmed, you have been summoned by Pharaoh. Come at once."

The warden poked his head out of his office. "Who is it this time?"

"It's Potiphar, you cranky old bat. I'm here for two of your prisoners."

The warden jumped, an increasingly common occurrence since the attack on the farm. "Yes, I should have known. Just a second." There was the sound of bolts being unlocked, and the warden emerged wearing a frayed bathrobe that was clearly not meant for a grown man. He bowed and scraped. "How good of you to visit us, Potiphar. You will see that we have taken excellent care of Pharaoh's special prisoners."

"I am most pleased to hear this, and I'm sure Pharaoh will be as well. But I'm afraid I don't have time for formalities. I will take the prisoners and be on my way."

"Of course, you are a busy man. Bring out the prisoners," called the warden.

Salim and Ahmed were quickly herded over to Potiphar, Salim striding along as if he was already a free man and Ahmed taking on a sickly, greenish hue that made him look like a wilting plant.

Joseph felt bad for Ahmed, but he couldn't miss this opportunity. "Remember me," he called, but neither responded as they were marched off.

"Well, that's that," chirped the warden as the gate swung shut. "They must be headed to Pharaoh's party. It's his birthday, you know?"

"I didn't," replied Joseph.

"Take my word for it. And Pharaoh knows how to throw a party— at least that's what I've heard. I've never been invited. Maybe one of these days."

"Maybe," Joseph said.

"Yes, he likes to make quite the public spectacle. Every year he celebrates his birthday by granting freedom to a prisoner condemned to die."

Joseph's blood ran cold. Had he misinterpreted Ahmed's dream? He swallowed hard before he spoke again. "Why would he take two prisoners then?"

The warden shifted uncomfortably. "There's another part to the whole birthday ritual. A little grotesque for my taste, but he always takes two prisoners: one to live and one to die."

Joseph's eyes grew big, and his heart pounded like a drum. Could this be confirmation that his interpretation was right after all? "Thank you for telling me," he said.

The warden waved his hand as if it was nothing. "Enough talk of such things. You are to go back to the farm today. Take the men who are fit to work and bring me a full report when you return."

Joseph gave the warden a generous bow, which seemed to please him greatly. The old man returned to his office humming a merry tune, and Joseph shook his head. The warden was a mystery, a half-mad mystery.

Only a handful of the prisoners who'd survived the attack were fit to work. With double the usual guards, they made their way out to the farm. Joseph's heart sank when they arrived. In the mad rush to escape the attack, the field had been trampled. The irrigation system had been crushed and riddled with bullets. What remained was a jumbled mess littered with dead plants. He'd have to start all over again.

Tears welled up in Joseph's eyes. After the brief joy of seeing Emmanuel, it was back to having his hopes and hard work dashed. What about his dreams and visions he'd received all those years ago? When would they be fulfilled? When would things finally work out for him?

Looking out over the ruined garden, this felt like some sort of cruel test. He still believed that God had a plan and purpose for his life, but why did it have to be so hard?

He felt the other prisoners watching him. This was no time to have a breakdown, but as much as he tried, he couldn't pretend to be cheerful. He felt too numb. Joseph heard himself saying things to the men. Words like, "rebuild, start over and just a setback," but he felt far from them. He wanted to go home. To cross back over the mountains and find his way back to the bunker. He wanted to hug his father and sleep in his old bed. He wanted to be anywhere but here. He felt a stirring to pray, but all he could muster was "help." Hopefully that was enough.

******

On the far side of Avaris, Mariam had been recruited for the day to be an extra server at Pharaoh's massive birthday celebration. She jumped at the opportunity to get away from Zuleika for the day and see what the palace was like.

It was strange to think that she'd lived in the shadow of the palace for years now but had never been inside it. The courtyard alone took her breath away. Giant blocks of carefully quarried stone gave the space a larger-than-life feel. Covered in ancient hieroglyphs, red stone colonnades seemed to grow out of the desert floor and rise high in the air. It was like stepping back in time a thousand years. Mariam marveled at how this structure had survived the fire that fell from the sky during the apocalypse.

There were plenty of touches of modernity with wires and floodlights, the occasional bit of graffiti on the wall, and plenty of manned machine gun nests. It was clear the palace doubled as a small fortress, but hidden within the hulking mass were touches of beauty with colorful tiles forming grand mosaics on the walls.

She and the other recruits were shooed up a flight of stairs guarded on either side by oversized statues of the ancient Egyptian gods. Mariam cringed at the sight of these wild creatures with wings and teeth and beaks.

Entering the main palace building felt like walking into a cave, and Mariam was instantly homesick for the Qumran caves where she'd been raised after the apocalypse. The air was cool and dark underneath the thick stone ceiling, and everywhere she looked there were guards. It seemed that Pharaoh employed a small army to protect this place.

Before long, Mariam was completely lost as her group wound its way through the palace. They finally emerged into a small courtyard where they were briefed on how to be a server. Apparently, they had to dress in fancy black-and-white attire and carry around trays of finger food to the guests. This was apparently a throwback to olden days when such parties were the norm for the elites of society. Mariam tried to take in all of the instructions: dress nicely, don't talk to the guests, avoid eye contact, don't draw unnecessary attention to yourself... Those seemed to be the big ones.

An hour before the party, Mariam was given a crisp white shirt and flowy black skirt that brushed the ground. She'd never worn anything so nice. There was a large mirror in the changing room along with a hairbrush, and she looked at herself while brushing out her long hair, trying to untangle the knots. She hadn't done this since she was back in the caves, borrowing her mother's brush. "Vanity is a sin," she heard her father say, but just for tonight it would be okay. God would understand. She wished Joseph could see her now. God bless Emmanuel for carrying that note from him. At least she knew he was alive and well.

She and the other servants were taken to some sort of staging room right next to the throne room. There were tables covered with assorted foods and drinks, the likes of which Mariam had never seen. It was difficult to imagine so much food in one place.

The attendant in charge pulled a small whistle from his pocket and gave it three shrill blows. Everyone in the room froze, and he began to speak.

"Let me remind you that tonight is a significant night as we celebrate our esteemed leader. It is the event of the year. The most important citizens of Avaris have been invited, and it is our job to ensure they have a wonderful evening. Remember your roles. If under any circumstance you find yourself in the Pharaoh's presence, you are to kneel before him. Do not rise until he bids you to do so. Any questions you have should be directed to your assigned palace staff. Now move with a purpose."

He gave another shrill blast of his whistle, and the room exploded into action. Mariam was swept towards a table of silver serving trays filled with food. Much to Mariam's amazement, the food seemed to have been turned into tiny works of art, but there was no time to admire the artistry. Following the lead of those in front of her, she snagged a tray and held it shoulder high as she stepped into the throne room.

Mariam had to remind herself not to gawk. The throne room was a world unto itself and seemed to stretch into eternity. The space was flooded with colorful lights that lit up soaring marble pillars and a floor that was as smooth as glass. Equally impressive were the people within. Mariam felt like she'd been transported back in time. The men wore fancy suits, and women wore extravagant gowns.

Mariam made her way nervously about the room. When she came to the far end, she found herself in front of a set of polished steps that rose to a high platform. At the top of the stairs sat a celestial golden throne, and on it was perched a middle-aged man with dark hair that hung around his shoulders like a lion's mane. He wore a pinstriped suit that hinted at a muscular frame beneath, and in his right hand he held a gold walking stick topped with a ruby the size of a chicken's egg.

Pharaoh.

Even from this distance he oozed power. Pharaoh seemed to carry the strength of his ancestors, and Mariam could instantly understand why people used to believe the pharaohs were divine. This man was somehow more than all the rest of them.

On her second lap around the room Mariam ran into Zuleika. Mariam hated to admit it, but the woman knew how to dress for the occasion. She wore a ravishing red dress and carried herself with such extraordinary confidence that Mariam immediately grew self-conscious. Potiphar stood stiffly at the edge of her aura. He was nothing more than a well-muscled prop.

Zuleika was in the middle of a forced social laugh when she spotted Mariam and beckoned her to come over with the food tray. As Mariam drew near, Zuleika gave her a quick look over before speaking.

"Well, well, well, I almost didn't recognize you outside of your regular rags."

Nothing like a little backhanded insult, thought Mariam. "Thank you, Mistress. Might I compliment you on how beautiful you look this evening?" *Play to her vanity.*

"You may, but make it quick as I'm quite sure I can still smell you even in your borrowed attire."

Mariam bit back a scathing retort. "I am sorry, Mistress. You are a vision to behold tonight."

Zuleika snatched an hors d'oeuvre and took the tiniest of nibbles before dropping it back on the serving tray. "I'm afraid your presence has spoiled my appetite. Leave, and do not come near me again this evening." Then she took Potiphar's arm and moved towards the crowd forming at the base of the stairs. Pharaoh was making his descent; God coming down to mingle with mortals.

CHAPTER 19

Starting Over

Later that day, Joseph sat dejectedly in the warden's office, admitting that they had to start all over on the farm.

The warden frowned. "One in the hand is worth two in the bush. Looks like they went ahead and blew up the bush."

Joseph wasn't entirely sure what the warden was getting at, but he tried to play along. "Of course, sir, we'll do our best to get back up and running as soon as we can."

"That's what I like about you, Joseph. You're resilient. Like a duck, you let it all roll off your back."

Again not entirely sure about the warden's analogy, Joseph decided to take it as a compliment despite feeling far from resilient. "Sir, we don't have the manpower we did before the attack. We're running a half crew, but we will make do. One day at a time."

"That's the spirit! Now go ahead and let yourself out. I've got to feed my cats."

Joseph glanced at the two glass cat figurines on the desk as the warden rummaged in his top drawer. Better leave before this got too strange. He ducked out and went to check on Sticks, who was in one of the two cells that had been converted into a makeshift infirmary.

When Joseph entered he was surprised to find Sticks propped up in one corner, his face gaunt with dark circles beneath his blank eyes. Beads of sweat clung to his forehead, and his skin had taken on a yellowish tinge. He'd clearly taken a turn for the worse. The room smelled sickly, and Joseph put his shirt over his nose and mouth to try and block it out. He walked across the room and knelt next to his friend.

"Sticks, it's Joseph. Can you hear me?"

Sticks' eyes moved ever so slightly, then he closed them as if the small effort had been too much for him. Joseph grabbed his hand and leaned in.

"I'm here, Sticks. You're going to be okay." Joseph knew it was a lie. He sat for a long time holding Sticks' skeletal hand and watching his rib cage rise, rattle and fall. Each breath was labored. There would be no miraculous recovery for him. It would be a mercy when Sticks took his final breath and returned to his Maker.

As he waited for the inevitable, Joseph's mind wandered back to his first days in prison when he'd met Sticks. What was it that had caused this skinny man to extend kindness to him? How had he maintained his compassion and humanity amid so much suffering and cruelty? He was different from the other prisoners, and Joseph was desperate to know why.

It was humbling to be with a person teetering on the precipice of death. Joseph had never experienced anything like it. There was something sacred and intimate about it, a silence that spoke volumes. Each breath was a declaration of life's fragility. Joseph could almost see the life force ebbing out of Sticks. Water leaking from a cracked basin. As the final drops dripped out and Sticks' breathing grew short and ragged, his eyes suddenly went wide. Perhaps it was Joseph's imagination, but the room seemed to grow momentarily brighter. Sticks squeezed his hand and looked off into the distance with a smile.

Then his hand went limp, and his spirit was gone. All that remained was a festering shell. Joseph lowered Sticks' bony hand onto the floor and closed his eyes for the last time. "From dust we came, and to dust we will return. May light perpetual shine upon you."

Joseph stayed for a long time. How easily it could have been his body lying there or in a well or killed by Cain. He'd narrowly avoided death so many times. Maybe it was more than that? Maybe he'd been saved by an invisible hand, or the bony hands of a good man like Sticks. Maybe they were one and the same? There would always be a reason not to believe, not to see God's hand at work. There would always be the choice to grow bitter and angry in the face of his own suffering, but there was also the choice to see the good and look for the light. To choose hope. To choose to see the humanity of others. To stop sipping the slow poison of bitterness and revenge and truly live.

That's what he wanted to do. He gently covered Sticks with a sheet and whispered in his ear. "Thanks for showing me the way, friend."

CHAPTER 20

Dreams or Lies?

That night, Joseph woke abruptly from a deep sleep. His dream had returned as intense as ever. He'd seen his brothers bowing before him, small and fragile, while he sat in power over them. It was a strange feeling when he lived most of his days feeling powerless.

His mind drifted to other dreams, to Ahmed and Salim, and he wondered what had become of them. Had his interpretations come true? Had Salim lived? Would he remember Joseph? Months went by, and it seemed the answer was no. Joseph lost hope that an entourage from Pharaoh was coming to set him free. He'd been forgotten, but this time he refused to lose hope.

Slowly, he began to rebuild and go about the work of living. His old dreams kept coming back, stronger and stronger. He took them as a sign that God had not abandoned him.

He was out overseeing work on the farm when a prison guard came running towards him, waving his arms and hollering at the top of his lungs. "Joseph, come quickly! You have a visitor from the palace!"

Joseph's heart rose. Could this be it? He took off toward the prison. By the time he arrived, the guard was well behind him. He dashed through the gate and skidded into the courtyard. There sat a well-dressed man waiting with his hands folded while the warden sat in the shade sipping a cup of tea. The man looked vaguely familiar.

Remembering himself, Joseph bowed low. The man stepped towards him, extending his hand.

"Joseph, it has been too long. It is good to see you." There was a moment of confusion, and then Joseph realized who it was.

"Salim, it's you. The dream. It must have come true!" said Joseph excitedly.

"It did."

"Thank God. When I never heard from you, I kept wondering what had happened."

"I was restored to my former position, just as you prophesied."

Joseph was nearly giddy with excitement until he remembered the *other* dream he'd interpreted.

"And... Ahmed?" he asked.

Salim nodded. "Executed for treason, just as you predicted. Pharaoh had his head put on a spike and paraded through the city."

Joseph's stomach rolled and he had to take a deep breath to quell his nausea. He'd believed his interpretation would come true, but it was a whole different thing seeing Salim here in front of him—and getting confirmation that Ahmed was dead. He wanted to reach out and touch Salim just to be sure this wasn't another dream, but he held back.

"Why are you here?" he asked.

"Pharaoh had a strange dream that no one can interpret. I told him I knew someone who might be able to help."

"You want me to go to Pharaoh and interpret his dream for him?"

"Yes, and if you succeed, then perhaps Pharaoh will set you free, but I make no promises."

The thought of being free made Joseph giddy, but he did his best to remain calm. "It's God who provides the interpretations, but I'll come and see what I can do."

Salim nodded approvingly at Joseph, who suddenly noticed that he was now taller than the wispy man. He even had more facial hair than Salim and his scraggly pointed beard.

Salim turned up his nose ever so slightly as he responded. "Whatever you say, but we need to get you cleaned up first. Don't take this the wrong way, but you look like a mess and smell even worse."

Joseph laughed. "You've been at the palace too long. I remember when you looked and smelled the same way."

Salim grimaced. "Let us not speak of those times. I stuck my neck out to get you this chance. Don't mess it up, or I'll look like a fool wasting Pharaoh's time with a meager slave. Do you understand?"

Joseph grew serious. "I understand."

"Good. Now let's get out of this hell hole. Pharaoh is not the most patient of men."

As they rushed through the city Joseph couldn't help but think how fitting it was that his world would once again turn on a dream. Dreams, these strange snippets of the Divine waiting to be understood; foggy glimpses into the future for those who had ears to hear and eyes to see. They'd shaped the trajectory of his life, and now they were bringing him before the most powerful man on the planet.

Give me eyes to see, God. Help me find favor with Pharaoh. Please don't let me get put back in jail.

He could hear his father quoting from the book of Proverbs. "Trust in the Lord with all your heart and lean not on your own understanding. In all your ways acknowledge Him, and He will make straight your paths." They were good words. Words that had stood the test of time.

I will give you all the credit, God. Please make my paths straight.

When they arrived at the palace, two armed guards whisked him away. He craned his neck trying to take in his opulent surroundings. The palace was bigger and more majestic than he'd thought possible. Doubt crept in. Who was he to stand before the ruler of all of this?

A trio of muscular men nearly drowned him in an overflowing tub. The hot water felt so good he couldn't even be mad as they vigorously scrubbed him from head to toe and commented loudly on how filthy he was. One of them took his clothes away, never to be seen again.

Another man entered the room as Joseph was being pulled from the water and wrapped in a towel. He was unlike anyone Joseph had ever laid eyes on. He had bright red hair, and seemingly every inch of his skin was covered in tattoos. His eyebrows were pierced, and he wore some type of makeup to elongate his eyes. He held a large pair of scissors and an oversized razor in his hands as if they were extensions of his lanky arms. With intense yellow eyes, he gave Joseph a quick look over and then shook his head in disapproval.

"Come with me," he sighed dramatically. "Just a simple trim, I was told. More like a shearing. They expect me to work miracles with a pair of dull scissors and a dented razor." He stared at Joseph, waiting for him to respond, but Joseph was too slow.

"Don't just stand there, move!" The man waved the scissors at Joseph. "I haven't accidentally killed anyone yet, but if you stand around much longer I might."

"I'm sorry," said Joseph. Holding onto his towel, he followed the strange man into an adjacent room with a large chair and tall mirror. Snapping scissors directed him quickly towards the chair, and a cape of some sort was draped over him, covering his torso. Joseph sat as still as a corpse.

Putting the razor down, the man ran his hand through his thick red hair. "First, introductions. My name is Cyasi. Personal stylist for Pharaoh. And who, might I ask, are you?"

Joseph was still processing the fact that Pharaoh had a personal stylist. "I'm Joseph." How should he describe himself? "I'm a...prisoner."

Cyasi's pierced eyebrows shot up.

"I was unfairly sentenced though," Joseph added, trying to keep the defensiveness out of his tone.

Cyasi put up his hand. "I'm sure you were. Why Pharaoh wants a private audience with a prisoner, I have to know, but it sounds like a long story. You can tell me while I work. This is going to take a while." The barber wielded his scissors with a skilled fury that left Joseph in a mixture of awe and fear. "Anytime now, Prisoner Joseph. I want to hear this," Cyasi said between snips.

Joseph related how his brothers sold him into slavery, how Ishmael dragged him across the desert to Avaris, and how he wound up in jail for a crime he didn't commit.

"I met Salim when he was in prison for a little while," Joseph said, "and I interpreted a dream for him. You could say he owes me."

"Mhmmm. Little piece of friendly advice. Salim does not do anything for free. That man is calculating. Let me guess, he bailed you out of prison to interpret Pharaoh's crazy dream?"

"Yes. Is that a bad thing?" replied Joseph as he watched chunks of his hair fall to the ground like shrapnel.

"That depends. Can you really interpret dreams, or are you just an overly hairy con artist?"

Joseph sighed. "I can't exactly interpret dreams, but I'm not a con artist."

"Now you gotta spill the beans, because I don't really see another option." Cyasi stopped cutting and fixed all his attention on Joseph.

"Apparently interpreting dreams is a gift that I've been given. A gift from God."

"Ooooh, so you're like one of those old fancy mystics. Like the Dalai Lama or something?"

"Not like that. I'm just a normal guy who happens to interpret dreams."

Cyasi raised his eyebrows. "Hate to break it to you, but there's nothing normal about that."

Joseph shrugged. "Look, it's not something I chose. It started when I was a kid. I'd dream every night. Lots of dreams. I'd wake up and remember them clear as day. I never shut up about my dreams, so my brothers called me 'Dreamer Boy.' Not the most original nickname, but then if you met them, you'd understand.

"My father told me to stop dwelling so much on my dreams. He thought they were childish. A desperate cry for attention and all that. He assumed they'd pass as I got older, but they didn't. One day he told me to pray for wisdom to understand my dreams. He said that God had communicated with our ancestors through dreams, so why not me too?"

Cyasi twirled the scissors on his index finger. "You know this all sounds a little crazy right?"

Joseph tried to stay calm next to the whirling blades. "I do, but I swear it's true."

"Well, you figure out Pharaoh's crazy dream, and I'll be a believer. In the meantime, watch out for Salim. If you succeed, he'll try and use you. If you fail, he'll throw you right back where you came from. Now we have to take care of that mess you call a beard. Stay nice and still."

Cyasi pulled out the razor and began to work. Joseph felt the cold, metal edge sliding along his skin. One slip, and he was done for, but Cyasi had a steady hand. When he was done, he spun Joseph around so he could see himself in the mirror.

Joseph gasped. It had been well over a year since he'd seen his reflection. He guessed he was just past his twentieth birthday, and he barely recognized the man staring back at him. The little string bean from the bunker was gone. He ran his hands through his curls and admired the straight line of his beard. He couldn't help but smile. Who would have thought he'd make it this far?

"You clean up nice for a prisoner. Just don't let it get to your head. I wish you all the best with Pharaoh, Dreamer Boy."

"Thank you. This is definitely a better haircut than my brothers used to give me."

"I should hope so! I'm not just some run of the mill hair cutter. I'm a hair artiste. If you get past Pharaoh, I might even give you another haircut. Time for you to get going. I'm sure Salim is lurking somewhere in the hall and won't be hard to find. Off with you now."

Cyasi was right. As soon as Joseph opened the door, Salim pounced.

"At long last. I was beginning to wonder if—"

"If Cyasi was working his magic and giving your prisoner pal an impressive look after years of bad grooming?" asked Cyasi.

Salim frowned and immediately folded his hands in front of him. He clearly did not like the phrase "prisoner pal." There was some serious negative energy between the two men.

Salim spoke to Cyasi, his voice dripping with condescension. "Of course, thank you for your help. You have once again outdone yourself. You are the da Vinci of hair."

Cyasi gave an exaggerated bow. "It is nice to be appreciated by one with such a refined artistic eye as yourself."

This little barb made Salim's nostrils flare. "Do not mock me," Salim warned. "You may cut Pharaoh's hair and fill his ear with gossip, but I am his right-hand man. You would do well not to forget that, Cyasi. Now come, Joseph. Leave the poor artist to his sweeping."

Salim turned and headed for the door. Cyasi flipped him the bird, and for a second Joseph wondered if he might throw the broom at Salim. Joseph didn't like being caught up in the middle of their power struggle. There were dynamics at play here that he was not familiar with: alliances, grudges, and long histories. He would need to make some allies, and quickly, if he was going to survive in the palace. He just had to figure out whom he could trust.

Salim glided down the hallway as Joseph tried to keep up with him. The farther they went, the more guards there were, all heavily armed and standing at attention. At last they came to a set of large brass doors, each with half a glistening sun etched into them. There was no doubt who dwelt within. Salim came to a halt before the doors, dwarfed by their magnitude, and then turned to Joseph.

"Welcome to Pharaoh's throne room. Please him, and your life will be forever changed for the better. Disappoint him, and you will not see the sun rise again."

Meeting Pharaoh

No pressure, thought Joseph as the doors swung open, revealing a sprawling space made up of quarried blocks that must have weighed a couple tons each. The whole room seemed to bow in reverence before the figure sitting on the high-backed throne at the top of a towering marble staircase. Two guards blocked Joseph's path before he could even step into the room.

"Name and reason for admission?" they growled.

Joseph suddenly felt very small. *Lord give me strength.* "My name is Joseph, and I am here at the request of Pharaoh."

The two guards looked at each other. They had clearly not been briefed about his impending arrival. Salim obviously saw this as his cue.

"I will take it from here. I assume you both know who I am?"

They nodded.

"Excellent. You've done your part now. I'm sure Pharaoh is very impressed at how well you're protecting him, so it's time to let us through so we don't keep Pharaoh waiting. As you know, it has been a difficult day for him."

The guards exchanged glances again and stepped aside. "Very good," said Salim as if he was talking to a pair of well-mannered puppies. Joseph was surprised Salim didn't pat the men on the heads as he slithered by. They crossed the long hall, their steps echoing around the chamber until they were standing at the base of the steps that seemed to rise into the heavens.

Salim whispered to him. "Breathe. Bow. Be quick to listen and slow to speak. If you do speak, always refer to Pharaoh as 'Your Greatness.' Up we go now."

Breathe. Joseph focused on his breath as he climbed. In and out, nice and easy. He needed to release the anxiety coursing through his body. He could do this. They finally made it to the top, and Joseph found himself standing on a circular golden dais. Just a few feet away sat Pharaoh, and behind him was a throng of his advisors, but they paled in comparison to Pharaoh. The man was a lion, powerful and somehow larger than life. His piercing gaze made Joseph feel small and exposed. He bowed low, his face nearly touching the floor as he waited for permission to rise.

Inhale. Exhale. Sweat coursed down his back. Then, after what felt like an eternity, Pharaoh spoke.

"You may rise."

Joseph got shakily to his feet but kept his gaze cast down as Pharaoh spoke again.

"Salim, you have done as you promised and brought me the young man from prison."

"Yes, Your Greatness. We came as quickly as possible." He nudged Joseph, who looked up.

"I'm sure you did. You are nothing if not efficient," said Pharaoh as he shifted his gaze to Joseph. "Step forward and tell me your name. No need to look so scared. I promise I won't eat you."

Joseph gave another bow as he stepped forward. He could feel the power radiating from this man like heat from the sun. "My name is Joseph, Your Greatness."

"Joseph. A good Jewish name, if I'm not mistaken."

"You are not, Your Greatness."

"You are a long way from home then, I take it?

"Indeed, Pharaoh. Mine is a long story, which I would not hope to bore you with. I am here only to serve."

"Very good. Straight and to the point. I like that. You are here because I was told that you can interpret dreams. Is that correct?"

This is where things get interesting, thought Joseph. "Yes and no, Your Greatness. It is God who interprets dreams. I am just a humble mouthpiece."

Pharaoh leaned back in his throne. "Very curious. I was under the impression that God was long dead, and yet here you are, claiming otherwise."

"I do not seek to contradict Your Greatness. I only speak of what I know from my experience," said Joseph, fighting to keep his teeth from chattering with nerves.

"Let us put your God to the test then and see if you are more helpful than my useless collection of advisors. Listen to my dreams and see if you receive any divine inspiration."

Joseph bowed a third time. "Your servant is listening, Your Greatness."

Pharaoh took a sip of water from a glass and then began. "The vision came in two parts. In the first part I saw Avaris, as if from a drone. We circled the city and landed on the bank of the Nile. As I stood there, five majestic stallions came up out of the water. Their coats were black and sleek with manes like pure silk. They stomped and pranced, and their hooves shook the ground like thunder. They stared at me with eyes as brilliant as the sun. One came over and nuzzled my hand while the others grazed along the water's edge. As soon as it touched me, there was a flash of light, and it suddenly became dusk. The dark waters of the Nile began to boil and were covered with a thick oily smoke."

Joseph listened carefully to every detail and nodded as Pharaoh continued.

"Five new stallions emerged from the river. These creatures were bent and broken, their bodies mutated beyond belief. Covered in scars and eyes red like dripping blood, they stood before the five majestic stallions. There was a peal of thunder, and a strike of jagged lightning tore through the sky. Suddenly, the mangled stallions attacked their counterparts and devoured them. Lightning lit up the sky again, and all that remained were the five disfigured stallions. They stared at me and began to approach. That was when I woke up the first time."

Pharaoh looked at his advisors with disdain, and they shrank into the shadows. Pharaoh was clearly displeased with them, but Joseph didn't have time to ponder that because Pharaoh continued.

"When I fell asleep a second time, I was once again swept up over Avaris and deposited on a farm on the outskirts of town. There was a series of greenhouses, and an invisible hand pushed me inside. There I found a giant stalk of grain, and it gave off a fresh, powerful scent. On it were five healthy heads of grain unlike anything seen since before the Great War.

"I reached out to pluck a head of grain, and as I did the sky became overcast. Thunder shook the greenhouse and lightning struck nearby. In the distance I heard bombs being dropped and the smell of smoke drifted in on the east wind, carrying with it the scent of death. At my feet, a plant snaked its way up from the ground. Like a vine from the pits of hell, it rose, charred and black. Its leaves were shriveled and pockmarked, and the writhing vine began to climb the base of the grain plant. Like a python, the vine wrapped around the heads of grain.

"The grain plant withered. As if by poison, the life was sucked from it until all that was left was a blackened husk. The terrible plant remained and sprouted five skinny heads of wheat. I pulled back my hand, afraid to touch them, but they stretched toward me, chasing me as I backpedaled. I tore from the greenhouse only to wake." He sat back in his throne again, his gaze fixed on Joseph. "Those were my two visions. What do you make of them?"

The room fell silent, and Joseph watched the advisors exchange nervous glances. He closed his eyes and prayed. Dreams were like a foreign language that only God spoke. He would have to unstop Joseph's ears for any of it to make sense. At first it was chaos, but then out of chaos came order. Thus was the nature of God. This time was no different.

Joseph sensed God's spirit swirling around him and whispering into his soul the truth of the dream. Then the spirit swirled away, as uncontainable as the wind. Joseph opened his eyes and took a deep breath.

"The dreams are two parts of the same message. God has seen fit to give you a glimpse into the future. What you choose to do with this warning will determine the outcome of many lives. You hold in your hands the power over life and death."

Pharaoh leaned forward, and Joseph noticed Salim creeping closer, one ear cocked toward Joseph.

"The five black stallions and the five heads of healthy grain represent five good years of peace and prosperity for Avaris. But then will come a season of desolation—five years of terrible famine and fighting, and the memories of abundance will be as if from another lifetime. The doubling of the dreams is a sign from God that all you have seen will assuredly come true. There is no time to waste, for this very day the season of abundance has begun."

Joseph bowed his head and waited for Pharaoh to respond. Pharaoh took his time, and Joseph fought off the anxiety creeping in around the edges of his thoughts.

"If your interpretation is true, then what should be done?"

Time to take a leap of faith, thought Joseph. "Your Greatness, you should select someone you trust, someone wise and discerning, and name them as your second-in-command. Let them oversee the mass production, collection, and storage of food. You will need to enact a twenty-percent tax on all food that is grown and build giant silos to store it all. If you do not, even you will perish."

Pharaoh stood from his throne and began to pace. "If I don't listen to you, I'm going to die? Those are bold words. I've had men killed for less."

"You may kill me if you like, but it will not change the truth of what I have spoken."

"You have put me in a complicated situation, Joseph. If I listen to your advice and levy a heavy tax on my people, they will grumble and wonder what I am up to. But if I ignore your interpretation and what you have said comes true, then we are all doomed."

"I do not envy you, Your Greatness," replied Joseph quietly.

Pharaoh stopped pacing and turned to Salim. "What do you think, Salim?"

Salim's chest puffed up. "It would seem to me that Joseph has provided you with a win-win situation. Should the interpretation prove correct, then you will be viewed as a savior. If the interpretation proves false, then you will have increased your power and control of Avaris and its goods. Placing a second-in-command to take care of these matters will ensure it has little impact on you and let someone else be the face of the new order."

Pharaoh scratched his cheek, looking strangely human and vulnerable as he wrestled with the decision. "You make a good point. We will need a strong leader to oversee this project, someone with vision and wisdom who I can trust completely."

"I agree, Your Greatness," Salim crooned. He had the look of a proud peacock ready to strut, and it sickened Joseph.

"It is decided then," declared Pharaoh. "Salim"—Pharaoh's personal assistant stepped forward with his face suddenly a mask of false humility—"You have served me well for many years, but I hereby declare Joseph as my second command."

Salim staggered backwards as if he'd been punched.

Joseph stood stunned, trying to wrap his head around what had just happened, but Pharaoh continued speaking.

"I know you are disappointed, but this new position must be someone removed from the politics of Avaris. Someone who will say what needs to be said and do what needs to be done. Someone incorruptible on a divine mission to save Avaris and its citizens, and you are not that man."

Salim had already regained his composure and nodded his head as if everything Pharaoh said made complete sense and didn't bother him in the least, but Joseph could see the fiery hate in his eyes. Joseph had made an enemy, and a dangerous one at that. But there was no time to dwell on such things now. Part of him wondered if all of this was just some strange dream and he'd wake up any second back in the prison.

Pharaoh turned and addressed Joseph. "This may be the rashest decision I have ever made, but so be it. There is something about you, Joseph, that compels me to trust you and believe that you are the man for the job. There is more to you than meets the eye. I would say it is no coincidence that you are here for such a time as this. Maybe your God is not quite as dead as I had thought."

God may be unseen, but that is not the same as dead, thought Joseph. His mind flashed back, and he could see the long hand of God at work in his life. From the pit to the palace, God had protected and prepared him for this very moment. Joseph kneeled on the golden dais, but little did Pharaoh know that it was not before him that Joseph kneeled. Joseph kneeled before one greater than Pharaoh, the true and living God.

With tears in his eyes, Joseph spoke. "I place myself in your service, Pharaoh. I swear to serve as you see fit as long as I am able."

"Rise, Joseph. I receive your promise to serve. In Avaris such things must be done in the correct manner. An appointment like yours must take place in public for all to see. You have much to learn about life here, which is why I have decided to make Salim your assistant. He will help you navigate whatever hurdles come your way," said Pharaoh happily.

A ball of icy horror solidified in Joseph's stomach. *More like put hurdles in my way,* he thought. He knew this new appointment was the last thing Salim wanted.

"Salim, collect my council and advise them to meet us here at once," commanded Pharaoh.

Salim slinked down the stairs, clearly licking his wounds. When he returned with the council members, Joseph noticed that they were all men, strong and proud. Chairs were brought, and they sat in a circle with Pharaoh towering over everyone from his throne. Joseph sat silently at Pharaoh's right hand, an arrangement he was sure was not lost on those present.

Pharaoh stood and looked around the circle, making eye contact with each member. These were men he knew well.

"Esteemed members of the council, thank you for coming on such short notice. I have done so because fortune has favored us."

Joseph could tell that Pharaoh was picking his words carefully. This was a delicate situation. To give away power to one not in the inner circle was an unexpected move.

"I have led you well for many years. We toiled together and fought side by side. By sheer willpower we built this city in the aftermath of the Great War, but all our hard work is now in danger."

The council members murmured, but Pharaoh pushed ahead. "This week I received a troubling dream, a miraculous warning of what is to come. We must begin at once to prepare ourselves. There will be five years of plenty followed by five years of devastating famine and fighting. We cannot afford to be idle or argue amongst ourselves, or all will be lost. It is a time for unity and action. You have grown complacent these past few years as you enjoyed the fruits of your labor. No more!"

More murmuring, but it didn't faze Pharaoh in the least. "I am hereby appointing a new second-in-command to lead, and his name is Joseph."

The council members turned and stared at Joseph. He wanted to shrink under their gaze but knew he had to look confident.

"It is he who interpreted my dream," Pharaoh continued, "He alone has shown the qualities necessary for this role. Joseph, kneel before me."

Joseph did as he was commanded. Pharaoh stood over him with his ruby-encrusted walking stick and tapped him once on each shoulder. Joseph had a vague recollection of this being something that was once done to those becoming knights. He could hear his father quoting Ecclesiastes. "There is nothing new under the sun." How the man loved his ancient proverbs. If only he could see Joseph now.

The sound of Pharaoh's voice brought him back to the present. Pharaoh spoke as if there was a thunderstorm inside of him. "Joseph, from this day forward, I place you in command of the great city of Avaris. You will be second only to me, and your word will be law. All that you ask for, you will receive. This I declare and seal with my very own signet ring. Rise and serve to the best of your ability, Commander of Avaris."

Joseph stood, and Pharaoh removed a large ring embossed with a bright red ruby and placed it on Joseph's finger. It was far too large for him. Pharaoh leaned in and whispered, "Don't worry, you'll grow into it."

He spun Joseph around to face the circle of hardened faces. This picture was strangely familiar, like staring at his older brothers back in the bunker on the day Abba gave him the jacket that started him on this path. He'd had plenty of preparation for this moment. This time he'd try to do a better job being a peacemaker.

After meeting each of the cabinet members and engaging in small talk for a while, Joseph was ready to be alone for a bit, if only to give his head a moment to stop spinning. The cabinet members politely excused themselves. Only then did Salim slither over with a message for him. "Pharaoh has a formal dinner invitation this evening and has asked for you to accompany him. If my memory serves me correctly, I believe the invite will be of some interest to you. Tonight, we dine at the home of Potiphar."

Joseph's stomach did backflips.

He was going to see Mariam.

CHAPTER 22

In Potiphar's House

Salim led Joseph to his quarters and then disappeared, most likely to gossip with the other members of the council. Joseph would have to earn their trust, and fast. His new room in the palace was lavish. It had a connecting bathroom and study, making it nearly the size of the bunker. Joseph felt guilty having so much space to himself. He even had a real bed! A suit coat was carefully laid out on the mattress with a handwritten note in loopy cursive that read:

Better make a good impression this evening. You're already the talk of the town. Pharaoh himself requested this jacket for you. Best of luck
—Cyasi
P.S. Let me know when you need another haircut.

Joseph held up the jacket and smiled. There was only one person he wanted to make a good impression on tonight, and it wasn't Potiphar. As he put on the jacket, the symbolism of this moment wasn't lost on him. It was a jacket that had started this wild and crazy adventure. This was a new jacket for a new beginning.

He, Pharaoh, and Salim were ushered into an armored vehicle and driven the short distance to Potiphar's house. Joseph knew that fuel was an extraordinarily valuable commodity, but apparently there was a special supply for Pharaoh. His father had always said that the rich had their own rules, and apparently, he was right.

When they arrived at Potiphar's house, Joseph was a mess on the inside. All his emotions were on high alert: excitement, fear, anxiety. It had been two years since he'd seen Mariam, and he was desperate to get to her, but the thought of having dinner with Zuleika made him feel sick. It was all happening so fast. The car door opened. There was no backing out now.

Joseph nervously buttoned his jacket and stepped out of the car. Time slowed to a crawl. There was Potiphar standing at attention along with his men. He saw the looks of surprise and confusion pass across their faces, the unspoken question ringing loud in his ears. *Is that Joseph? What is he doing here? Why is he with Pharaoh?*

He looked around for Mariam, but she was nowhere to be found. He wanted her to see his victorious return, but it would have to wait. Potiphar stepped forward and bowed before Pharaoh.

"Your Greatness, I am honored that you would grace my house with your presence. We are honored to have you and your guests come and dine with us."

"The pleasure is mine," replied Pharaoh. "Your lovely wife can be quite convincing."

"That is very true," said Potiphar. He shot a quick glance at Joseph but said nothing else.

Pharaoh motioned for Joseph and Salim to step forward. "Let me introduce my two guests—Salim, who you know well, and Joseph, my new second-in-command."

Potiphar's eyes grew wide, and Pharaoh looked at him curiously. "Why the surprise, Potiphar? Such a response is unlike you."

Joseph shifted his weight. Things were about to get interesting.

Potiphar managed to find his voice. "I am sorry, sir. It is just that... I am well acquainted with your new second-in-command, and his presence here comes as somewhat of a shock."

"Why is that?" asked Pharaoh.

Joseph wasn't sure, but he thought he could see Potiphar sweating. That was certainly something he'd never witnessed before. This was a delicate situation.

"Your Greatness, Joseph served as a slave in my house for some time, and it was I who had him placed in prison."

The night grew deathly quiet as Pharaoh processed this new information. Before Joseph knew what he was doing, he began to speak.

"Your Greatness, I would ask that we leave the past behind us. I hold no anger in my heart toward Potiphar. He did what he thought best, and God used it for good. This is not a time for seeking revenge. Avaris needs every good man, and there is none better than your faithful servant Potiphar."

Pharaoh looked back and forth between the two men. "Most men jump at the opportunity to use their power to destroy their enemies— enemies who have done far less than Potiphar has done to you. Instead, you have offered forgiveness. Surely, you are the right man to lead Avaris. A man of character is more rare and more valuable than diamonds. Joseph, let it be as you have requested. From this day forward there will be no animosity between Joseph and the house of Potiphar."

Potiphar knelt before Joseph, the world turning upside down. "I and my entire household are at your service. I will not forget the kindness you have bestowed upon me this day. May you prosper in all you do, and Avaris with you."

Doing what he had seen Pharaoh do, Joseph extended his hand, and Potiphar kissed the ruby signet ring. The two of them were formally bound together. He had made an ally of his former master. Potiphar would be a good man to have on his side as he navigated his new position. Now it was time to face Zuleika.

Joseph walked through the garden toward the house, his heart rate increasing with each step. He replayed his last fateful hours in this house like some terrible nightmare: Zuleika's advances, the sound of his cloak tearing, running, overwhelming fear, the tears in Mariam's beautiful eyes as he surrendered himself...

Then Zuleika appeared, and a shiver ran down Joseph's spine. This was not a dream. This was the woman who'd ruined his life. Who'd lied to save her own skin. She was a beautiful, poisonous snake, and he was prey returned from the dead. But this time he was not defenseless.

Zuleika held out her arms in a warm welcome and opened her mouth as if to speak when their eyes met, and recognition flashed across her expression. He watched the blood drain from her face and swore he detected a tremor in her hands, but she was a true predator. She gathered herself, and her red-painted lips spread into a dangerous smile. He'd surprised her, but she would not be intimidated. She was still the hunter.

She shifted her gaze gracefully to Pharaoh. "Welcome, Your Greatness. Thank you for receiving my invitation for dinner."

Pharaoh smiled. "A most gracious offer, which I could not refuse."

Zuleika smiled. "You are too kind. I have had your favorite dishes prepared, and"—she paused for effect—"we are to be served by my very own handmaiden who will certainly be to your taste as well. All you need is to ask."

Joseph's cheeks grew hot with anger. *How dare she?* Thankfully Potiphar intervened. "Your Greatness, what my wife wishes to say is that all that we have is yours. We only wish for you to be comfortable here."

But Joseph knew it was more than that. Zuleika sent a clear message. She had the one thing she knew he valued over anything else, which meant she was still in control. One word from her, and Mariam would be lost to him forever. He needed to tread carefully.

Potiphar turned to his wife. "Let me introduce Pharaoh's esteemed guests this evening. Salim, Pharaoh's personal assistant, and I imagine you recognize Joseph, Pharaoh's new second-in-command."

Zuleika's mouth twitched as if to speak, but Potiphar quickly took her arm, and she was forced to hold her forked tongue. Joseph could tell that Potiphar was doing his best to keep the peace.

"Joseph and I have reconciled our past," Potiphar said. "We wish him all the best in his new position. Should he manage Avaris half as well as he did our estate, then the city is bound to flourish. Now enough talk of bygone days. Let us enjoy the evening." Potiphar quickly ushered them all into the dining room.

This would be a dinner to remember. Fortunately, awkward dinners were Joseph's specialty, but all hopes of being at the top of his game went out the window when he caught sight of Mariam.

She stood there with her big brown eyes and lips ripe for kissing. She was the embodiment of sunshine and laughter and everything that was right with the world. Joseph wanted to run, take her in his arms, and kiss her until he ran out of breath.

Zuleika sniffed as if she could smell the attraction and found it nauseating. Joseph had no hope of keeping a poker face, and neither did Mariam. She was so radiant that Zuleika nearly gagged, which made it all the better. But, of course, the moment could not last forever, and Zuleika was not one to be outshone at her own party. She barked at Mariam to leave the tray of food and return to the kitchen. Then she turned to Pharaoh.

"Poor thing, pretty to look at, but not the brightest bulb in the box, as they used to say."

Pharaoh nodded sadly. "Indeed, she is rather exquisite."

"I am glad you find her to your liking," cooed Zuleika.

Joseph lost his appetite as he watched Pharaoh's eyes linger on Mariam as she exited the room. What was he supposed to do? He needed to come up with a plan, and quickly. The five of them sat at the large dining table with Pharaoh at the head, flanked by Zuleika and Potiphar. This left Joseph across from Salim. Servants came and went with food, but each time Mariam entered, Zuleika remarked on her beauty and ensured that she served Pharaoh personally. By the time they reached dessert, Pharaoh was practically drooling over Mariam, and Joseph knew that he had to act.

There was a momentary lull in the conversation. Up until now, Zuleika had kept up a steady stream of flattery in Pharaoh's direction, so Joseph seized the opportunity. If there was anything he'd learned from being a younger brother, it was to speak up when the chance arose.

"Your Greatness, it seems that our esteemed hostess has provided us with such a rich array of foods that I find myself in need of a small break. What would you say to joining me for a brief stroll to see the property's magnificent garden before we finish with dessert?"

Pharaoh's face lit up. "That sounds most excellent."

"Very good. Potiphar, would you care to lead us?" asked Joseph. He needed to get Pharaoh away from Zuleika.

"Most certainly," replied Potiphar. "Zuleika, I think perhaps we will venture forth with just the men. We will return shortly." Zuleika frowned but didn't protest, and Joseph could see how much it pained her. Now he would see if Potiphar was an ally to be trusted.

As they walked out to the garden, Joseph gathered his words. It was now or never.

"Pharaoh, I am afraid there is something I must tell you. It might make you angry, but I must tell you nonetheless."

Pharaoh stopped in his tracks. "Out with it then. Bad news only gets worse the longer you wait."

All Joseph's carefully crafted words disappeared, and instead he blurted out, "I am in love with Mariam, the serving girl."

There was a moment's silence, and then Pharaoh began to laugh. "In love with the serving girl. I can't blame you. You have good taste. So, what would you have me do?"

Keep your hands off her, thought Joseph. Instead, he looked Pharaoh in the eye, and, with a fire in his belly, he spoke the words that had long been hiding in his heart. "I'd like to marry her."

Pharaoh gave Joseph a surprised look. "I'm afraid she's not mine to give. What would you say, Potiphar?"

Potiphar massaged his furrowed brow. "I'd say that Zuleika will not be pleased."

Joseph's heart sank.

"But... I would say you have my blessing. You are a good man, Joseph. Let this be proof of my commitment to you." Potiphar held out his hand, and Joseph shook it. This was the happiest moment of his life. Here, in the garden, God was restoring to him what had been lost.

Pharaoh clapped Potiphar on the back. "I will offer you a generous sum for her to ease the loss, and I insist that you take it."

"Then I accept," said Potiphar.

"Excellent," gushed Pharaoh. "Joseph, it is only fitting that a man of your status has a wife, but there will be many sad women across Avaris. I imagine that schemes were already being set in place to try to seduce you."

Joseph hadn't even thought of this. What a strange world he was now living in, but if he had Mariam by his side then everything would be okay. "I am sorry to disappoint them, but once they meet Mariam, I have no doubt they will understand my choice."

Pharaoh smiled. "This is true. No one will doubt that you have an eye for beauty. Now let us return to your new bride, so you can tell her the good news."

Potiphar's shoulders sank low. "And I will break the news to my wife."

Joseph floated on air as they made their way back into the house, and the rest of the world faded away when he saw Mariam standing quietly in the shadows. Somewhere nearby Potiphar was talking quietly to Zuleika. She stormed out of the room, but Joseph didn't care. The only person who mattered was just a few feet away.

Joseph practically ran across the room and could see the startled look in Mariam's eyes. She looked even more surprised when he took her hands in his, but she didn't pull away.

"Mariam, I have wanted to say these words to you for a long time. I love you, and I want to spend the rest of my life with you." He squeezed her hands and could feel tears welling up in his eyes. "I promise to care for you every day, as long as I live. You are more beautiful than the sunrise. You are more than I deserve. I will never stop loving you. I couldn't, even if I tried. Mariam, will you marry me?"

Mariam hesitated just for a second. Then she intertwined her fingers in his and looked up into Joseph's hope-filled eyes. "Yes! I love you, Joseph, and I always will. I want to be your wife."

Bolts of electricity shot through their fingertips, and Joseph swore that somewhere up above them fireworks from the olden days were exploding across the sky. He looked at Mariam's perfect lips, and he knew what he wanted to do. He leaned in and whispered. "May I kiss you?"

Mariam laughed. "I thought you'd never ask."

Her lips were like honey, sweet and delicious. When they finally parted, Joseph took a breath, and it was filled with the delicious fragrance of her.

"How was that for a first kiss?" Joseph asked, feeling rather good about himself.

"Why do you think it's my first kiss?"

"What?"

"Just teasing. It was good," she said with a twinkle in her eye.

Joseph leaned in for another kiss. It wasn't just good. It was great. A taste of Heaven. He was about to kiss Mariam again when Pharaoh cleared his throat nearby. Joseph pulled back.

"I apologize, Your Greatness. I got caught up in the moment."

"No need to apologize, but let's save round two for another time. Preferably when I'm not around."

"Of course," said Joseph trying to hide his boyish grin. He couldn't wait for round two.

CHAPTER 23

New Beginnings

The sky seemed somehow less gray than usual as Joseph stood next to Pharaoh in the back of an open-bed truck as they drove through the streets of Avaris. Salim shouted into a bullhorn, his voice oppressively loud and garbled.

"Come and see His Greatness, Pharaoh, and his new second-in-command, Joseph, the commander of Avaris! Come one, come all."

And come they did. People poured out of every nook and cranny in Avaris. All of them were clearly curious to lay eyes on this new mystery man who had risen to power. Potiphar and his men did their best to keep the crowd from crushing the truck as people swarmed around trying to get close enough to touch Pharaoh and Joseph.

Joseph watched Pharaoh bask in the limelight, feeding off the energy of the people. He smiled ear to ear, reaching out and shaking hands and patting heads. He was like the politicians of old. Joseph was not nearly as comfortable, but he did his best. The two of them were quite the spectacle, but Joseph knew this was precisely what Pharaoh wanted: the powerful coming down amongst the commoners. Pharaoh wanted to be both touchable and untouchable, both loved and feared. It was a fine line to walk, and Joseph would have to learn to walk it as well. This was his new life.

Joseph was exhausted by the time they returned to the palace. It felt like they'd driven down every side street and alleyway and shaken every hand in Avaris. As soon as the truck came to a stop, Salim disappeared. Having to tell the whole city that Joseph was the new second-in-command had clearly taken its toll on his ego.

Pharaoh stepped down from the truck looking as fresh as when they'd started. The man was a machine. He gave Joseph a grin. "You'll get used to it. The fame. The adoration. The endless line of people who want to talk to you. It's all part of the job. We have dinner in an hour. I've invited the cabinet. We need to discuss our strategy for storing food." He looked up at the sky. "It seems your prediction may already be coming true with weather like this."

Joseph felt a moment of panic at Pharaoh's words. If he was correct, that meant the great famine was coming, and he was responsible for keeping them all alive. He tried to push aside his dread and fatigue. "I will clean up and be ready right away."

"Excellent." Pharaoh waltzed off, leaving Joseph to slump back to his room.

Joseph opened the door, ready to throw himself onto his bed for a catnap, but Cyasi was waiting for him and shot to his feet when Joseph entered.

"Please pardon my intrusion. I'm here to help prepare you for dinner."

Joseph rolled his eyes. "No rest for the weary."

"I'm afraid not. Now change out of those clothes and put on the fresh ones that I hung in the bathroom. Then the real preparation for the dinner begins."

"What do you mean?"

Now it was Cyasi's turn to roll his eyes, his many piercings rippling like a small tidal wave across his face. "You need to be ready for tonight. It's one giant test. The members of the cabinet will be watching your every move and analyzing your every word. Even your attire will be judged, but I've taken care of that for you."

Joseph groaned and flopped onto the bed, but forty-five minutes later he was dressed in a dark suit, complete with a sky blue handkerchief made of fine silk for the front pocket. More importantly, thanks to Cyasi, he had a basic bio of each of the council members. Cyasi was a gift from God, a red-haired tattooed angel who seemed to know everything about everybody.

Cyasi straightened Joseph's tie and patted him on the shoulders. "I declare that you are ready. Time to go."

Just then, there was a knock on the door. Cyasi opened it, and there stood Salim. He gave the slightest of bows. "I am here to escort Joseph to dinner."

"Of course," said Cyasi as he ran his hand through his hair, "but I believe that you should give your superior the honor he is due by referring to him with his proper title, Avaris City Commander."

Salim gave Cyasi a small sneer before turning to Joseph. "I apologize most profusely. I meant you no disrespect, Commander."

Joseph watched him warily. "No offense taken, but from now on you will use my formal title, even when we are in private." He needed to make it clear that they were not equals, and he made a mental note to thank Cyasi later for drawing his attention to Salim's intentional slight. He was sure it would not be the last from Salim and from others who believed him unworthy of his new position.

Cyasi gave him a wink as he walked out the door with Salim. It was clear there would be no pleasant small talk, so Joseph went over the names of the council members in his head instead. He'd met them once, but it had only been for a few minutes. He also needed to learn his way around the palace. The place was a labyrinth!

Finally, they arrived at a bronze door that seemed to mimic the one into the throne room. Salim pushed it open and called out in his nasally voice, "I present Joseph, newly appointed Avaris City Commander." Then he motioned for Joseph to enter the room in front of him. Joseph stepped in and saw five sets of eyes staring at him. All conversation stopped. Glasses in hand, the members of the council were milling about the table, but no one was seated. Pharaoh was nowhere in sight. *Probably waiting to make a grand entrance,* thought Joseph.

It did Joseph's heart good to see Potiphar. He at least had one advocate amongst the cabinet. Now it was time to charm the others. As Joseph crossed the room, Potiphar stepped forward to greet him.

"Welcome, Joseph. May I introduce you to my fellow cabinet members?"

"That would be most appreciated." All eyes were on them as Potiphar steered him toward the largest man in the room. Joseph couldn't help but notice that all the cabinet members were well armed with knives and guns strapped to various parts of their bodies. He made a note to acquire some sort of knife so he could fit in. He had no idea how to shoot a gun, so that wouldn't do him any good.

Potiphar made introductions until the doors burst open, marking Pharaoh's arrival. Joseph half expected to hear trumpets blaring, but apparently that was a lost art these days.

Salim stood at attention and called out. Joseph couldn't help but notice his voice was suddenly much less nasally and depressing. "All rise for Pharaoh, the great ruler of Avaris."

On cue, Pharaoh swept in. His presence filled the room, making everyone else seem small compared to him. They all waited for Pharaoh to speak, which, of course, he obliged.

"Gentlemen, thank you all for coming. Before we are seated, let me re-introduce our new city commander, Joseph. I believe that he will be a valuable addition to our new team." He paused and looked at each of them, seemingly daring them to question his choice. No one moved a muscle.

"Well then, we have much to discuss after the events of the last few days. Let's eat, and then we will hear from Joseph about his plans for Avaris."

Joseph was seated at Pharaoh's right hand. Pharaoh was making his new status abundantly clear. Joseph didn't have much of an appetite, but he forced himself to eat and give the appearance of calm. He remembered Cyasi's words. *They will be watching your every move and listening to your every word.* Well, if there was one thing Joseph was good at, it was words. When the plates had been cleared, Pharaoh invited him to share his plan.

Joseph stood. The council members looked up at him unimpressed. He tried not to let it unnerve him as he began.

"I am honored to have been put in this new position, and I do not take it lightly. There is much work to be done if we are to survive. I believe that each of us in this room is here for a purpose. Now let me share my plan for Avaris."

He laid out a verbal blueprint for his vision, and the others hung on his every word. They asked all sorts of questions as he discussed greenhouses, irrigation systems, and storage silos. By the time they were done, it was late, but Joseph sensed a shift in the mood in the room. He'd gained their respect. Time would tell if they could pull off his massive plan.

Joseph and Pharaoh were the last to leave. Pharaoh clapped him on the back.

"Well done! I knew you were the right man for the job. Most of this lot are hardened fighters, not city planners or thinkers like you Joseph. You're exactly who we need. It's almost like God dropped you right out of the sky. Imagine that. Anything you need, you let me know."

God hadn't exactly dropped him out of the sky. It had been more like a long, painful dragging process, but Joseph wasn't about to correct Pharaoh. He was just grateful to be here.

"Oh, and I arranged to have Mariam come to the palace tomorrow. Tonight's your last night as a single man, you lucky dog."

Joseph gasped. The day had been so busy he hadn't had time to think about Mariam and their impending wedding. "Will there be a service?" he asked.

Pharaoh laughed, and then realized Joseph was serious. "You really were raised in a bunker, weren't you? The old wedding services have mostly gone out of style, especially if you are looking for a religious service. There aren't any rabbis or priests that I know of in Avaris. I can throw you a feast, though, if you'd like one. I'm always up for a good party."

Joseph thought for a second and then knew exactly what he wanted. "It doesn't seem right to have a grandiose affair since we're about to increase taxes and start saving food. Something small would be better, and I know just the person to perform the ceremony."

"Whatever you want, it will be done," said Pharaoh.

******

Joseph woke the next morning to the sound of someone knocking on the door. Why did someone always need him? Still groggy, he rolled out of bed and opened the door.

"Rise and shine sleepyhead." It was Cyasi, and he seemed far too awake for Joseph's liking.

"What do you want?"

Cyasi gave him a mock pouty face. "Did someone get woken up from his beauty sleep?"

"I would remind you that I'm the second-in-command of all of Avaris," said Joseph.

"Yeah, yeah, I don't really play by those rules. The joys of being a true artiste. We make up our own rules. You don't like it, then I don't help you look good on your special day."

"What do you mean?"

"I mean it's not every day you get married; in fact, most people don't even bother anymore. Before the Great War divorce was at an all-time high, but I have a feeling that's more information than you wanted."

Joseph nodded as his brain caught up with the words spewing out of Cyasi's mouth.

"Got it, I'll spare you the history lesson."

"Thanks. How did you know I'm getting married today?" asked Joseph.

Cyasi grinned mischievously. "It's my job to know. I don't ever give up my sources, but let's just say my information came from the very top."

"So, Pharaoh told you?"

"I can neither confirm nor deny that, but I did give him a little trim up this morning..."

"Remind me never to give you any top-secret information if this is how you protect your sources."

"You owe me big time and you don't even know it," said Cyasi. "You have no idea how much I've been offered for dirt on you."

"Like whether my hair is thinning and what type of clothes I like?"

Cyasi laughed. "It's good you have a sense of humor about all this, and you'll be happy to know I've told everyone that you have a fine head of hair."

"That is a huge relief. I'll still be able to show my face in public, but that type of curiosity is exactly why today's wedding is going to be a private affair."

"I completely understand. I promise that people's curiosity will die down in time, but for the moment it's good to hold your cards close to your chest. I can always leak a little information here and there if you like. Think of it as tiny breadcrumbs to keep people happy. Then you control the narrative that gets out."

"That makes sense. We can plan a breadcrumb strategy later. Today I only want to think about one thing."

"As you wish, but first let me give you a quick trim, Great Commander of Avaris." The words sounded so unnatural coming from Cyasi that Joseph couldn't help but laugh. The man defied all convention. Like a time traveler who'd accidentally shown up in the wrong period of history.

Cyasi completed his artistry and let himself out. Joseph was left alone with his thoughts and a stretch of hours that felt like an endless chasm. Around lunchtime there was a knock on the door.

"Who is it?" called Joseph.

"An old friend," came a familiar voice.

Joseph leapt from his chair and threw open the door for Emmanuel.

"I heard there was a wedding today," the old man said.

Joseph wrapped him in an embrace. "Now that you're here, there will be. Can you believe it?"

"I can, Joseph. I can. God has taken care of you. I always knew He would."

"Then you had faith even when I did not."

Emmanuel squeezed his shoulders. "That's how faith works. Sometimes we hold onto it for each other."

"Today we'll hold onto it together," said Joseph.

"Yes, we will. Now if I'm not mistaken, we have some details to plan. I've never officiated a wedding before."

CHAPTER 24

Until Death Do Us Part

A few hours later, Joseph waited with Emmanuel in a small chamber, the walls of which were covered in ancient hieroglyphics. At the front of the room was a stone basin filled with water, and he dipped his fingers into the water nervously.

The silence in the room was finally broken when Cyasi peeked his head inside the door.

"Sorry to keep you waiting, Joseph, but I am pleased to tell you that your bride is here."

Joseph's chest tightened with a mixture of fear and excitement, and he felt the need to pinch himself to make sure this wasn't just another one of his dreams. This was really happening. Mariam was here, and they were getting married. He looked over at Emmanuel who gave him a thumbs up and walked to the door to escort Mariam to the anxious groom.

All the air rushed out of Joseph's lungs when Mariam stepped into the room on Emmanuel's arm. She wore a rich cream-colored dress adorned with beautiful beadwork that shimmered like diamonds, and her dark hair perfectly framed her face and fell down around her shoulders like a waterfall.

When Joseph locked eyes with her, the room was suddenly aglow with love. It was as if Heaven had come down, and for a brief second all the pain and hurt in the world disappeared. This was not what he and Emmanuel had planned, but Joseph was so overjoyed to see his bride that he ran over and embraced her. He had to touch her and know that she was real. And she was. Beauty incarnate, she was his future. His everything.

Hand in hand they made their way to the front of the room and stood beside the stone basin. Emmanuel, his eyes already watery and his voice warbling with emotion, began to speak.

"This is a most wonderful day. A day I never thought I'd see. My meager faith could barely imagine such a gift from God, and yet here we are. Today, by the grace of God, we are here to celebrate two wonderful people being married. I am honored that you have asked me to guide this service." Emmanuel paused to wipe away a tear.

"You must forgive an old man his tears. Let us begin. Marriage is a sacred covenant between a man and a woman. Today, we gather before God to uphold this covenant. As God has cared for both of you, so may you care for one another. May you love one another well as long as you live. And now a reading from Sacred scripture.

Set me as a seal upon your heart,
 as a seal upon your arm,
 passion fierce as the grave.
Its flashes are flashes of fire,
 a raging flame.
For love is strong as death,
many waters cannot quench love,
neither can floods drown it.
If one offered for love
all the wealth of one's house,
it would be utterly scorned.'"

Joseph nodded, his heart filled to overflowing with this vast, unquenchable love. Emmanuel paused to catch his breath and wipe away another tear.

"May it be so for the both of you. May you love each other well all your days. In a broken world, may your love bring healing to one another and to those around you. Now, Joseph, you have some words you would like to share with your lovely bride."

Joseph squeezed Mariam's hands and looked deep into her eyes. He wanted to remember this moment for the rest of life. "Mariam, in the midst of my darkness, you brought me light. When I thought all hope was lost, you brought me hope. You are beautiful inside and out. You are strong. You are smart. You make me laugh. You are full of surprises. Through the ups and downs of life, I promise to love you with all that I am and all that I have."

Emmanuel turned to Mariam. "Do you have anything that you'd like to share?"

Mariam paused, then took a deep breath. "Joseph, you are like the warmth of a fire on a cold night. You protected me when I was vulnerable. You were persistent when my guard was up. You have brought me so much joy. Thank you for seeing me, for treating me like an equal. I can't wait to spend my life with you, and above all else, I will always love you."

Emmanuel was crying again, but he didn't wipe away the tears this time. "In our world where so much has been lost, let it not be said that love is dead. Joseph, do you take Mariam to be your wife from this day forward?"

"I do!"

"Mariam, do you take Joseph to be your husband from this day forward?"

"I do!"

"Then I pronounce the two of you husband and wife, and I leave you with this blessing. May your love be as beautiful each day you share as it is on this day of your wedding. May the Lord bless you and keep you; the Lord make his face to shine upon you and be gracious to you; the Lord turn his face towards you and give you peace. At long last, Joseph, you may kiss your bride."

Joseph leaned in and kissed Mariam, trying to pour all his love into that single action in case the world suddenly ended and he never got another chance. She kissed him back with the same intensity. In that moment, he knew with every fiber of his being that the best was yet to come.

When they finally came up for air, Joseph opened his eyes and saw that Emmanuel had found a handkerchief and was dabbing at his red, runny eyes. Cyasi had disappeared. The palace was quiet, and the rest of Joseph's life seemed to stretch out before him, filled with the knowledge that he was no longer alone.

CHAPTER 25

In the Blink of An Eye

Five years flew by in the blink of an eye. Joseph remembered his father telling stories about when he was a young man waiting to marry Joseph's mother and how his seven years of courtship felt like little more than a day. Joseph had always chalked up those stories to his father's overzealous nostalgia, but now he understood. His life with Mariam was so rich. Each day was a gift. His work was tiring and the hours were long, but he had no complaints. So, the years whisked by, and Avaris prospered under Joseph's leadership. Even those who were skeptical of him at first became believers. He won them over, all except for Salim. The man was as bitter as the day was long.

It helped that as Joseph took office there seemed to be a healing of the land, as if the world itself had been waiting for just the right moment to begin coming back to life after all the damage it had suffered. Some marveled how this coincided with Joseph's rise to power. He was a constant topic of conversation. Some thought the timing was simply blind luck or chance, others began to see Joseph as a sort of talisman, a lucky omen for Avaris. Wherever he went, people prostrated themselves before him. Mothers wanted him to touch their babies, but Joseph did not allow this treatment to go to his head. He knew the simple truth to his success: God. His job was merely to be a faithful servant.

With Mariam at his side, they worked together for the good of Avaris. It didn't take long for Mariam to be as beloved as Joseph. She was heralded as the most beautiful woman in all the world, but her beauty was matched by her strength. Much like her husband, she was a force to be reckoned with, and the two of them proved to be a world-changing duo.

While the time flew by, Joseph never forgot Pharaoh's dream and the impending destruction that loomed over Avaris, thought the people did. They reveled in having enough food to eat and clean water to drink. There were even vineyards planted to make wine, and plants emerged that had long been thought extinct. It seemed as if Avaris had become the second Eden.

Then the whole Earth seemed to explode at once. The ground shook, giant fissures formed, and cracks spread across the Earth like lightning. People went temporarily deaf from the noise. The sky grew black, a colossal ink spill spreading across the heavens, and the air was filled with the smell of sulfur as a giant volcano erupted nearby, spewing lava. Twisting rivers of magma surged into the valley where Avaris sat vulnerable and alone. Huge chunks of stone sprayed across the valley and into the sea beyond.

A smothering wave of ash rained down upon Avaris and across the land as the wind picked up, carrying it far and wide. All anyone could do was run for cover and wait. When at last the stones stopped pummeling and the ash had subsided to a dribble, Joseph went out to survey the damage with a heavy heart. This all felt strangely familiar, as he looked at fields of destroyed crops, obliterated water tanks, and houses smashed to pieces. It was like a rampaging giant had rumbled through Avaris.

The five years of famine and hardship had begun. "Lord have mercy," Joseph prayed. Then he ran into the chaos to help.

******

It took days to pull people from the rubble. Joseph oversaw the operations and refused to sleep. While he worked, he couldn't help but wonder about his family back in the bunker. Were they okay? Did he want them to be okay? Certainly Abba, but what about his brothers?

Maybe this was God's justice being meted out. He felt torn. One moment he wanted justice, the next he hoped and prayed they were all safe. It was all too confusing, and he threw himself into his work even more.

Finally, Potiphar came to him. "Pharaoh has commanded your presence. You must go."

Joseph looked at him with weary, bloodshot eyes. "Please, we are almost done."

Potiphar put his hand on Joseph's shoulder. "I will oversee the remaining work myself. You have done all that you can for now."

Joseph made his way back to the damaged palace. After standing for thousands of years, many of its pillars had crumbled, and large sections of the roof had caved in. Like the rest of Avaris, it would have to be rebuilt. He wove his way through the piles of stone until he arrived at the throne room, noting the jagged crack that now ran through the marble stairs leading up to Pharaoh's throne. As he climbed, his legs felt heavier with each step.

When he reached the top, he kneeled before Pharaoh. The man seemed to have lost his air of confidence, and he motioned for Joseph to rise. "I have been hearing reports of your tireless efforts on behalf of my people."

"Yes, Pharaoh. I and many others."

Pharaoh nodded approvingly. "You have done well. Not that I should be surprised by now. For five years you have gone above and beyond, but I fear that the long-anticipated day of reckoning has arrived."

Joseph rose and looked at Pharaoh, his eyes filled with sadness. "Yes, Pharaoh. Five years have flown by, but the vision you received from God has come true. Surely the five years of famine and destruction have begun."

Pharaoh slumped, and it was as if he were aging before Joseph's very eyes. When Pharaoh spoke, his voice was little more than a whisper. "All this time I secretly hoped that the second half of my dream would not come true. You are too young to remember what the first days were like after the Great War began, but I remember, Joseph. I remember, like a terrible nightmare that constantly haunts me. The thought of having to relive such a thing makes my very bones shudder."

Joseph did his best to be strong. "You are correct that I do not remember what it was like, but I believe that God helped us to be ready for this day. I already have reports that the food we stored remains safe and sound. We'll have enough food to provide for the people of Avaris while we rebuild. You were bold enough to envision Avaris as a place for the rebirth of civilization, and that is truer today than ever before. We must not lose heart."

The light in Pharaoh's eyes seemed to slowly turn back on, and he rose from his chair. "Thank you, Joseph. You are right. We cannot lose hope. I think it would do the people good to receive a visit from their leader. So, if you'll excuse me, I'll be taking my leave to join the efforts."

He swept past Joseph. Halfway down the steps he stopped and called back. "Go and get some sleep. That's an order."

Joseph happily obliged and headed to his room. He had to turn around twice to find a different route since the hallway had caved in. Finally, he made it back to his room and slept the sleep of the dead. He woke to the sound of Mariam's voice and the touch of her hand rubbing gently on his back.

"Wake up. You need to eat."

Joseph rolled over and opened his eyes. All the world was afire but seeing her made him smile. His only sadness was that they had not been able to have children. He knew she bore that burden more than he, but children or no children, he loved her more than life itself.

"Hello, Sunshine. How long have I been sleeping?"

She swept the hair back from his eyes. "Long enough. I was beginning to worry. Now let's eat together before you run off again to save the world."

"I would like nothing more." Joseph kissed her hand, and they sat down to eat a small breakfast.

"I'm surprised no one has come looking for me," said Joseph.

Mariam laughed. "Oh, they have a whole slew of people, but I put a guard at the door to keep them out. You needed to rest. Avaris cannot afford to lose you."

Joseph smiled. "What would I do without you?"

"We both know the answer to that. You'd work yourself to death," Mariam replied, but Joseph could tell her thoughts were elsewhere.

"Probably true," said Joseph. He reached across the table and took her hand. "Tell me what's on your mind?"

For a moment she didn't make eye contact. When she looked up, her eyes were filled with tears. "I can't stop thinking about my father and all the people in the caves. I keep imagining them buried alive by the earthquake."

Joseph scooted around the table and wrapped her in his arms. "I'm so sorry." He held her for a long time. There were no words to say. His mind drifted to his own family. Had they survived? But there was no time to dwell on such things. When he finally let go of Mariam, he kissed her. "I will be back tonight. I promise."

Outside the palace, the cleanup was continuing, and Joseph relieved Potiphar of duty. He set up distribution hubs so people could get a day's worth of food for their family. Enough people had died; there was no need for others to starve.

A week after the eruption, Joseph woke early in the morning. Dawn was just breaking, and Mariam was still asleep beside him. He kissed her softly on the cheek before rolling out of bed. A few minutes later, he met Potiphar, and the two of them went to survey Avaris's defenses which had been mostly left unattended while the wreckage inside the city was tended to. As Potiphar and Joseph walked along the border, it was clear there was much work to be done. Large sections of the chain link fence had toppled over, and almost all the lookout towers had collapsed, leaving behind a barrage of exploded sang bags and splintered beams and no sentries.

Joseph looked at Potiphar as he scanned the damage. "What do you think?"

"I think we are vulnerable until we get all this fixed. We should make it a priority to re-establish our defenses," said Potiphar in a matter-of-fact voice.

"I hear you. We will send a team today to start the work, but from what I can tell it'll take weeks, maybe months, to fix this." Joseph rubbed his temples.

Potiphar agreed. "Which means we should station a twenty-four-hour patrol along the border until the work is done. A storm is coming, Joseph. I can feel it."

The back of Joseph's neck prickled. "What do you mean?"

Potiphar sighed. "The kind of storm that leaves a lot of people dead. I've been a soldier long enough to read the signs and trust my instincts. A war is coming."

A chill ran down Joseph's spine. They weren't ready for war. "Are you sure?"

"As sure as you are that somewhere out there is a God watching over us. You better start praying because the militias and warlords will be coming."

Joseph shivered. Had there not been enough death? Enough killing? Why did humans never learn? That's when the first bullet flew by him. Before he knew what was happening, Potiphar tackled him to the ground.

"Stay down," Potiphar growled as he pulled out his gun and tossed Joseph a knife. "Looks like they're already here. Follow me if you want to see Mariam again."

Joseph pictured Mariam still asleep in bed, and he knew that he couldn't die here. He army-crawled behind Potiphar, and together they made it to the wreckage of one of the lookout towers. They rolled in behind a large pile of sandbags, and Joseph breathed a sigh of relief.

Potiphar peeked from behind the sandbags and ducked back as a barrage of bullets exploded right where his head had been. "Not good," he growled. "Looks like a full unit of militia."

"What do we do?" asked Joseph. His heart was racing, and his mouth had gone dry.

"We run and live to fight another day. Avaris can't afford to lose you, and we have to alert our troops." Potiphar paused, and Joseph knew he was coming up with a plan. "It's time for a little diversion." He pulled out a grenade.

"Why do you— Wait. How long have you had that thing?" asked Joseph.

Potiphar grinned. "Long enough. I've been saving it for a rainy day. When I throw it, cover your ears. As soon as it goes off, we're out of here. You got it?"

Joseph gripped his knife for dear life and nodded.

"Good. One, two"—Potiphar pulled the pin—"three!" He launched the grenade high into the air. Joseph covered his ears, but they still rang at the sound of the explosion. There was shouting and smoke, and the next thing Joseph knew, Potiphar grabbed his shirt and pulled him up. In the chaos, they sprinted toward the safety of Avaris. Joseph didn't dare to look back. His lungs felt like they were seizing up, but he kept running.

A bullet streaked by him like an angry hornet. Just ahead of him, Potiphar groaned and staggered as the bullet sank into his leg. He unleashed a string of expletives while his blood spattered on Joseph. The big man kept moving, but he was limping badly.

"Go without me," he grunted through clenched teeth.

"Not a chance," said Joseph. He put his arm around Potiphar's shoulders, and together they staggered forward. Bullets struck the dirt all around them, nipping at their heels. What he wouldn't give for another grenade right about now. Joseph looked up and saw buildings just a little way ahead. "Come on," he shouted to Potiphar. "We're almost there. Keep moving"

If they could just get to...

A squad of Avaris's guards burst from behind the buildings and sprinted toward Joseph and Potiphar. Providing the pair with cover fire, they shepherded them to safety. Joseph leaned against the wall, trying to catch his breath. Next to him Potiphar was bleeding something fierce. Joseph was amazed he hadn't gone into shock, but he guessed this wasn't his first time sustaining a major injury. One of the soldiers tied a shirt around Potiphar's leg to slow the bleeding, then turned to Joseph. "We need to get the two of you back to the palace at once. Can you walk?"

"I can," said Joseph, though he could barely hear himself over the ringing in his ears.

"Okay then. Let's move out," said the soldier. He gave a signal to the other soldiers, and from there everything became a blur in Joseph's memory.

CHAPTER 26

Under Siege

Joseph and Potiphar lay on cots in the palace's small infirmary when Pharaoh and the other cabinet members burst through the door.

"What in the world happened to the two of you?" asked Pharaoh.

Joseph was going to answer, but Potiphar beat him to it. "Your Greatness, we were attacked while patrolling the perimeter. It would seem Joseph has a forcefield around him, but I wasn't so lucky. I took a bullet to the leg. Hurts like hell, but I'll be fine."

There was plenty of hushed chatter amongst the cabinet members, but it was Pharaoh who said what everyone was thinking. "So, we are under attack."

Potiphar grimaced as he tried to sit up. "Yes. It was a small militia group. Maybe ten, fifteen soldiers from what I could tell, but there will be more. They're going to come out of hiding like rats looking for food, and we're the only ones around who have any."

The cabinet chorused its agreement.

"What should we do?" asked Pharaoh.

"Fix the perimeter, double the guard, and lock down all entrances except for the main gate. Everyone going in or out needs to be searched, and we have to be on the lookout for spies," said Potiphar.

"Those all sound good while we get things under control. How long until you can be up on your feet again?"

"I'll be up and about in a few days, but I won't be moving very fast for a good while. I've had worse. In the meantime, Joseph should be able to run logistics."

Pharaoh turned to Joseph. "Can you manage that?"

"I can," Joseph said. "There's no need for me to be cooped up in this bed."

"Good. Let's get to it. All citizens that are fit to work should assist with rebuilding the perimeter. Time is of the essence," said Pharaoh.

Potiphar was more right than he knew. Over the next few days, skirmishes took place all around the city, and there were many casualties. Even the jackals were desperate, and there were multiple attacks on those working to shore up the fence. Joseph barely saw Mariam. She was volunteering in Emmanuel's makeshift hospital in the main square. Each day, citizens were given a small portion of grain in exchange for their work. It wasn't much, but it was enough to keep everyone going.

It didn't take long before refugees started trickling in. They brought with them terrible tales from the eruption and ensuing earthquake. It seemed the whole world had been disrupted. Potiphar's men vetted every refugee before allowing them access to the city. As new citizens of Avaris they, too, were expected to work and were tossed right into the frantic rebuilding of the city's defenses. As the defenses rose, the attacks diminished, and Joseph prayed that they had withstood the worst of it.

When they finally went a whole day without any attacks, Joseph felt like he could breathe again. He and Mariam celebrated by sitting down to eat dinner together, something they hadn't been able to do amidst the chaos. They made small talk, not wanting to broach anything too heavy after days of wading through heaviness. It was just good to be together.

After dinner they decided to go for a walk to one of their favorite places in the palace. Climbing over piles of stone, they arrived at a small terrace with a clear view of the city. Mariam rested her head on Joseph's shoulder as they looked out over Avaris. It took time for their eyes to adjust to the thick darkness. Only a few lights dotted the windows of the jumbled mess of buildings down below. There was a sense that the whole city was hunkering down. It was a season of survival. The air had a tinge of sickliness to it.

Mariam broke the silence. "What will you do with the refugees that keep coming?"

It was a good question. For the moment they were helpful hands, and the city had enough food to feed them, but for how long?

"We'll take in as many as we can," Joseph said. "I fear that if we turn them away, they'll join our enemies. The famine is only going to get worse, and I won't have their blood on my hands. I believe that God has put me here for such a time as this."

Mariam leaned in and kissed him.

"What was that for?"

"For being you. For caring about others," said Mariam.

Joseph grinned like a schoolboy, but then he became serious. "We have to learn from the mistakes of the past. A house divided against itself will fall. We have to come together."

"I agree, but it won't be easy. Where there is difference there will be fear and doubt. I saw it all the time in the caves. Any outsider was a devil. These refugees will bring lots of different customs and beliefs with them."

Joseph pulled her in and gave her a kiss. "Then we must welcome them. We will need all their ideas and knowledge to survive. Let's channel that creativity towards solutions rather than war."

They stood there for a long time, just two people trying to make a difference in the world. As he looked out across the wrecked city, Joseph decided to welcome all refugees to Avaris. He would even sell grain to outsiders who came in search of food. Let Potiphar see to vetting and security and such things. He would do his best to see Avaris be a city with open arms.

CHAPTER 27

Facing Ghosts

Joseph was overseeing the dispensing of food when he heard the door open and looked up. A band of men entered the room. Their clothes were ragged from travel and their faces smeared with ash and dirt. Like most refugees who straggled in, they looked like they'd been through hell and back again. Then Joseph took a second look and nearly fell out of his chair with shock.

He was staring into the faces of ghosts, men he thought he'd never see again. Ishmael, his tempestuous tormenter, and his brothers who had sold him into slavery.

A long-simmering anger rose within Joseph, a dormant volcano ready to explode. Time froze as he stared at them, trying to decide what to do.

He was seated in his raised chair in his most formal attire, making it unlikely that any of them would recognize him. He wasn't the scrawny youth or half-starved slave they remembered. If he wanted to, he could exact his revenge right now. The thought of it was like the sweet taste of honey, and he beckoned them to step forward. They came and fell at his feet. Their faces touched the ground, and they didn't dare make eye contact with him. Oh, how the roles were reversed.

As they prostrated themselves before him, Joseph had a flashback. The scene in front of him was the exact fulfillment of what God had revealed so long ago: his brothers bowing before him. He was witnessing a miracle, but he also remembered how his brothers had mocked him and made fun of his dreams. They'd sworn they would never bow before him and that he'd never amount to anything. He could still feel the sting of their old insults. He carried the scars of being tossed into the well.

The question was, what should he do with these men groveling at his feet? These men who had caused him such suffering?

Joseph's anger was too great, and his wounds were too deep to simply let the past be the past. He wanted to see if they had changed and were deserving of forgiveness. What type of men had his brothers become? It was time to turn up the heat on them. Trial by fire was the best way to find out.

"On your feet!" Joseph commanded, his voice cracking like a whip. Ishmael and his brothers jumped to attention. He narrowed his eyes. "Where have you come from?"

Ishmael stepped forward, and the very sight of him made Joseph's skin crawl, but he controlled the urge to call for the guards and have him sent away.

"Your Honor, please forgive us if we have offended you in any way. We are but humble travelers come in search of food. We have journeyed a long way, from the land which used to be called Israel."

Joseph held up his hand to silence Ishmael. "Do you think I'm a fool? You come here and speak to me like a child. I am well aware of the old countries and the way things used to be." His voice continued to crescendo. "You will not come here as a guest and then disrespect me!"

Ishmael slowly retreated at Joseph's words, and a murmur of concern swept through the brothers. The guards at Joseph's side stepped forward, ready to attack at his command. Joseph glowered down at the men. "I do not believe your story. I received word just yesterday that spies were on their way to scout out our city. Spies from across the mountains. It's clear to me that you are the very spies I was warned about!"

Ishmael continued to backpedal, but Reuben flung himself before Joseph and cried out, "Please, My Lord, have mercy on us. We are not spies. I swear by Heaven and Earth that we are ten brothers. We were once twelve, but one is no more and our youngest is back with our aged father. We have come only to provide for our families. We are honest men. I promise this." Reuben's voice broke down, and he was on the verge of tears.

Joseph's heart leapt at the news that his father and younger brother were also alive. It took everything in him not to jump down from his high position and comfort Reuben. He had a soft spot in his heart for him, but he couldn't give up the ruse just yet. He pounded the arm of his chair and rose to his feet. His words were a tempest.

"I can smell your deceit from here, but I'm a fair man. I will give you a chance to prove your story is true. One of you must return to the hole you came from and bring back your youngest brother. Only if I see him will I know that you are not spies."

At this, Reuben tore his robe and the other brothers fell to the ground as well, and Joseph knew they were thinking how Abba would never allow his beloved youngest son, Benjamin, to travel to Avaris. Watching their grief, Joseph's heart ached, but he still didn't reveal his identity.

"Guards," he said, "take these men to the warden so they might consider my generous offer from prison. Let them return in three days."

The brothers didn't resist, but Ishmael was a different story. He lashed out at the guards trying to corral him, and his booming voice filled the room. "I demand a private audience, Your Honor. Do not lump me in with these traitors."

Joseph smiled to himself. This was about to get interesting. "I will grant you your audience, but not in private. You may speak here, and you had better make it worth my while."

The guards released Ishmael but continued to flank him with their hands on their weapons. Ishmael adjusted his robes before speaking. "Your Honor, I am here to share my own story of how I became mixed up with these unscrupulous men."

Joseph interjected. "Choose your words carefully, Bedouin. I do not take well to being lied to."

Ishmael swallowed. Clearly, things were not going according to plan, but he was committed now. "As you have pointed out, I am a Bedouin. We have quarrels with no man. Kingdoms rise and fall, and still we traverse the desert trading our wares. So it has been since the beginning of our people."

Joseph couldn't help but admire the man's ability to sweet talk. He was setting himself up nicely to somehow be the victim in all of this.

Ishmael looked down at the ground, a picture of contrition. "I came across these men while on my way to Avaris. I was unaware of their terrible plans. I meant only to be of help, seeing that they were starving and would surely die without my assistance."

"So, you are the Good Samaritan come back to life?" asked Joseph, his voice dripping with sarcasm.

Ishmael winced. "Perhaps I have overstated my position. The men did assist me by providing a large traveling group to deter thieves and bandits, but my intentions were pure. This is my story, and I stand by it."

"Very well," said Joseph. "You have given me much to think about. I will have you placed in your own cell, so that you're not forced to associate with such dangerous criminals, while I mull over what to do with you."

Joseph was sure that Ishmael had never done anything for another human being out of the goodness of his heart. Now to see if he could prove his hunch. He needed to talk to Cyasi. The man knew everyone and every rumor in Avaris.

Later that evening, Cyasi arrived in Joseph's private room. "I hear you need a trim. Is that correct?"

"Yes and no," said Joseph.

Cyasi grinned. "I thought that might be the case. Word on the street is there was a strange occurrence this morning at the grain dispersal site."

"Word travels fast."

Cyasi took out his scissors. "In the right circles, as I'm sure word has spread that you are getting your hair styled, so we would do well to make sure it looks perfect. What is said while I work will stay between us."

"I surely hope that people aren't concerned about my grooming habits, but your discretion is appreciated as always," replied Joseph as he sat in a chair.

Cyasi threw a towel around his shoulders. "What would you like to discuss then?"

Joseph filled him in about Ishmael, but he kept the identity of his brothers a secret. As much as he trusted Cyasi, he wasn't sure if the stylist could sit on such big information. When he'd finished telling of the morning's events, Cyasi took a break from snipping and pondered a moment before speaking.

"Here's my two cents. Never trust a man who's willing to sell other people for money. Such men have no souls. My guess is that your old pal Ishmael plans to double cross this group of brothers, if they are who they say they are, of course."

"That wouldn't surprise me in the least," said Joseph. "Is there any way we could check and see if he arranged plans to sell them?"

Cyasi played with his hands. "There's always a way if you know the right people."

"Let me guess, you might just know the right people?"

Cyasi grinned. "I might. There aren't too many people in Avaris who deal with slaves. I'll put out some feelers and let you know what I find. Until then, I suggest you let Ishmael and the others enjoy the hospitality of Avaris's prison. I hear the warden is a memorable host."

An image of the warden popped into Joseph's head, and he had to fight not to laugh. "He is indeed, if you call petting glass cats memorable."

"Now that I haven't heard. Care to share any more juicy details?" asked Cyasi with great interest.

"I think I will let the poor man exist in anonymity as much as possible."

"That's a shame," pouted Cyasi. "Then I believe we're done here until you're ready for a fresh shave in a day or two, if you catch my drift."

"I do. Thank you, Cyasi."

After Cyasi left, Joseph sat for a long time and tried to gather his thoughts. It had been a day of facing ghosts and staring into his past. He didn't want to admit it, but he'd been keeping himself busy so he didn't have to think about the past. It was easier to stay in the present than face the pain of all that had happened. In so many ways God had redeemed his trials, but his past still hurt worse than he wanted to admit. The pain of being abandoned was a perpetual wound.

Mariam found Joseph deep in thought when she got home. "Everything okay?" she asked with concern.

Joseph didn't even know how to answer that question. "Well... I saw my brothers today?"

Her eyes went wide with surprise. "Wait... What? How?"

"They came for grain. Things must be really bad back at the bunker."

"You didn't ask them? Okay, just start at the beginning," said Mariam. She came and sat right next to Joseph.

Joseph sighed and took Mariam's hand. He needed to touch her, to know that something was normal, unchanging. "I was just overseeing the daily grain distribution when suddenly my brothers appeared. It was crazy, and to make it all even weirder, our old friend Ishamel was with them." Joseph felt Mariam flinch, and he squeezed her hand gently. "I know. I felt the same way."

"What did you do?"

"It all happened so fast. They didn't recognize me, and at the last second, I decided to test them and see if they've changed."

"And how exactly did you do that?"

Joseph squirmed a bit. "I yelled at them, called them spies, and had them thrown into prison."

She glared at him. "You what? You're telling me that you didn't tell them who you are? If it was my father who'd walked through the door, I'd have run to him at once and hugged him until my arms fell off."

A wave of guilt washed over Joseph, leaving him sick to his stomach. "I know. I should have done that, but it's complicated, Mariam. The last time I saw them they beat me black and blue and then sold me as a slave. They treated me terribly my whole life!"

"So now you're getting back at them? Now the bullied becomes the bully? Joseph, how could you do that? That's not like you." Her conviction cut Joseph to his core.

Joseph knew she was right. *How could he?* His shoulders slumped. "I was angry. I wanted them to get a taste of what they'd done to me. I know it's not right, but in the moment, I just couldn't stop myself. I thought I'd forgiven them, but when I saw them, it all came rushing back. It felt so good to hold that power over them. To see the looks on their faces."

Mariam spoke in a kind but firm voice. "Forgiveness is more powerful than revenge, Joseph. I do not fault you for your actions, but neither do I want to see you trapped in a prison of bitterness. You need to face this. Don't run from it."

In that moment Joseph loved Mariam more than ever. She was the voice of truth that he needed. She wanted to bring out the best in him.

"Thank you for not hating me," he said. "I know what I did was foolish."

Mariam wrapped her arms around him. "It's not my place to judge you, and Lord knows I might have done the same thing or worse if I was in your shoes. There's a part of me that still wants to take Ishmael's whip and beat him with it, and don't get me started on Zuleika."

Joseph couldn't help but laugh. "I know exactly what you mean. I used to have dreams about giving Ishmael a good thrashing."

Mariam snuggled in. "Forgiveness is a process. I'm still working to forgive Ishmael and Zuleika. We can be on the journey together."

"I'd like that, but it might take me a little longer."

Mariam nodded. "I understand."

"There's more. My father and younger brother are alive. They're back at the bunker."

Mariam's face lit up. "That's great news. Your brothers can go and bring them to Avaris."

"We'll see."

They sat for a long time together, safe in the comfort of each other's arms. No matter what happened with his brothers, Joseph knew that he had Mariam.

CHAPTER 28

The Plot Thickens

Two days went by before Joseph received a note from Cyasi that read "Time for a shave. Noon today."

A man of his word, he showed up at exactly midday and pulled out a slender razor with a flourish.

Joseph sat and felt the razor edge sliding smoothly along the soft flesh of his throat. No matter how many times Cyasi gave him a shave, it always unnerved him. "You can tell the measure of man by how he responds when you put a blade to his throat," said Cyasi. It was almost like he read Joseph's mind.

"Is that right?" replied Joseph. He tried not to move his Adam's apple while he talked.

"It most certainly is. But you can also tell by whether a man tells the truth. It seems that Ishmael, the misunderstood Bedouin, is a liar."

If it weren't for the blade on his neck, Joseph would have jumped out of the chair to celebrate. Instead, he tried to remain calm. "I knew it. Give me all the details."

"The details are my specialty," said Cyasi as he wiped the blade clean. "Ishmael had no plans of helping the brothers. He had already arranged to sell them as slaves."

"And you have this on good authority?" asked Joseph.

Cyasi nodded. "Straight from the mouth of the man who was waiting for Ishamel to show up with ten unsuspecting slaves. He didn't really want to talk with me, but I have my ways."

"I won't ask," said Joseph.

"That's good because I won't tell. Think of me as a magician, and a good magician never reveals his tricks. Now stop talking and let me finish up before I cut you. Slicing you up will be bad for business."

Joseph wasn't about to argue. Cyasi really was a magician. With this new information there was no way he was about to let Ishmael walk free. The question was, what to do with him?

That afternoon, he called for the prisoners to be brought to him. When they arrived, Joseph's anger flared again. Three days in prison was nothing compared to what he'd been forced to endure. He'd have mercy on them, but he wasn't about to let them completely off the hook.

When he spoke, his voice was devoid of emotion. "I have considered your situation and reached a decision. What I say is final and cannot be refuted. You told me that you have one brother back home. To prove that you are the honest men you claim to be, you will return to your home and bring your youngest brother to Avaris so I may see him with my own eyes. Meanwhile, one of you will remain here as a prisoner until the others return. But do not think me cruel. I will allow you to take grain back with you for your family. Be warned that should you return without your missing brother, you will all be put to death as spies."

When the brothers heard Joseph's declaration, they immediately began to speak to each other in their tribal language, clearly believing Joseph couldn't understand them. Although rusty, he could make out the gist of what they were saying.

"God is punishing us for what we did to Joseph," cried Reuben. "I knew this would happen. His blood is on our hands, and today we must pay the price for our sins." The brothers clung to one another and wept, probably expecting a death sentence. Joseph knew their father would never part with Benjamin.

Their distress moved Joseph to the brink of tears because they seemed truly sorry for what they'd done to him all those years ago. But his plan had already been put into motion. Now he would see what they would do when another of their brothers was taken into captivity. How would they respond this time? Joseph looked around, deciding which one to retain as his prisoner. With a flicker of anger, he landed on Simeon. Simeon, the instigator and his longtime tormentor, would be the perfect choice. He called for his guards and pointed at Simeon.

"Tie this man up. Bind him hand and foot so he cannot escape and have him thrown into prison."

As the guards closed in, the other brothers crowded around Simeon, looking as if they might try to defend him. Joseph wanted to avoid bloodshed and called out, "Don't be foolish. You are greatly outmatched. This man is now my prisoner, and nothing you do can change that."

The guards waded into the throng of human limbs and pulled Simeon away as he clutched at the hands of his brothers. Joseph felt a small pang of guilt when he saw the fear in Simeon's eyes, but he didn't relent. The room grew silent except for the sound of Simeon whimpering as he was tied up and dragged away.

"The rest of you may leave, but do not forget your brother here in Avaris. Prison is not a pleasant place," said Joseph. His voice shook with emotion, but he somehow managed to pull himself together. "Your sacks have been filled, and your animals are outside waiting. Be gone, but you, Bedouin. I will speak with you alone."

The brothers filed out of the room. Never had Joseph seen them so sad. All the fight had drained out of them like water into the sand. Their response caused him a strange mixture of joy and sorrow. Surely, they had changed from the tormenting teenagers he'd known, but he needed to see how much. It pained him to put them through this gauntlet, but there was no other way.

Once his brothers had cleared out, Joseph spoke to Ishmael. As much as he tried, Joseph could not keep the venom out of his voice. "Growing up, my father would often say, 'You reap what you sow.' Today these words have come true for you. In the same way that I passed judgment over your traveling companions, so will I pass judgment on you. Ishmael, I hereby sentence you to a lifetime in prison. With your own life, you will pay the price for the lives that you have taken and sold as slaves, as well as for the innocent lives that you conspired to take. I am Joseph, Commander of Avaris, and former slave whom you beat and sold into slavery."

Joseph watched as this information sank in and Ishmael finally realized who he was. At that moment, Ishmael knew he was caught, and he lashed out like a cornered animal. He rushed towards Joseph and yanked the whip from underneath his robe.

"I'll kill you," Ishmael bellowed, and Joseph saw the unfiltered hatred in the man's eyes—no remorse, only hatred. Ishmael pulled back the whip to strike, but a bullet from one of the guards sent the whip flying from his hand. Blood flowed from where the bullet had pierced his skin, but still he kept coming. His giant hands were curled into fists ready to bludgeon, and there was bloodlust in his eyes. He was half man, half demon, and Joseph feared he would fight his way through the guards. But even demons fall. It took three guards to bring him down, and finally the crack of a cudgel silenced his terrifying howls of rage as he crashed to the floor.

Joseph stared down at him. "Can you hear me?"

Ishmael rolled over on his side and spat a mixture of blood and saliva, and Joseph noticed that he was now missing a few of his teeth. "I hear you, you dirty—"

One of the guards slugged him in the midsection, and Ishamel never finished his sentence. Joseph felt no sympathy for him.

"It is a stain upon the earth that you are even allowed to live, but I am not a violent man like you. Death is too good for you, so I will see that you are nursed back to health to serve your punishment in full—a life sentence."

Ishmael leered at Joseph, his face already swelling and turning a ripe shade of purple. "In this life or the next, I'll find you."

His threat sent chills down Joseph's spine and launched the guards into action. They gagged Ishmael and dragged him out of the room. Once they were gone, Joseph collapsed into his chair, exhausted. The day's events had taken it out of him, but he couldn't help giving a wry smile. He'd left a little surprise for his brothers, and he wondered how they'd respond when they found out.

CHAPTER 29

Waiting

Joseph paced his room like a caged lion.

"What's wrong?" asked Mariam.

"My brothers should have been back a month ago." Three months had passed since his brothers left. Far too long. They had to be nearly out of food by now.

"Any ideas why they might be delayed?" asked Mariam as she snagged Joseph's arm and pulled him to sit next to her. He obliged her, but his legs kept jittering.

"There are too many possibilities: they got lost, got attacked, were eaten by wild animals."

Mariam gently rubbed his back. "Take a deep breath. Assuming that none of those worst-case scenarios happened, why else might they not be back?"

"I don't know, but what if I sent them to their death? What if they don't come back? For so long I assumed I'd never see any of my family again and had come to grips with that, but then they appeared, and the thought of losing them a second time is too much to bear. I should never have sent them away. I'm such a fool." Joseph hunched over like someone had punched him in the gut.

Tears formed in Mariam's eyes at the sight of Joseph's anguish. "They'll make it back. Just be patient and don't lose faith."

Those were the last words Joseph wanted to hear right now. Filled with restless energy, he hopped back up and started pacing again.

"All the waiting is killing me. I have to do something. I'm going to go check with Salim and see how preparations are coming for Pharaoh's celebration." As he was about to leave, Joseph turned around to look at Mariam. "I know you're right, and I know you're trying to help. I'm sorry for being angry."

"It's okay," she whispered. "I still love you. Don't forget that."

"I won't." He blew her a kiss and left the room.

Joseph threw himself into his work to try to take his mind off his brothers when one of the guards barged in. Annoyed at being interrupted, he looked up. "What is it? Can't you see I'm busy?"

The guard bowed low. "I apologize for the interruption, Commander, but I was stationed at the front gate when a group of men arrived seeking an audience with you."

Joseph snapped up straight. "How many men were there? Were they related? Did you catch any of their names?"

"Yes, Commander." The guard was like an eager puppy. "There were ten men. All brothers, and the leader was named Reuben."

Joseph's heart started pounding. *Deep breath*, he told himself.

"This is excellent news, soldier. Please be sure that these men relinquish all their weapons and are brought to the granary at once. I will meet them there."

"As you wish, Commander." The man bowed and left as quickly as he'd come.

Joseph could hardly believe it. After months of waiting, they were finally here. All ten of his brothers had arrived safely in Avaris. Now he had to decide what to do with them. First things first, he needed to prepare himself for the audience.

An hour later Joseph was dressed in his formal attire and seated at the end of the granary hall on his elevated chair. The time had finally come. He gripped the armrests of the chair until his knuckles turned white.

The brothers were brought inside, flanked by several heavily armed guards. Their footsteps echoed in the empty hall as they walked solemnly towards Joseph. He watched them shoot nervous glances back and forth, and he relaxed his hold on the chair. He was in the position of power.

When he saw his brother Benjamin, Joseph was nearly overwhelmed with emotion. Benjamin was no longer the toddler Joseph remembered. He'd grown into a young man. It was like looking at a younger version of himself, just paler. He noticed the way that Reuben held Benjamin's arm protectively, his body tensed like a cat about to spring.

Then as if they'd rehearsed, the brothers prostrated themselves before Joseph. There was no social grace to their action. This was a full-fledged act of desperation, not the gamesmanship of the Avaris upper class. Joseph was moved.

"You may rise. Show me this brother of yours," declared Joseph.

Reuben helped Benjamin up and dusted him off like a piece of fine china. "Thank you for welcoming us back to Avaris, Commander. I have brought you my youngest brother Benjamin as you requested. I bring him as proof that we are not spies."

Joseph inclined his head toward them. "I must admit there is not much of a family resemblance."

Reuben pressed on. "Yes, Your Greatness. We share the same father but have different mothers."

"That is very interesting." Joseph dragged out his words.

Reuben, on the other hand, was clearly trying to move things along as quickly as possible. "We have returned and fulfilled our end of the bargain. Now may I ask you to release our brother, Simeon so that we might be on our way."

"You may not. These things must not be rushed," rebuked Joseph.

"But—"

Joseph held up a hand. "You would do well to remember your place. I will release you when I am convinced that the man standing here before me is indeed your brother, as you claim." He turned to Salim, who stood silently at his side. "Take these men to the palace. There are too many eyes and ears here for my liking. Have a meal prepared, and I will join you at midday to question this Benjamin."

"As you wish," replied Salim.

The brothers followed Salim out of the room looking shell-shocked, and Reuben brought up the rear, looking the worst of the lot. Joseph felt a twinge of guilt as he watched them go, but he pushed it away. It was for the best. This needed to be handled as a private affair. Once they were gone, he slipped after them to the palace and stood with Salim outside the door where he knew Simeon waited for them. A smile tugged at the corners of his mouth as he heard the happy reunion on the other side of the door. He gave them a moment before sending Salim inside.

"All kneel for the Commander of Avaris," Salim announced.

The brothers did more than kneel. Again, they prostrated themselves on the floor before this man who held their lives in his hands. The moment was not lost on Joseph. Here they were, all twelve brothers in the same room for the first time in over a decade. One by one they presented him with a small gift. Benjamin was the last, and when he kneeled at Joseph's feet, Joseph caught his scent and was filled with memories of long ago. He wanted to hear his younger brother's voice, so he asked, "How is your aged father?"

Benjamin didn't make eye contact. "He is doing well, sir. His eyesight has left him, but he is mostly in good health."

Joseph put his hand on Benjamin's shoulder. "You may rise. There is no need to be afraid of me."

Benjamin gulped but did as he was told. Joseph could sense the anxiety of the brothers as they watched the interaction, but he returned his attention to Benjamin. It was so strange to see him. His face was the same, only stretched out and with a faint shadow of stubble, but there was no question that it was him.

The sight and sound and smell of Benjamin brought up deep emotions that had long been dormant within Joseph. He'd never thought he'd see this day. Everything in him wanted to swallow Benjamin up in a giant hug, but he couldn't bring himself to do it. Instead, he turned and walked out of the room without a word. He needed space. He fled to his private rooms and locked the chamber behind him before dropping into a chair and sobbing. Mariam sat next to him and patted his shoulder, clearly uncertain what to do to comfort him. When his sobbing finally subsided and he could breathe again, he looked up at Mariam, knowing his eyes must be red and puffy.

"What is it, my love?"

Joseph wiped the snot from his nose. "I don't know if I can fully capture it, but it's like I'm being pulled in different directions at the same time. It feels like my soul is being torn apart. Part of me wants to tell my brothers who I am so we can be reconciled and just put all the hurt behind us. But there is the other part of me that is still angry and bitter and wants to punish them and teach them a lesson. It's like I'm trying to carry two weights at once and am being slowly crushed."

Mariam leaned in and kissed him gently on the cheek. "I'm sorry, love. In time you will know what to do and will make the right decision. Be patient with yourself. In the meantime, make sure you wash your face with cold water unless you want everyone in the palace to know you've been crying."

A small noise from outside the door to his rooms made him turn his head, but he didn't hear it again. With all the emotional turmoil today, he wouldn't be surprised if his mind was playing tricks on him. He turned back to Mariam with a faint laugh. "That's good advice. I'd better get back to my guests before they think I've had a psychotic breakdown. I made quite the dramatic exit."

He splashed cold water on his face until he looked normal on the outside, but the inside was a different story. Things were tense when he strolled back into the room where the brothers were milling about, but Joseph ignored the discomfort. He turned to Salim, whose usually impassive face seemed to be doing something curious.

"Seat our guests, and have the food served at once." Then he took his seat at a small, raised table and watched with interest while his brothers were seated below him. He wondered how long it would take for them to realize what he'd done.

A minute went by before Joseph saw Judah freeze and go pale. He leaned over to Reuben and whispered something in his ear. Then Reuben looked around, and his jaw nearly hit the table. The two brothers shot a quick glance at Joseph—just long enough for Joseph to catch the mixture of wonder and fear in their eyes. Then they returned to their whispering, which now spread to the other brothers.

Joseph couldn't make out what they were saying, but it was clear they'd picked up on the fact that he'd seated them at the table in order of their age.

Watching their response was quite enjoyable. Joseph just wished he could turn the volume up, but Simeon helped him out with that. Never much of a whisperer, Simeon was failing miserably at having a secret conversation with Reuben. Joseph couldn't make all of it out, but he heard enough to know that Simeon was passing along some of the popular gossip that had turned Joseph into a living legend. This only seemed to unnerve Reuben.

Just then, the food was served. It was a meal fit for a king, and Joseph had yet another surprise in store. He'd ordered that Benjamin receive a portion five times as large as all the other brothers. Benjamin's meal came out on a massive platter, while the rest of the brothers ate off regular plates.

Again, Joseph watched with great interest to see how the brothers would respond. Benjamin, to his credit, did his best to eat everything he'd been given, but it was a truly ridiculous amount of food. When he seemed to think the commander wasn't watching, he tried to covertly share his portion with those nearest him, but Joseph saw it all—the way the brothers shared the food to ensure that Benjamin didn't offend their host. It was touching.

When they finally finished, Joseph stood and raised his silver drinking glass. He had one last trick up his sleeve. "The hour is late, and you have a long way to travel tomorrow, for you are free to leave Avaris. Let our sharing of a meal be proof that you are no longer considered enemies of Avaris. You are welcome to return if you need food. Now I bid you a blessing for the road. May God lead you in peace and direct your steps and cause you to reach your destination. May you be safe from every enemy and ambush, from robbers and wild beasts on the trip. May God confer blessing upon the work of your hands and grant you grace."

There was a moment of shocked silence in response to Joseph's blessing, for he had blessed them with the very words their father used to pray over them whenever they left the bunker.

At last, Reuben spoke. "Thank you for your generous hospitality and for keeping my brother Simeon safe. We are sincerely in your debt and pray that there might be good relations between us from this day forward."

"May it be so," said Joseph. Then he excused himself and motioned for Salim to join him. Out in the hall he gave Salim specific instructions. "As you did last time, place each man's silver in the mouth of his sack of grain." Salim nodded, though Joseph knew he was not a fan of simply giving away money, especially to strangers.

"Then, do one more thing, Salim. Take my silver cup and place it in the youngest's grain sack."

Salim's mouth turned up into a wicked smile. "As you wish," he said.

Joseph bit back a smile of his own. Salim clearly believed that Joseph was truly trying to frame Benjamin. Such a conniving act was out of character for Joseph, but Salim would love it. Salim wrung his hands gleefully and headed off to have the grain sacks prepared for the brothers.

CHAPTER 30

Lost and Found

Joseph looked like he hadn't slept a wink all night when he called for Salim. The sun was just beginning to rise when Salim arrived with a generous bow. Joseph wasted no time.

"Go at once to Potiphar. You are to travel with him and a small company of his best men to chase down the brothers who left early this morning. Tell Potiphar that the men and all their belongings are to be searched."

"Right away. What shall I say to the brothers?"

"Tell them that you have been sent by the Commander of Avaris who demands to know why they would repay his kindness with evil. Why would they take his sacred cup which he uses to divine the future for the good of the people of Avaris?"

"It will be as you have requested, Commander."

"Good. Now make haste," commanded Joseph.

Salim left with a glint in his eye and a giddy-up in his step.

The hours ticked by slowly as Joseph waited for news from Salim. Had he found Joseph's brothers? Had they tried to fight? He paced back and forth wondering if this latest test of his brothers' character was one too many. Should he have just forgiven them like Mariam suggested? Why was it all so complicated in his head? All these questions wore him down as he wore a path in the floor with his continuous motion.

At long last there was a knock on the door. Unable to contain himself, Joseph ran and threw open the door. Salim stood before him.

"What news do you bring?" demanded Joseph.

Salim bowed low. "I bring you good news. The brothers were arrested without bloodshed. They are on their way here as we speak."

Joseph nodded, relief flooding through him. "You have done well, Salim. Meet Potiphar when he arrives and bring the men to meet me."

Joseph made sure that by the time his brothers were ushered into the room where he awaited them that he looked the part of the mystic they'd come to believe him to be. His hair was disheveled and his eyes were wild. Even Salim seemed unnerved and stepped back from Joseph.

Joseph turned on his brothers, his voice a condensed thunderstorm, "What is this you have done? Surely you must have heard of my secret powers, and yet you still tried to steal from me? Did you wish to make a mockery of me?"

Reuben stepped forward with a look of defeat. "We did not, Your Greatness. I cannot explain how the cup made its way into our belongings. There are no words I can say to prove our innocence. We will be your slaves as promised."

"Never. I would not have it said that I am a cruel man. An eye for an eye. Only the man who was found with the cup will be my slave, your brother Benjamin. The rest of you may go without harm and return to your aged father."

"No!" Reuben seemed to surprise even himself with his sudden response, and the room went deadly quiet. "Take me as your slave. Let the rest go. I will be a substitute for my brother. I will be the eye that you gouge out to have your vengeance. Were my brother to remain here, my father would die of a broken heart. I could not bear to watch that. It would be worse than death itself. I beg you, please take me in his place." He fell to his knees before Joseph.

Joseph looked at Reuben on the floor in front him, willing to give his life for his brother. He couldn't help indulging in a moment of self-pity. Where had Reuben been when he needed him all those years ago? But the moment passed. Joseph glanced at his other brothers who had returned to Avaris to support Benjamin. These were not the brothers he'd once known. They'd changed, and what they had at one time intended for evil, God had used to save Joseph and now his whole family.

As this reality hit him, an avalanche of pain and anger broke free from his heart, and Joseph finally knew what to do. It was time to forgive. No, it was long past time.

"Potiphar, you and your men leave the room. Salim, you join them. I would speak with these men in private."

No one dared question Joseph, such was the intensity in his voice. When the room was clear, Joseph stepped down from his pedestal. He'd wanted to tell his brothers the truth for so long, but now he didn't know what to say as they huddled together, cowering in fear.

He cleared his throat. "Don't be afraid. It's me, Joseph, your long-lost brother."

Their eyes went wide, but none of them responded. They probably thought this was some kind of cruel joke. How would the Commander of Avaris know about their brother? Joseph stepped toward them.

"Really, it's me. Come close and see."

Benjamin was the first to step forward, followed closely by Reuben. Joseph held out his hands. "Look, here is the scar from when I fell off the top bunk in the bunker, and this one is from where Simeon threw a butter knife at me."

The truth of Joseph's words slowly dawned on Reuben's face. "Could it really be? After all these years? Joseph, is it really you?" asked Reuben, his voice filled with hope.

"Yes!" Joseph felt tears flow as he showed them another scar. "This one is from when you threw me into the well before you sold me to the Bedouin slave trader. Ask me anything, and I'll prove that I am your brother Joseph."

Reuben's eyes began to glow. "It's you. It's actually you. You were dead and now you're alive again," he cried.

"It's me," wept Joseph, and he did something he'd never thought he'd be able to do again on this earth—he hugged Reuben. He wrapped his arms around him and squeezed him with all his might and felt Reuben do the same.

"I'm so sorry," said Reuben as his tears splashed onto Joseph's back. "I'm so sorry for everything. We failed you."

The other brothers joined in. Enfolding Joseph in their arms and apologizing profusely for what they'd done. Their words washed over Joseph like a healing balm, giving him strength to do the last thing that needed to be done.

The words long trapped in Joseph's soul finally were set free. "I forgive you."

Their tears turned to laughter and shouting as they all tried to speak over one another all at once. There was a lifetime of stories to catch up on. The room was filled with noise.

Remembering there were people waiting outside, Joseph flung open the door and looked into the confused faces of Potiphar and his men. Joseph laughed. "It's okay. Come in, come in! I want you to meet my brothers." Salim and Potiphar followed as Joseph introduced them to his brothers. The whole thing was wild. The most unexpected reunion of all time. After making the rounds, Joseph sent Salim to share the good news with Pharaoh.

He couldn't be sure over all the noise his brothers were making, but as Salim left the room, Joseph thought he heard the man cackling.

CHAPTER 31

A Party to Remember

Pharaoh's party was always the highlight of the year. While things would be a little leaner this year, it would still be quite the spectacle, and the sudden arrival of Joseph's brothers only added to the buzz. As soon as Salim had told Pharaoh of the arrival of the brothers, Pharaoh immediately invited them to the party, and all of Avaris was curious to see them.

The palace was filled with energy, but no one was as excited as Joseph. He'd managed to find a secluded room to use for the little breakfast he'd arranged so his brothers could meet Mariam. He couldn't wait for them to see firsthand just how amazing she was.

Joseph and Mariam strolled arm in arm to breakfast, while people rushed all around them, running errands and moving items. Joseph tried to block out the chaos, but he couldn't stop his anxiety. It was like a swarm of butterflies had hatched in his stomach and were trying to escape. Mariam must have sensed it because she put her head on his shoulder. "Everything's going to be great. Meeting your brothers will be a piece of cake."

Joseph laughed. "Easy for you to say. You haven't met my brothers."

"Considering you just spared their lives, I imagine they'll be on their best behavior."

Joseph grinned. "You have a point."

"I usually do," replied Mariam.

"I know. That's why I married you."

"Good answer."

They stopped to let a man carrying a stack of chairs go by. Once the path was clear, they started walking again, only this time without speaking. After a while Mariam broke the silence. "I have something important that I want to tell you."

"Please don't tell me you're leaving me. That would be really bad timing," joked Joseph.

Mariam hit him on the arm. "Don't even kid about that. This is quite the opposite. I was waiting for the right time, but I guess this is as good as any." She paused. "I'm pregnant."

Joseph stopped dead in his tracks, unable to fully process the words he'd just heard. "What!" They'd been trying to have a baby for years. This was a miracle. Overwhelmed with joy, he picked Mariam up and spun her around. "That's the most amazing news. How long have you known?"

"Not too long."

"Do you think it's a boy or a girl?"

"I don't know," laughed Mariam. "Either way will be wonderful."

"Let's hope it's a girl. Twelve brothers is a lot of boys. We could use some more women in the family."

"That's true. I'm a bit outnumbered."

"Yes, but not outmatched." He shook his head, trying to grasp all the good news he'd received lately. "My brothers are here, my father is still alive, and now a new baby on the way. It's more than I deserve."

"Just receive it as a gift from God," said Mariam.

"I'll try," replied Joseph with utmost sincerity. "Now you have to try and make a good first impression on my brothers."

"Oh, I will. How else will I get them to share all their old stories about you?"

Joseph shook his head. He knew it wouldn't take much prodding before embarrassing stories would start spilling out. Not even being the Commander of Avaris could help him now.

Joseph's brothers were already in the room when they arrived, all waiting to be introduced to Mariam.

"Good morning," Joseph said. "I believe we have some long overdue introductions to attend to. Everyone, This is Mariam, my brilliant, beautiful, resourceful, funny, amazing wife. The only thing she can't do is sing, so she'll fit right in." There were a couple of chuckles, and Joseph turned to Mariam. "Any descriptive words I missed?"

Mariam rolled her eyes. "A couple, but I'll let it slide. Should I tell them all the things you can't do? I'd be happy to."

"No need. I'm pretty sure they are aware." Joseph winked at his brothers and then spread his arms out. "Mariam, these are my long-lost brothers. Though, I guess it was really me who was lost, but anyway: Here they are in all their glory."

Reuben stepped forward and introduced himself, and the others followed suit. A good twenty minutes later, Mariam had met the whole gang, and Joseph motioned for them to sit down. Before they ate, Joseph raised his silver cup to get their attention. "What a gift it is to be together and share a meal, but I have yet another reason today to rejoice. I wanted you to be the first to hear the good news. Mariam is pregnant!"

These words were met with a raucous response. Fists pounding on the table, shouting, and lots of hugs. Reuben stood on his chair and called for everyone's attention. "Brothers, join me in raising a toast to Joseph, his beautiful wife, and their unborn child. May God's favor be upon them, this day and forevermore."

The room resounded with clinking glasses and "amens." Then they tucked into breakfast with a ravenous appetite and equally ravenous conversation. Mariam asked a million questions, as did the brothers. Joseph's heart filled with more joy than he knew what to do with. Today was a beautiful day.

Too soon Joseph was called away. He promised Mariam and his brothers that he would see them at Pharaoh's party in the evening. As he headed off, he tried not to think about the stories that would be told about him in his absence.

It killed him not to be able to stay, but Pharaoh had demanded his presence, and that was an order he could not disregard. Joseph stepped into the throne room to find Pharaoh directing traffic. Pharaoh saw him and waved him over.

"Welcome, Joseph. It seems that both of us have much to celebrate today."

"Yes, Your Greatness, I never dreamt that I would see my brothers again."

"In these times, I would say it's nothing short of a miracle. But then such things tend to swirl around you from what I have seen."

"God has been good to me." Joseph replied modestly.

"You are too humble. I say that we make our own luck, but enough of such talk. On to business. It will be good for morale for the people to see your brothers. A good, heartfelt story has been hard to come by recently."

"As you wish, Pharaoh."

"A free tip for you. People love it when they get a glimpse into the lives of their leaders. It humanizes us. You are quite the man of mystery, so this will be good for you."

"Thank you. My brothers will all be in attendance. Having grown up in the bunker, it's fair to say they are excited to see a real party, especially my youngest brother, Benjamin."

Pharaoh gave a small frown. "This won't be my best party, but I will make sure they are not disappointed."

Just then Salim emerged from the shadows, as he tended to do. *Rather unnerving*, thought Joseph. Salim gave a deep bow and looked expectantly at Pharaoh.

Pharaoh sighed, clearly annoyed at having been interrupted. "What is it, Salim?"

"I apologize, Your Greatness. It was not my intent to interrupt. I am here to advise you that the two prisoners have been selected and moved to the palace."

"Very good. I assume you have their files for me as well?"

"I am afraid I do not. They are with Potiphar as he is in charge of the prisoners, but I will happily retrieve them for you."

Joseph thought that was odd but didn't say anything.

Pharaoh nodded. "That would be good. Will there be anything else?"

"I am most eager to know the order for this evening's program so I can make the necessary preparations as the master of ceremonies. I want to make sure everything runs like clockwork."

Salim is nothing if not meticulous, thought Joseph. Apparently, Pharaoh agreed. "Yes, yes, dot your i's and cross your t's. I have an order set. You will note there is a late addition. We are going to present Joseph's brothers."

"A most excellent decision. The people will be pleased to meet them. Such a reunion should not be kept private."

"Precisely. You've played the political game long enough to understand. There is a list of their names, so be sure to practice the pronunciations."

"I will, Your Greatness. Everything will be perfect," promised Salim.

I hope so, thought Joseph as he watched Salim make a hasty exit.

******

An hour or so later, Joseph was waiting for Cyasi to arrive for a quick trim before the big event. Normally he didn't mind Cyasi's commitment to being fashionably late, but today was another matter. Cyasi appeared with an apologetic grin on his face.

"Sorry I'm late, but I had to make sure those brothers of yours looked good for this evening. From the look of their hair, none of them knows their way around a pair of scissors."

Joseph's annoyance at being kept waiting disappeared. How could he be mad at Cyasi?

"You don't know the half of it," he said.

"I know a whole lot more than I did this morning," replied Cyasi. He sat Joseph down and covered him with a towel. "A few well-placed questions and your brothers shared all sorts of gossip-worthy information. Might be good to address that before tonight."

Joseph groaned. "We are feeding them to the wolves tonight, aren't we?"

"Possibly. Don't tell dear old Pharaoh this, but I think people are more excited to meet your brothers and pump them for information than they are about his party."

"I guess I'll be on babysitting duty all night. Any other choice pieces of information that I should be aware of?"

Cyasi paused from his careful trimming and looked Joseph in the eye. "I think it's me who should be asking you that."

"What do you mean?" asked Joseph.

"Not to be too forward, but when were you going to tell me that Mariam's pregnant?"

Joseph nearly fell out of the chair. "How do you know that? I only just found out myself."

"The walls have ears around here," said Cyasi with a grin.

"A reality I'm only too aware of. You haven't told anyone, have you?"

"No, as much as it has pained me to keep such a juicy secret. Congratulations by the way."

"Thank you, Cyasi. I really mean it."

"You are most welcome. Let's get you through tonight's big family introduction before we announce another new family member."

"I agree. One step at a time."

"Good, now stop talking so I can finish up and make sure you sparkle like a diamond. Can't have your brothers outshine you."

A few minutes later, Joseph looked in the mirror. Cyasi was a miracle worker. A true "artiste," as he liked to remind everyone. "As usual, I am in your debt," sighed Joseph.

"There are no debts between friends," replied Cyasi, his tone suddenly serious.

Joseph turned around. He sensed tension in Cyasi. "I'm honored to consider you a friend, Cyasi. The world would be a better place if there were more men like you. Here's to being friends." Joseph stuck out his hand.

All the tension went out of Cyasi's body, and he grinned. "Where I come from, friends don't shake hands, they hug." And hug Joseph he did.

The Lord will provide. Abba had always said that, and he was right. The Lord had provided this tattooed hair artist to help him navigate the complexities of life in Avaris. Without him, Joseph would have been sunk. Not quite the guardian angel he'd been expecting, but an effective one, nonetheless.

Just then Mariam came into the room. She raised an eyebrow but didn't say anything at the sight of the two men hugging. Cyasi pulled away and gave her a gracious bow.

"He's all yours now. I took care of the trim, but I recommend you help him with his suit. You know how he is…"

"Thank you, Cyasi. I think I can take it from here and make sure he doesn't embarrass himself."

"That would be much appreciated. Can't have him tarnishing my reputation."

Joseph butted in. "The two of you talk like I'm not here. I'm not a child who can't dress himself."

They both laughed, and Cyasi headed for the door calling over his shoulder, "Like I said, you pick his suit."

"What's that all about?" asked Joseph.

"Well, honey, it's just that you don't have much sense of style. It's probably not your fault growing up with ten older brothers in a bunker. I imagine there weren't many new clothes coming your way, and probably not a lot of emphasis on fashion."

"It's true," admitted Joseph, then he chuckled. "How long have you and Cyasi been secretly helping me with my clothing?"

She patted his arm. "A long time."

"Good to know the two of you are scheming on my behalf."

"Always, my love. Always."

A short while later, Joseph and Mariam emerged in their best attire. Mariam looked stunning in a royal blue dress, and Joseph cut a fine figure himself. His tie even matched her dress, but not by his own design. They strolled down the hallway toward the throne room. After all these years Joseph still didn't enjoy these types of events, but it was better with Mariam at his side. She navigated them with such ease. Years of being the prophet's daughter had trained her well in the arts of schmoozing and politics.

When they entered the throne room, only a handful of the guests had arrived, and Joseph was astonished to see the warden was one of them. The poor man was dressed in the most ragged suit imaginable, a ruffly shirt that was probably white in a former life, and a lopsided bowtie. Never had he seen a man so out of place, and yet the warden was grinning ear to ear. He held a glass in one hand and a serving platter in the other, which he must have wrestled from some poor waiter. When he saw Joseph, he waved so vigorously that he splashed the entire contents of his drink onto the floor. Joseph gave him a small wave but didn't go over to him. He felt a pang of guilt about it, but there were optics to maintain.

Pharaoh had not yet arrived, but Joseph knew he was waiting to make his grand entrance once everyone had arrived. The room itself looked incredible; Joseph tried not to think about all the resources that had gone into making tonight possible. It had been easy to justify the cost and the food usage when crops were good, but now it felt like an unnecessary extravagance. He had not mentioned this to Pharaoh, though, afraid of what his response would be.

As he looked around, he did note a few things that had been scaled back, and he was grateful for that. Even the throne room itself bore the scars of the past year. While it had survived the giant earthquake, fissures and cracks ran through most of the large blocks. A few of the statues had toppled over and been smashed beyond repair, and they were noticeably absent. The most prevalent eyesore was the large crack running the length of the glorious marble staircase. Some of the stairs had shifted, and now one had to climb them carefully to avoid tripping and looking like an uncoordinated dunce.

Despite it all, there was still a festive atmosphere, although the smiles seemed a little drawn and the laughter a little more forced. Joseph noted that some people were wearing the same attire as last year. Even amongst the upper class, people were pinching pennies; a funny old saying that always made Joseph smile.

He and Mariam did the rounds, making small talk about all manner of superficial things. Joseph let Mariam do most of the talking while he tried to look interested. Joseph knew that Cyasi would give him any notable gossip tomorrow; who was on the outs with each other, who was having an affair and so forth. There was always some sort of drama. The world may have changed, but people were still the same.

Joseph tipped his head to Potiphar as he and Zuleika made their entrance. Mariam had told Joseph that Zuleika always made sure to arrive just before Pharaoh so all eyes would be on her. This evening she was dressed in a scarlet gown that fit her like a glove with a high slit up the side. Joseph's eyebrows shot up as a murmur rumbled through the crowd. Zuleika always pushed the limits, but this was scandalous even for her. Somewhere Cyasi was probably silently applauding her for her bold style, but there were plenty of others who disapproved. Of course Zuleika didn't care about that. In fact, she fed off it. She waltzed into the room daring anyone to challenge her. There were no takers.

As if he'd been waiting for Zuleika to make her entrance, Salim stepped onto the first stair. Joseph looked back at Zuleika. Why did she seem like some sort of signal for Salim? Joseph shrugged. He was probably just imagining things. He turned his attention to silently hoping Salim would trip, but no such luck. Salim raised his hands and clapped three times to get the people's attention. Everyone knew the drill. The crowd fell silent, and Salim annoyingly cleared his throat.

"Good people of Avaris. It is my pleasure on this fine evening to welcome you to our great Pharaoh's birthday celebration. And now, without further ado, I present His Greatness, the ruler of Avaris and the Savior of Humanity."

The people applauded, and Pharaoh appeared, as if by magic, at the top of the dais. Pharaoh did not disappoint in a perfectly cut suit of powder blue with a pink shirt. He looked like he'd stepped out of an old movie from the days of Hollywood. He smiled and waved as he glided down the marble steps, and as always, the people were caught in his spell. They mobbed him as he descended, desperately trying to get a word or even a handshake. Pharaoh looked over the fray and winked at Joseph.

"He's a smug one all right," whispered Mariam.

"He's a sight more than that," replied Joseph, but he didn't dare say anything else as he was surrounded by glassy-eyed Pharaoh worshippers.

"When do you think he'll present your brothers?"

"Probably after he's soaked up the first round of adoration from his loyal subjects."

Mariam's grip tightened on his arm, and he knew that could only mean one thing: Zuleika was approaching.

He could sense Mariam trying to calm herself in the presence of her former owner. Mariam handled everyone else with delicate ease, but not Zuleika. Joseph had to deal with her.

Zuleika dangled Potiphar on her arm as she snaked towards them. He was the arm candy, not her. People conveniently got out of her way, and there was no doubt she was headed toward Joseph and Mariam. Joseph cringed. Speaking with Zuleika always felt like a game of chess, and he was always a few moves behind. If she'd been a man, she would have been the Pharaoh.

Zuleika stopped a few feet away and acted as if she hadn't noticed them until now. This was all part of the game: move, counter move. She tilted her head, clearly waiting for Joseph to say something, but he wouldn't give her the pleasure. The silence stretched on until people began to notice. Finally, Zuleika caved. One point for Joseph.

"Good evening. Lovely party, isn't it?" asked Zuleika. Her eyes were filled with disdain as she looked down on them.

"It is," replied Joseph stiffly. He shifted his gaze to Potiphar. "How are you?"

Before he could answer, Zuleika slipped in. "He's as miserable as ever. He hates these things."

Who doesn't, thought Joseph, but he didn't dare admit that. Instead, he replied, "I'm sorry to hear that. They can be a bit much at times. Certainly a security nightmare."

Potiphar nodded, and his head swiveled around, scanning the room.

"Don't feed his paranoia, Joseph," Zuleika said.

She used his name so casually. No one else dared to, but Joseph was afraid to make a scene. Of course Zuleika knew that. She smiled mischievously. One point for her.

Then she continued, "A little bird told me that tonight is not just a big night for Pharaoh, but also for you."

Joseph wasn't surprised that she knew. "You'll just have to wait and see," he said, trying to sound mysterious.

Her eyes lingered on him uncomfortably. "I'm waiting with great anticipation. I have no doubt this will be a night to remember."

The way she said it sounded like a threat. Before Joseph could respond, Zuleika tapped Potiphar on the arm. "Could you please take me to the refreshments table? I'm parched." Then she whisked him away without a final word. No polite goodbye, nothing. She'd made it clear to everyone around them how she felt about Joseph. Meanwhile, he could feel Mariam's anger boiling.

"That bitch," she whispered. "I'd love to—"

"Not here," said Joseph. "Everyone is watching."

"Of course they are," said Mariam. "They're watching to see how you will respond to her insult."

"What am I to do?" whispered Joseph.

"I don't know," replied Mariam with a defeated sigh. "As usual, that horrible excuse for a woman has backed us into a corner. If you call her out on her rudeness, she'll merely say it was a misunderstanding, and then you'll look like a self-conscious egomaniac. Say nothing, and she wins. Say something, and she wins."

"She has us in checkmate."

Mariam nodded. "I say we head over toward Pharaoh. That way we can avoid another ambush." Together they strolled in Pharaoh's direction, trying to look as casual as possible. Once they arrived, he waved them over much to the dismay of those pressed in around him.

"Joseph! It's good to see you, and your beautiful wife as well. I was beginning to wonder if you were ever going to come over and say hello to the birthday boy."

"You are very kind. I apologize for not coming over sooner to wish you a happy birthday," said Joseph.

Mariam followed up at once. "And may the year ahead be filled with joy and blessings, Your Greatness."

"Thank you. I, too, hope it will be so. Now I believe the magic of my grand entrance has worn off, so it's time for our big introduction. It's not often I share the spotlight, so you should feel honored."

"We do," they both said together.

Pharaoh chuckled. "How cute. They used to say that in marriage two would become one, but I don't think they were talking about speaking the same words, if you know what I mean."

"We do," said Joseph, but this time it was only him as Mariam was busy blushing.

Pharaoh leaned in and whispered to Joseph. "From what I've heard the two of you have figured out how that all works with a little one on the way. Is my information correct?"

Joseph tried not to look around to see if anyone was eavesdropping.

"You have heard correctly. I'd planned to tell you personally after your party."

"No offense taken. It would seem the walls have ears these days," said Pharaoh.

"I found myself saying those exact words earlier today."

"Good words for politicians to remember, but let us put such things aside. We have some exciting news to announce, and we have a crowd eager to pretend that they do not already know it." Pharaoh grinned. "Now, where is Salim?"

Salim seemed to appear out of thin air. "I am right here, Great Pharaoh. How may I be of service?"

"Bring Joseph's brothers to the top of the dais through the private entrance. Joseph and I will meet you there for the announcement."

"As you command," replied Salim in his oily tone.

Joseph and Pharaoh mounted the steps, knowing full well that the crowd was watching them. "The drama. The intrigue," sighed Pharaoh. "You have to appreciate the political theater, Joseph."

"I can't say I do. I appreciate a well-run garden that provides food for hungry people."

Pharaoh shook his head. "Of course, of course. You're always so boringly practical. Hopefully your brothers are a little more exciting."

"They'll be the life of the party if you let them," replied Joseph.

"That's what I like to hear. We need somebody to get things going. Everyone is politely somber tonight."

"You can be assured my brothers do not have the social graces to be politely somber."

"Excellent! I think I'm very much going to enjoy the second half of my birthday celebration then," replied Pharaoh with far too much glee for Joseph's comfort.

They'd barely reached the top of the stairs before Salim once again seemed to materialize from nowhere. "The brothers are ready to be announced, Your Greatness."

"Very good, Salim. I will share the good news and then leave it to you to announce them by name."

Pharaoh turned and held up his hands. The people had already collected around the base of the steps like fish waiting for crumbs to be dropped in the water. "My people, on this special day I am pleased to announce some wonderful news. You all know my right-hand man, Joseph. Fate smiled upon us by bringing him here, and now fate has smiled upon him. It is my great pleasure to share that after years apart, Joseph and his brothers have been reunited right here in Avaris!"

The people cheered, but Joseph could tell it was half-hearted. It was the casual cheering of people who already knew the good news, but at least they tried. Pharaoh didn't let it stop him. "Here to introduce

Joseph's brothers, the most eligible bachelors in Avaris, is Salim. Let's give him a round of applause."

This round of applause was even less impressive than the first. It was clear Salim was not a fan favorite, but he stepped forward and began to introduce the brothers one by one, going from oldest to youngest. Once all the brothers were standing on the dais, looking dazed by their surroundings and all the people staring up at them, Pharaoh raised his hands again.

"Please give our guests a warm welcome and see that they enjoy the party." Then Pharaoh, Joseph, and the brothers descended the steps to meet the throng of overzealous partygoers. Joseph held onto Benjamin and looked for Mariam. She was waiting at the bottom to help manage the inevitable chaos. He looked back up and felt a pang of jealousy as he saw Salim slip out of the room. Lucky stiff, getting out of this madness.

People pressed in to talk with the brothers. Everyone wanted to shake their hands and ask them questions. There was nothing Joseph could do to stop them. It was like trying to hold back the tide. He did his best to keep them away from the worst of the gossip hounds, but he could only be in so many places at once. After an hour, the tide began to let out, and Joseph felt himself breathe normally again. They had weathered the worst of it. The crowd gradually lost interest, and Joseph uttered a silent prayer of gratitude when Pharaoh made his way back onto the steps and signaled for the people's attention. Joseph stood with Reuben and Benjamin on either side of him as they watched.

Pharaoh smiled warmly at the crowd, his gaze a ray of sunshine illuminating the room. Except for Joseph's brothers, everyone knew what was going to happen next, but that didn't stop Pharaoh from having his moment. "Thank you all for coming to celebrate my birthday. I am honored by your presence here tonight. As we all know, we are living in difficult times. After years of plenty we once again find ourselves scraping for survival. Each day that we draw breath should not be taken lightly. Yet even in the darkness, there is hope. Long lost brothers have emerged from the desert, our food stores are still high, and we have managed to rebuild our defenses. We have proved ourselves to be a resilient people. As the leader of Avaris, I commend you for your efforts."

There was a smattering of applause and a few clinking glasses, then Pharaoh raised his hands for silence. "But not all news is good news. There has been an increase in threats from the outside, raiders and bands of militia testing our defenses. If that were all, I would say we are in good shape, but the threats are not just from the outside, they are from within. Crime is up, gangs are on the rise, and there are even whispers of illegal dealings done by some in this very room. So let me remind you that Avaris is watching us. It is up to us, the leaders of Avaris, to maintain the peace and keep people united. Things are only going to get more difficult. I give you this fair warning because I will not extend mercy even to you. I am Pharaoh, and I hold in my hand the power of life and death. Do not test my patience."

This time there was no applause. People looked side-eyed at one another, wondering who the Judases in their midst were. Joseph's brothers seemed thoroughly confused, which only made sense since they did not know the prophecy and the years of hardship ahead. To them Avaris seemed a paradise, but Joseph knew that it was no Eden.

Pharaoh broke the uncomfortable silence. "As a sign of my power, I present to you two prisoners. One shall live, and the other shall die. Let this be a reminder to you all. Bring forth the prisoners."

The people on the far side of the throne room parted as two guards pulled the shackled prisoners through the crowd. Joseph couldn't see them until they emerged from the crowd right in front of him, and when they did, he nearly passed out. Just a few feet away stood Ishmael, glaring at Joseph with the venom of a thousand vipers.

Joseph's blood froze. How could it be that he'd been chosen as one of the prisoners? He'd only just been placed in prison.

Something is wrong here, thought Joseph.

But before he could do anything, Ishmael roared in anger and pulled a gun from the folds of his robe. In the blink of an eye, he shot the two guards escorting him. People shrieked and yelled, and the room fell into a wild pandemonium, but Joseph was frozen to the spot as Ishmael approached. Time slowed down. Joseph could hear his own heart beating. This was the end.

Ishmael raised the gun and leveled it on him. It was impossible to miss from this range. Joseph closed his eyes and thought of the people he loved: Mariam, his unborn child, his dear friend Emmanuel, and Abba all alone in the bunker. Joseph had cheated death before, but not this time. He braced himself. Once, twice, three times. Joseph's ears rang from the sound of the gunshots. He fell to the ground. There was blood, so much blood.

But surprisingly there was no pain. He always imagined that death would be much more painful. He opened his eyes and screamed. Reuben lay at his feet, his chest a mass of bullet wounds and his eyes glassy. Reuben looked up at him, his face contorted in pain.

"No!" cried Joseph, realizing that Reuben must have flung himself in front of Joseph. "No, please, no."

As he wept, another gunshot went off, and Ishmael fell to the ground. Joseph barely registered Potiphar standing over Ishmael, checking for a pulse. He threw himself on Reuben, gathering him in his arms. His brothers surrounded him, weeping and wailing.

With great effort, Reuben reached up and gently caressed Joseph's face. Chest heaving, and struggling for breath, he fought to speak. "This time I saved you," he whispered.

Then Reuben's hand slipped from Joseph's face. His chest gave a final shudder, and he went still. Joseph sobbed and sobbed. He felt Mariam's arms wrap around him, trying to console him, but he couldn't stop. How could this happen? He didn't care that everyone was watching. His brother was dead. Reuben was gone.

He had no idea how long he and his brothers sat there weeping, but by the time their tears gave way to numb shock, the throne room was empty except for a few guards and Potiphar, who stood nearby with his gun drawn and his eyes scanning the room.

Joseph looked around at his brothers. Their faces were a mixture of shock and grief. "He gave his life for me," said Joseph. "Why did he…"

Judah put his hand on Joseph's shoulder. "Because he loved you. Receive it. It was his final gift."

Joseph felt the tears beginning all over again just as Potiphar drew close and spoke. "I am sorry for your loss. I don't want to interrupt your grieving, but it would be best if we took you to another location in case there is another planned attack. Clearly, the person capable of making this happen had high-level connections."

"Was anyone else hurt?" asked Joseph.

"No, I believe you were the primary target. I eliminated the prisoner before he could do any more harm."

"Thank you," whispered Joseph. He could barely get his words to come out.

"I'm just sorry I wasn't able to save your brother," said Potiphar. His voice betrayed a rare swell of emotion.

"I know." Joseph reached out and took Potiphar's hand. "You're a good man, Potiphar. Thank you. I do not blame you for this."

"Don't thank me. I will be tendering my resignation later this evening. Such a thing should never have happened on my watch."

"Please don't. Avaris needs all the good men it can get. If there's any hope for us, we're going to need you."

"You are very kind, Joseph. Your rise to power has not changed that about you. I will let Pharaoh decide what to do with me. I serve at his behest. For now, let me get you to safety, and we will see what tomorrow brings."

Joseph nodded. He was in no condition to argue. Potiphar led him and Mariam to their quarters while the brothers were escorted to theirs. Two guards were stationed outside their door, and once inside, Joseph collapsed onto the bed. Mariam lay next to him, and for the longest time they just held one another.

Finally, Mariam spoke up. "I think you should get cleaned up. Then we can talk if you want to, or you can try and get some sleep."

Joseph knew it was good advice, but he didn't want to wash the blood off him. It was all he had left of Reuben.

"Come on. I'll help you," said Mariam, and she took him to the bathroom. Joseph caught a glimpse of himself in the mirror. He was a bloody mess. Mariam helped him out of his ruined suit and tossed it into the corner. Then she began to wipe the blood from his hands and face with a towel and water. By the time she was done the towel was red. The cold water revived him somewhat. He looked at his hands. There was still blood under the nails, but the rest of him was clean.

"Thank you," he said to Mariam, but he couldn't find any other words to say.

Mariam put her finger on his lips. "I understand. You don't have to say anything. Let's try and get some rest."

She led him back to the bedroom where Joseph fell into a fitful sleep. He was haunted by Ishmael's face and the sound of gunshots.

CHAPTER 32

The Day After

Joseph was startled awake. His hands were caked in blood, and he gagged. Stumbling in the darkness, he made his way to the bathroom to wash them. The water ran clean. It had just been a dream. But he continued to scrub, unable to get rid of the sensation. There was no going back to sleep now. He sat for a while and listened to Mariam's gentle breathing as she slept.

He tried to tell himself that it was all just a bad dream and Reuben was sleeping nearby, but he knew it wasn't true. Somewhere in the palace lay Reuben's cold, dead body. Joseph's hands shook as the memories from yesterday flooded over him. He took deep breaths to try to calm himself. Today was going to be a long day. He needed to hold it together.

"Lord, give me strength," he prayed. Then as quietly as possible he got dressed and stepped into the hall. The two guards were still in place, and they snapped to attention.

"At ease, men. Thank you for keeping watch. Was everything clear during the night?"

"Yes, Commander. No other signs of trouble that we've heard of."

"Very good. Would one of you escort me to find Potiphar? I want to know if there is any more information about last night's shooting."

As they walked, Joseph forced himself to replay the events from last night in his head to pick up any details that might serve as clues. By the time they reached Potiphar, he hadn't come up with anything.

Still in last night's bloodstained clothes, Potiphar looked like he'd had a rough night as well. He rose from his chair when Joseph entered.

"Do we have any leads on who was behind my brother's murder?" Joseph asked.

"Why don't we sit?" Potiphar motioned towards a chair for Joseph to use. Once they were settled, Potiphar continued. "We have a suspect."

"Who?" asked Joseph with iron in his voice.

"The prison warden."

"It can't have been him!" shouted Joseph. "He's half mad, not some criminal mastermind."

Potiphar nodded. "I thought the same thing, but the signs point to him. He had a forged invitation to the party on his person, and, more importantly, he had access to the prisoner."

"I want to talk to him," said Joseph.

Potiphar sighed and rubbed his temples. "You can't. He's dead."

It took a second for this news to sink in. "How?"

"A self-inflicted gunshot wound. The weapon he had matched the one we found on the killer. Same make, same bullets, everything."

"Who found him?"

Potiphar shifted uncomfortably in his chair. "My wife. She fled the scene and stumbled upon the warden while trying to find a place to hide. He was already dead on the floor. Needless to say, she's quite shaken and has taken to her bed."

Joseph stared at Potiphar and thought for a moment before he spoke.

"Do you think the warden could have been framed?"

"In my experience the simplest explanation is usually the correct one." Potiphar paused. "But in this case, my gut tells me there's more than meets the eye."

Joseph took a deep breath, not sure how Potiphar would respond to what he was about to ask. "Could Zuleika be involved?"

Potiphar dropped his head into his hands, clearly distressed. "I've been asking myself that all night, and I just don't know."

Joseph put his hand on Potiphar's shoulder. "You're a good man, and I trust you. We won't speak of Zuleika anymore for now. Where do we go from here?"

Potiphar sat up and massaged his brow. "Pharaoh will want justice, and he'll want to put the people at ease. The warden is an easy scapegoat—a deranged old man who snuck his way into the party to try to get back at those in power who secluded him to a life as a prison warden. It makes for a tidy little narrative."

"It does, indeed. The warden is dead, so dragging his name through the mud won't do him any more harm. Go ahead and tell Pharaoh that he was the culprit, but as far as you and I are concerned, the investigation is still ongoing."

Potiphar nodded. "Whoever did this will make a mistake at some point, and when they do, we'll be ready."

"Thank you. Now I'm going to return to Mariam before she wakes up and starts to worry about me."

"I will share the news with Pharaoh before returning to my wife as well. We will talk soon."

******

By mid-morning Pharaoh went public with the news that the man responsible for the attempt on Joseph's life was dead. Shortly afterward, a messenger arrived inviting Joseph, Mariam, and all the brothers to a private luncheon in honor of Reuben.

Reuben's absence was painfully present as Joseph greeted his brothers, and everyone made awkward small talk before heading to the luncheon. The brothers were like a flock of sheep without a shepherd. They milled about waiting for someone to take charge. Mariam nudged Joseph and whispered. "They are waiting for you to lead them."

"It should be Judah or Simeon. They're the oldest," he whispered back.

She shook her head adamantly. "It must be you. You may not be the oldest, but you are the wisest. Besides, you're the only one of them who knows how to get to lunch."

Despite himself, Joseph laughed. Everyone looked at him, and Joseph explained Mariam's joke.

Like sheep, the brothers fell in behind Joseph. He looked at Mariam, and she shrugged. It was the loudest non-verbal "I told you so" ever.

In the small dining room, a couple of tables had been pulled together so they could all eat together. Pharaoh sat at the head with Joseph to his right, and the rest of the brothers arranged themselves around the table. Before any food was served Pharaoh raised his glass and clinked it with a fork like they did in the olden days. The table grew silent.

"Gentlemen, let me express my sincerest condolences for your loss. I cannot emphasize enough how grieved I am that this tragedy occurred under my roof. Your brother was a good man, for only a good man would give his life for another. Such acts of courage and love are rare indeed. He will be remembered as a hero. Please raise your glasses and join me in a toast to your dear brother, Reuben. May he rest in peace."

"May he rest in peace," said the brothers softly, and many had tears in their eyes as they looked at Joseph, waiting for him to respond to Pharaoh. Joseph felt the words stick in his throat, but he managed to force them out.

"Thank you for your kind words, Pharaoh, and for your hospitality. Please know that we do not hold Reuben's death against you. If my father were here, he would say that life is but a breath. Like grass we wither and fade. Reuben lived a good life, and he died a brave and honorable death. Let us choose to focus on those things and not take our own lives for granted. Each day is a gift."

Joseph raised his glass, and the others followed suit. "To Reuben, until we meet again," he said. The others joined him, and Joseph couldn't stop the tear that ran down his cheek and spilled onto his chest. Reuben was gone, but he would not be forgotten. Joseph would make sure of that.

Lunch was served, and thankfully conversation turned to things other than Reuben. As the meal was coming to an end, Pharaoh pushed his plate back and brought the conversation full circle. "I do not wish to shine the light again on your sadness, but I do have two recommendations that I would have you consider. First, I think that you should have Reuben buried here in Avaris. Whatever you need will be provided. Secondly, I think that you brothers, except for Joseph, should return to your father and bring him back to Avaris. I will send a handful of soldiers with you to ensure your safety. I invite you to make Avaris your home. We could use more good men like all of you."

Joseph looked at his brothers and could tell they all knew that Pharaoh's words were good. First, they must bury Reuben, and then return to their father before he ran out of food. The news of Reuben's death would be crushing, but word of Joseph's miraculous survival would ease the pain. After all these years, it was time to leave the bunker, and where better to go than Avaris?

"We accept your kind offer, Pharaoh. Thank you," replied Joseph.

Pharaoh was clearly pleased. "It is settled then. Ask for whatever you need, and it will be provided."

There was a little more small talk before Pharaoh excused himself to attend another engagement. Joseph left Mariam in charge of planning the details of the funeral with his brothers. With her background as the priest's daughter, she was quite the expert on such things. As for him, he had an inkling to go see the room where the warden died to look for clues. Then he needed to find Cyasi. If anyone had information about who was behind Reuben's death, it would be him.

The room where the warden had died was small, a good place to hide. The body had been removed, but the blood had yet to be cleaned up properly. Joseph walked around, carefully examining the floor. On the far side of the room was a closet. Joseph opened the doors and was hit with the faint smell of perfume. He'd know that perfume anywhere. It was Zuleika's. Strange that her scent should be in the closet if she'd come into the room only to hide and had unexpectedly stumbled across the dead warden on the floor.

Kneeling, Joseph looked in the dim closet. He felt around, and his fingers found a small piece of cloth snagged on an exposed nail in the back of the closet. He gently pried the cloth from the nail and moved to the middle of the room where the light was better. He held up the cloth. It was the color of blood—the color of Zuleika's dress the night before.

Joseph felt his heart speed up. He held a shred of proof that Zuleika was lying. She was hiding something, and he intended to find out. He went back and checked the closet again but found nothing else. He definitely needed to talk to Cyasi now, but he had to be subtle. Zuleika wouldn't have had access to Ishmael, which meant she must have been working with someone, and here in the palace, the walls had ears.

On his way back to his room, Joseph ran into Salim, who bowed and put his hands over his heart. "My most sincere condolences, sir, on the death of your brother. What a terrible tragedy."

Joseph wanted to throttle him. He knew Salim didn't care a fig about Reuben, but now wasn't the time to call him out. "Thank you, Salim. It was indeed. Might I ask you where you were when the incident occurred? I'm interested in gathering firsthand accounts."

"Of course," Salim replied, seeming a bit flustered. "I was at the edge of the crowd when it happened. I'd been tasked with bringing out the two prisoners and had only just made it back into the room when the gunshots went off. While I'm not proud of this, I panicked and ran for safety. I am grateful that Potiphar killed the man before he could do any further damage. Now is there anything I can do for you, sir?"

Joseph thought about asking him if he'd seen Zuleika while he was fleeing the scene, but he didn't want to raise the slimy man's suspicions. But he did have a favor to ask. "Find Cyasi and have him brought to my chambers. We'll be hosting a funeral for my brother tomorrow, and I need his assistance."

"Very good, sir. I will go and find him at once. If you need anything else, please don't hesitate to ask. I know this is a difficult time. I hope it brings you solace that your brother's killer and his accomplice are both dead and cannot do you any further harm."

"Thank you, Salim, that does bring me comfort," Joseph lied.

Joseph watched Salim walk away. Interesting that he'd been as far away from the danger as possible, *and* he'd been the last person to have access to the prisoners before they were brought to Pharaoh. Joseph filed all this information away and headed for his room. Hopefully Cyasi would arrive quickly. He laughed at the thought. The man never hurried for anything or anyone.

But Joseph was pleasantly surprised. He'd barely had time to sit down when there was a knock on the door. It was almost as if Cyasi had been waiting to be summoned.

"Come in," called Joseph.

Cyasi stepped inside and locked the door behind him. "I hear you need my services for the funeral."

"We do. Have you ever worked your magic on the deceased?"

"I have not, but for you I am willing to try. I assume you would like me to assist with your brother. Reuben, correct?"

Joseph nodded. "If you could make him look presentable for the funeral, I would be most appreciative."

"I will do my best. Might there be anything else you'd hoped to discuss?"

"You and I both know there is. What I'm about to tell you, you must promise to keep secret."

"Although it pains me, I promise," replied Cyasi sorrowfully.

"Good. I don't think the warden was the mastermind behind my brother's death. I believe the architect of this atrocity is still at large, which means my life is still in danger."

Cyasi nodded. "Continue, if you would."

Joseph filled him in about the red fabric and Salim's access to the prisoners. When he was done, Cyasi rubbed his chin and stared up at the ceiling. His response was measured. "This corroborates what I have heard from others, servants who saw the whole thing and so forth. Zuleika likes to be the center of attention, but she was on the fringes of the crowd near the warden. He was too busy stuffing his face with food to really notice what was happening, if my sources are correct. As far as Salim, you know how I feel about the man. I wouldn't put it past him to try to have you eliminated. He is a snake, slithering around in your shadow waiting to strike."

Joseph brightened, encouraged that he wasn't the only one connecting the dots. "What do we do next?"

"First, we see Reuben properly buried. Then I have an idea regarding Salim. Zuleika is more difficult. If we can get our hands on her red dress —which was stunning, I must add—then we could try to match the material you found. Both Salim and Zuleika are powerful, so we need to be careful. We cannot afford to accuse them without proper evidence." He paused. "Do you trust Potiphar enough to turn against his wife if she is guilty?"

Joseph pondered before answering. "I do. He, Zuleika, and I have a long history. The real reason I was sentenced to prison was because Zuleika attempted to have an affair with me. I never attacked her, in fact, I did just the opposite. I resisted her advances."

Cyasi's eyebrows shot up. "Oh, I can only imagine that didn't go over well."

"You can say that again! But Potiphar caught her in the lie, putting him in a terrible position. In the end he chose to preserve his wife's name and had me thrown in prison. He could easily have had me killed, but he extended mercy. That's when I knew that he was a good man; A good man married to a terrible woman."

Cyasi let out a low whistle. "Now that right there is a story. It's going to hurt to keep that one to myself." Joseph gave him a look, and Cyasi chuckled. "Don't worry, I will. It makes sense then why Zuleika isn't your biggest fan."

Joseph nodded. "Find Salim and have him show you where my brother's body is being kept so you can prepare it for burial. The rest can wait until after that."

"An excellent plan, and... I'm so sorry about your brother. He must have loved you deeply to protect you the way he did."

Joseph let the words sink in. "I guess he did. It feels so unfair. He'd just come back into my life, and now I'm trying to wrap my head around the fact that he is gone. Life can be cruel sometimes."

"It can, but it can also be good. Don't lose sight of the good. Now I better be going."

After he left, Joseph sat down in a chair, grateful for the silence filling the room. He just wanted to be. He was still sitting deep in thought when Mariam found him. She went over and gently put her arm around him. "I love you," she whispered.

Her words brought him up out of the depths of his grief and back towards the light. He looked at her, eyes filled with sadness. "I love you too."

"We're going to make it through this," she promised.

Joseph nodded. "I know. It just hurts like hell right now."

CHAPTER 33

Goodbyes

It was still early when Joseph and his brothers made their way out of the palace toward the Nile, and already the sky was a gray ashtray. The faint beams of light that filtered down were ragged and weary. They carried Reuben's body in a wooden casket underneath this somber expanse.

The burial was a family affair. Joseph had requested Emmanuel's presence as an honorary member of the family, and Potiphar had granted him leave to join. No words were spoken as the mourners made their way to a small plot a little way from the banks of the Nile where the water moved slow and sludgy. A shallow grave had been dug, and the brother gently placed the casket by the human-sized hole.

Joseph removed the lid from the casket and looked at Reuben's face. Cyasi had done good work. He looked as if he was only sleeping and might sit up and climb out of the coffin at any moment. The others gathered around, their faces peering down at Reuben. The shirt he wore hid the holes in his chest, and his face looked peaceful. Joseph hoped that was what he'd felt when he'd died, peace.

Emmanuel was the last to join the circle. He'd seen more death than the rest of them combined, but Joseph watched tears form in his eyes. So much death, and yet he had not grown numb to it. The silence hung thick over the small group as the water churned behind them and the sun struggled above. The earth awaited its prize, but there they stood, unready to relinquish Reuben to the ground.

Finally, Emmanuel put his hand on Joseph's shoulder. "If you don't mind, I will say a few words." Joseph nodded, and Emmanuel began.

"There is no greater love than this: that a man lays down his life for his friend. The essence of being human is to love. In his final act, Reuben proved this to be true. He sacrificed his life out of love for his brother. This was a most sacred act which will never be forgotten. As we gather to mourn his passing, let us also honor his life; a life well lived. Now let us commit his body and spirit to God. Let us be reminded of the frailty of our lives and our brevity in the face of eternity. For it is from dust that we came, and to dust we will return. If anyone has any final words, let them speak them now."

Mariam spoke first. "Thank you for saving my husband, Reuben. If I am blessed to bear a son, I will name him after you. Your legacy will live on in him."

One by one the others paid their final respects: words of gratitude, stories, thank-yous. They shared until their words filled up the casket and spilled over. Joseph went last. He kneeled and put his hand on Reuben's head. "If Abba was here, he would say a blessing over you. The same one that he said over each of us a million times, but receive it one more time, dear brother. May God bless you and keep you. May He cause His face to shine upon you. May God grant you peace now and forevermore. Amen."

Then Joseph slid the lid of the casket back in place. He and his brothers carefully lowered it into the grave. One by one they threw handfuls of dirt onto the casket, and Mariam began to sing softly in the background. It was a haunting tune that swirled about them as they covered the casket until it disappeared beneath the earth. They placed a few small stones to mark the grave, and the final notes of Mariam's song drifted into nothingness as the work came to an end.

They trudged back to the palace, and Joseph knew the goodbyes were only just beginning. After a hurried breakfast, the brothers prepared to leave. Abba was waiting, and they feared they might need to perform his funeral next if they didn't get home quickly. A small group of soldiers stood nearby as Joseph and his brothers said goodbye. Joseph came to Benjamin last.

"Be safe. Don't do anything stupid, and stay away from man or beast that wants to harm you. I expect to see you again soon. You're going to be an uncle after all."

"I promise I'll return so I can be the best uncle ever," said Benjamin.

"Good, I'll hold you to that. Now get moving."

Joseph put his arm around Mariam's shoulder as they watched the brothers disappear. Then he said goodbye to Mariam as well and told her he'd meet her in their rooms later. Once everyone else was gone, he turned to Emmanuel.

"Thank you for being here."

"Of course. I'm grateful you asked."

"Let me walk you out. I have a favor I need you to do for me."

Emmanuel raised an eyebrow. "Yes?"

"I need you to find something."

"That is rather mysterious of you. What exactly am I finding?"

"A red dress."

Emmanuel laughed. "Now that is a first."

Joseph looked at him seriously. "I know this might sound strange, but it's important. Zuleika wore a red dress to Pharaoh's party when my brother was killed. That's the dress I need."

"Where might I find this red dress?" asked Emmanuel.

"That is the million-dollar question. I'm guessing that Zuleika hid it somewhere in her chambers, which is why you need to try and find it right away before she gets rid of it."

"I'll try my best. Pray that God might grant me favor."

"I will. Thank you, old friend. I know I'm asking you to take a risk."

"What is life without a little risk taking? I need something to help keep me young these days. Nothing like a top-secret mission to make one feel alive again. Now if you'll excuse me, I have important work to do."

"God be with you," said Joseph.

"And also with you," replied Emmanuel as he headed back to Potiphar's house.

Joseph watched him go, another one of the many goodbyes. The last twenty-four hours had been a soul-crushing whirlwind. It felt strange to just stand here, but now all he could do was wait. If all went well, his brothers would be back in a few months, and by then he'd have the evidence he needed to prove who was really behind Reuben's death. But for now, he had to try to go about business as usual.

CHAPTER 34

News

In the days following Reuben's burial, the weather took a turn for the worse. Massive dust storms pounded Avaris and turned everything gray and dreary. Anyone with good sense stayed inside. The sky was filled with giant bolts of lightning both day and night. There were tremors, and at one point hail the size of a child's fist pelted the city with a ferocity unlike anything Joseph had ever seen before. It was like the second coming of the ten plagues.

During the day, Joseph oversaw the distribution of grain to the citizens. The portions were small and people grumbled, but at their current pace they would have enough to keep the population alive. Joseph prayed that his brothers were okay traveling in this weather. Hopefully it meant that raiders and militias were holed up and would leave them alone. On the other hand, it meant that Zuleika probably hadn't left her residence, making it difficult for Emmanuel to complete his mission. Joseph waited anxiously for a message from Emmanuel, but none came. Cyasi had also been strangely absent. Perhaps he'd hit a dead end as well.

Joseph knew this process was going to take time, but that didn't stop him from wanting it to be done right away. He wanted justice for Reuben. Now, all he had were theories based mostly on a scrap of red fabric and coincidental proximity. Certainly not enough to take to Pharaoh and make an accusation.

It had been exactly a week since Reuben's death, and despite the terrible weather, he'd made a point of venturing out to his brother's burial site each day. He was on his way out when a messenger arrived for him. He took the note, thanked the man, and stepped back inside his room to read it in private.

Dear Joseph,

I have located the item you requested me to find, although it was no simple task. I was nearly caught, but that is a story which can wait. Having carefully surveyed the item, I believe that your suspicion was correct about the cause of damage. I also found a brief communication stored along with the item, and I believe it will be of some interest to you as well. I will not say more in this letter, but know that I am able to procure the items as needed.

Sincerely,

E

Joseph felt a surge of adrenaline at this news. His hunch had been correct about Zuleika. She was caught up in the thick of this somehow. Now came the tricky part. He had to draw her out, but Zuleika would not easily be caught off guard. She was a poisonous snake, always ready to strike. Disregarding decorum, Joseph ran to Reuben's grave to tell him the good news. Soon he would avenge his brother's death. The pieces were falling into place.

Later that day, Cyasi stopped by to trim Joseph's beard.

"Don't make me suffer through a gauntlet of small talk," Joseph said. "Tell me straight. Do you have any information about my brother's death?"

Cyasi nodded. "I do believe you are the first person to describe my conversation as a form of suffering, but I'll do my best to get past that. I received word from a friend of a friend who works in the prison that Salim paid an unexpected visit to the warden just over a month ago."

Joseph raised his eyebrows and was about to speak, but Cyasi silenced him.

"That's not the most interesting part. He also visited one of the prisoners while he was there."

"Let me guess," interrupted Joseph, ignoring the annoyed look on Cyasi's face. "Ishmael."

"Correct. They held a brief interview before Salim made a hasty exit. The whole visit took no more than an hour."

Joseph struck the desk with his fist and winced at the pain. "Salim set this whole thing up. I should have known. No, I should have gotten rid of him years ago."

"Men like Salim are more difficult to get rid of than you would think," said Cyasi. "You can't blame yourself."

"Easier said than done," replied Joseph as he rubbed his throbbing hand.

"Still, you must try. There is one small silver lining in all of this. It seems that Salim has overestimated his own cunning. He assumed we'd all buy the story that the warden was the culprit and let it go at that."

"His pride will come before his fall. I will see to that," growled Joseph.

"What do you plan to do next?" asked Cyasi.

Joseph's face was as hard as stone. "I plan to go hunting for snakes."

"Then, may that which dwells in darkness be brought forth into the light."

"Thank you. Now if you'll excuse me, I have some planning to do."

"Of course." Cyasi bowed and showed himself out while Joseph sat down to think.

An hour later, Joseph had written and sealed three carefully crafted letters. He dispatched them with a courier he trusted and then sat back. The trap was set. Now he just had to wait until tomorrow evening to see whether he would catch anything.

The letters arrived as expected; one to Pharaoh, one to Potiphar, and one to Salim. They contained an invitation to an exclusive dinner Joseph was hosting to honor his deceased brother. Joseph knew none of them would be able to refuse. He made a special request that Potiphar bring his wife, and within the hour all three guests had responded affirmatively.

Joseph sent one final note to Emmanuel asking him to please come at once and bring his medical kit to check on Mariam. Emmanuel would understand the true nature of the request, and carrying his medical kit would give him a way to smuggle out the items he'd found.

Joseph and Mariam were in their quarters later that evening when Emmanuel arrived. He seemed to move slower and slower each time Joseph saw him, like a windup toy that was nearly unwound. He was possibly the oldest man in Avaris. The apocalypse and subsequent years had not been kind to the elderly population. Joseph shuddered to think what the average human lifespan was now.

But his heart swelled with gratitude for the old man. He was a wise sage and a second father. A constant source of kindness amid the cruel world. Maybe someday things would be different, and there would be a place again for people like Emmanuel. People with souls like oak trees whose roots tapped into the deep waters of wisdom and understanding. Joseph prayed that someday there would be more than the daily fight for survival. That was the type of world he wanted to build for his unborn child.

All these thoughts rushed through him, and he gave Emmanuel a long embrace. Emmanuel sighed contentedly. "You don't realize how important human touch is until you don't have it."

"I'm sorry," replied Joseph.

"It is one of the many curses of getting old, but it is not your cross to bear."

"I'm still sorry. I would have freed you from Zuleika years ago if it was within my power, but even I have my limits."

"I know," said Emmanuel. "It is better that way. No man should be above the law. Such men existed in the old world, and their selfishness and greed led to the destruction of humanity."

"That's why I need to destroy Salim. His hunger for power knows no bounds."

Emmanuel's face grew stern, as did his words. "As you seek to find those who killed your brother, you must take care not to become like the very people you despise. Do not let yourself be ruled by the unquenchable thirst for revenge. Instead seek justice. Try to find compassion in your heart even for those who oppose you, and trust that God will take care of the rest. Do you hear me?"

Joseph knew that he had been rebuked, but even worse was that he knew Emmanuel was right. "I hear you. Loud and clear."

"Good. The world needs more men like you, more leaders who lead with humility." He patted Joseph gently on the back with his frail fingers.

"The Lord knows I'm trying my best," replied Joseph, as he sat down.

"That's all He asks of us. Now, I've been around long enough to know that tonight's meeting is not about the health of your lovely wife, but seeing her does my heart good," said Emmanuel.

Mariam came over and gave him a hug. "It is good to see you as well. The baby and I are both doing fine."

"Yes, you look the picture of health. If you'd like, I could listen to the baby's heartbeat just to make sure."

"I would like that very much. Thank you."

"Let me finish the more unsavory business first, and then I will attend to you." Emmanuel opened his case and pulled out the red dress along with a folded note. He handed them to Joseph. "I believe these are what you are looking for."

Joseph leapt to his feet. "Yes!" This was the evidence he'd been looking for.

"I think you'll find the note particularly interesting. Give it a read," said Emmanuel.

Joseph unfolded it and read aloud:

Dear Z,

The dreamer does not sleep
The unsuspecting slumbers
All is not lost.
Remain steadfast.

Justice will be served

At the bottom of the note was a small hand-drawn symbol that Joseph had never seen before. It was curious, but Joseph was more focused on the message itself. He looked up at Emmanuel. "While I don't consider myself a great poet, I think I can figure this one out. It certainly seems to implicate Zuleika."

"Yes, but there is more. Look at the symbol. Does it look familiar?"

Joseph studied it again. "No. Do you know what it means?"

Emmanuel shook his head. "It's not the meaning that matters. When I first read the note, I had a faint memory of having seen that same symbol before. It took me a while to remember where, but then it came to me. I'd once seen that symbol as a tattoo."

"On whom?" asked Joseph eagerly.

Emmanuel locked eyes with Joseph. "Salim. I saw it while he was in prison, and I was asked to tend to him. It is on his right shoulder blade. The exact same symbol."

Joseph felt a deep sense of relief. "So now we have proof that both are involved. I knew it."

"I wouldn't go so far as to say we have proof, but we certainly have enough dots for Pharaoh to connect to make a verdict. You should have everything you need, but for the moment let's put that aside. We have more important things to tend to. I would like to check on your wife."

Joseph knew Emmanuel was right, but it was hard to not fixate on seeing Zuleika and Salim brought to justice. He watched as Emmanuel carefully withdrew a stethoscope from his bag and blew on it, warming the metal with his breath. Then he gently placed it on Mariam's belly. He instantly broke into a smile and motioned for Joseph to come over. "Do you want to hear your child's heartbeat?"

He wanted nothing more. This was his little ray of sunshine amid the darkness. "Of course."

Emmanuel got him situated with the stethoscope and showed Joseph where to place it. At first he heard nothing, and then there it was—a magnificent little heartbeat. It was the most beautiful thing he'd ever heard. Joseph grabbed Mariam's hand, and she laughed at his excitement. "Soon you'll be able to feel him move too. This one doesn't like to sit still."

Joseph grinned. "I can't wait for that."

Mariam laughed again. "All in good time, my love. All in good time."

Emmanuel took that as his cue. "I won't keep you two. Everything looks good, Mariam. I will pray for you both in the days to come. May God bless you and keep you and protect you from all harm."

"Thank you," they replied in unison. With that, Emmanuel ambled out of the room, quietly singing an old hymn to himself.

"When peace like a river attendeth my way,

When sorrows like sea billows roll,

Whatever my lot, Thou hast taught me to say,

It is well, it is well with my soul..."

CHAPTER 35

The Trap Closes

Peace was not easy to come by as Joseph waited for the evening's festivities. He'd arranged for the dinner to be served in the room right next to where the warden had been killed. He wanted Salim and Zuleika to have to walk past the scene of the crime. He wanted them to be nervous.

When the time came, he placed the dress and letter in a leather satchel and made his way down the long hallways and through the giant throne room that echoed with his footsteps. His body tensed as he walked by the marble steps where he'd held Reuben as he died. Being back in this space made Joseph feel small and vulnerable, as if another gunman might jump out at any moment and take him too.

He kept walking, refusing to run from ghosts that didn't exist. Each step was an act of defiance, an act of faith. Once outside the throne room, he couldn't help imagining the crush of people screaming and running and shoving to escape as they ran for their lives on that ill-fated night. And then there was the warden; the poor, hapless warden happily munching on hors d'oeuvres, naive to the danger that lurked nearby. Joseph stopped to peer into the space where he'd been killed. The blood stain still lingered on the floor, and Joseph wanted to vomit.

He took a deep breath and kept walking. This was no time to lose his cool. Thankfully, he was the first to arrive. No one had seen him go weak-kneed and ashen. There were a few servants inside in the dining room tending to the final touches. A large table had been set. Joseph noticed one or two of the plates were chipped. Even the fine china had seen better days, but the fact that an entire set of china still existed was somewhat miraculous. The silverware didn't exactly shine, but none of the forks were missing tines, so that was good. He'd specifically requested no knives, just in case things went south.

Potiphar and Zuleika were the first to arrive. Potiphar looked grave, even for him, which made Joseph wonder if he sensed a storm was brewing. Zuleika's true feelings were hidden behind dollops of makeup and a plastic smile. They both bowed to Joseph. "Thank you for inviting us to this special occasion," said Potiphar, and Joseph could hear the anxiety in his tone.

"Yes, we are honored to be able to join you in commemorating your brother, and we are oh so sorry for your loss," crooned Zuleika.

Joseph swore he even saw tears in her eyes. She was a master actress. "I am grateful that you both have come. Thank you for your condolences."

From there they made small talk until Salim slipped in. He was dressed all in black with his hair slicked back and his face as stoic as a corpse. He bowed stiffly and addressed Joseph. "Sorry for your loss, sir. What happened was a terrible tragedy."

"Thank you, Salim. My brother was a good man. He did not deserve to die." Joseph gave Salim a penetrating stare until he looked away. The tension in the air increased just a little, as if someone had turned up the heat a few degrees in the room.

Last to arrive, as usual, Pharaoh strolled in cool as a cucumber. He gave Joseph a quick nod and spoke. "Thank you for the invitation to celebrate the life of your brother."

"I am honored by your presence. Thank you for coming, Pharaoh."

"Is there anyone else coming?" asked Pharaoh.

"No, just our small, hand-picked group this evening, but now that we are all here, let's be seated." Pharaoh was, of course, seated at the head of the table with Joseph at his right hand and Potiphar at his left. Zuleika and Salim were strategically seated across from one another. Joseph motioned to the servants, and they filled everyone's glasses and brought out the first course of food. Then Joseph raised his glass. "I would like to give a toast." The others joined him and raised their glasses.

"To Reuben, the blood of the innocent is not soon forgotten. May you rest in peace, and may you receive justice either in this life or the next."

His words hung heavy in the air as glasses clinked awkwardly around them. Potiphar stiffened in his seat, and Joseph noted with pleasure the hasty eye contact between Salim and Zuleika. He felt the tension crank up another notch. By the time dessert was served it would be unbearable.

After the clinking stopped Joseph had a few more things to say. "I would like to thank you once again for coming. I know my request was made on short notice, and you are all very busy people. A special thanks to Zuleika. I know the experience of that night has caused you great anguish. I am sorry for your suffering, and I hope this evening will be a balm for your spirit."

"You are too kind," replied Zuleika. Her heavily lipsticked lips stretched into a fragile smile.

Joseph continued. "While I wish to celebrate the life of my brother, I also wish for this to be a chance for us to look forward. My brother's death has unsettled the people of Avaris, but we cannot allow it to deter us from our important work. That is what my brother would want."

"I'll drink to that," said Pharaoh, and he raised his glass. "Wise words. Life is for the living. We will honor your brother by living well. To Reuben." There was another round of clinking glasses and then polite chatter as they began to eat the first course.

When the plates were cleared, Joseph decided to turn up the heat another notch. "Tell me, Salim, how have you been faring since that unfortunate night?"

Salim gave a strained smile. "You are gracious to ask me such a question after all that you have lost. I would say that I am holding up as best as possible under the circumstances."

"I'm glad to hear it. I would love to pick your brain on something pertaining to that night, if it's okay."

"Ask away, sir," replied Salim through gritted teeth, which he quickly turned into a fake smile.

"Thank you. One of the things that's been bothering me is how Ishmael managed to get his hands on a gun, considering the thoroughness of Potiphar's security. Do you have any ideas?"

An awkward silence descended on the table. Salim's eyes darted back and forth, as he clearly scrambled for an answer. "You have asked a most difficult question. I am afraid that I am quite as baffled as you are. I know Potiphar to be the most vigilant of men. How such a thing occurred is truly beyond me."

Joseph leaned in. "So, you admit that it is rather remarkable that the prisoner smuggled in a gun?"

"Yes... I mean... It's possible." Salim hesitated and looked at Potiphar uncomfortably. "I mean you no disrespect Potiphar, but we must consider the possibility."

Joseph could see the tempered rage behind Potiphar's eyes. The big man's whole body was tense, like a wire ready to snap. He gave Salim such a terrifying glare that Salim sank into his chair. When Potiphar spoke, his words cut like a dagger. "I take the utmost offense at what you are insinuating, for I checked both prisoners myself. You know that because you were there."

"Yes, but somehow the warden fooled us all," squeaked Salim.

"Or the weapon was provided after the prisoners were searched and placed in the holding room," said Potiphar.

Pharaoh's eyebrows had been creeping upward throughout the exchange, and now he joined in. "Who had access to the prisoners after they were in the holding room?"

An excellent question, thought Joseph.

Potiphar spoke up at once. "Only a handful of people, Your Greatness. The four guards and Salim. Not even I had access to them after they were searched, because I went to join my lovely wife for the event."

Salim had grown pale. "Your Greatness, I can assure you that I had nothing to do with this. It was clearly the warden. We all know the man was half mad and hated you and Joseph. They even found an empty gun safe in his mess of an office."

He's covering his tracks, thought Joseph irritably.

Pharaoh's words were carefully measured. "This evening has taken a most unexpected turn. No one is accusing you, Salim. We are simply trying to make sense of one of the greatest tragedies in the history of Avaris. You cannot fault Joseph for wanting to understand how such a thing could occur."

"Of course not," sputtered Salim. "It's only that I had thought the matter concluded."

"Me as well, but what Potiphar has said has made me wonder. If the warden did not have access after the prisoners were searched, could it be that we have not caught the actual killer? And if that is the case, then Joseph is still in danger," said Pharaoh.

"But then why would the warden kill himself?" asked Salim, trying to shift the conversation. "Clearly the man was guilty."

Joseph seized this moment to interject. "Please forgive me, but in the past few days I did some investigating of my own, and I stumbled across something very interesting."

Pharaoh leaned forward eagerly, a hound who'd caught the scent of the hunt. "What might that be?"

"I inspected the room where the warden was killed, and I stumbled upon the most curious thing. You see, there was a small closet in the room where he died. A closet just big enough for a person to hide, and in that closet, I found a scrap of bright red cloth." Joseph reached into his satchel, pulled out the piece of red fabric, and slid it over to Pharaoh to examine.

"And why does that matter?" asked Pharaoh after he'd looked at the fabric. Zuleika shifted uncomfortably in her seat, and Joseph had to bite back a smirk.

"It matters, Your Greatness, because the scrap of cloth is the same color as Zuleika's dress. According to her story, she ran into the room to hide and stumbled upon the warden's dead body. If that is the case, how did the scrap of cloth get into the closet? If she did hide in the closet, why did she lie about it?"

"Those are excellent questions," said Pharaoh. "Zuleika, can you shed some light on this for us?"

Zuleika unleashed her most captivating smile, the sort of smile that made men swoon. "I am sorry, Your Greatness, but this conversation seems to be moving very quickly, and I'm struggling to keep up."

Pharaoh's eyes flashed with irritation, but his voice remained calm. "Of course, let me ask the question another way. Do you have any idea why a piece of your dress might have been in the closet?"

"I am afraid I don't know. I ran into the room to hide and suddenly found myself staring at a fresh corpse. It was the most horrifying moment of my life." Zuleika put the back of her hand to her forehead as if she might faint. "I have had the most terrible nightmares every night since then. I see the warden's face and the blood. Always the blood. So much blood." She closed her eyes.

"I am very sorry. I did not mean to bring up such a painful thing. We will not speak of it anymore," said Pharaoh.

"I insist that we do," said Joseph. "She has not answered the question, and I must know for the sake of my brother and for the sake of my own life. For as you said earlier, if we have blamed the wrong man, then I am still a target. So tell us, Zuleika, why was there a scrap of your dress in the closet?"

Zuleika looked at Joseph with malice in her eyes. "I do not know what you found in that closet, but it was not mine. I stand by what I shared. Please don't make me relive it."

"I'm afraid that's not an option." Joseph reached for his satchel a second time and withdrew the red dress and placed it on the table.

Zuleika gasped and Joseph turned to Pharaoh. "As you can see, Your Greatness, the scrap of fabric matches perfectly with the dress. Ask anyone what Zuleika was wearing that evening, and they can attest she was wearing this very dress. The story she has been telling us is a lie!"

Pharaoh looked at the dress and the piece of fabric. There was no question they were one and the same. He looked up at Zuleika. "Why would you lie about such a thing?"

Zuleika paused for a second, then blurted out, "It was Salim! He made me do it. He told me that if I didn't do exactly what he said, he would kill me and my husband. He stashed the gun in the closet and made me—" She burst into tears.

"How dare you!" roared Salim. "I have no idea what she is talking about. I would never do such a thing. I—"

"Actually, you would," shouted Joseph. "And I can prove it."

"That's impossible," declared Salim.

"We'll see," said Joseph as he dipped into his satchel a third time and produced the note, sliding it across the table to Pharaoh. "This is in Salim's own hand, and if you need more proof, I have it."

Pharaoh read the note and then looked up "What other proof might you add to this?"

Joseph tried to keep his voice calm, but it was difficult with all the adrenaline pumping through him. "Look at the symbol at the bottom of the letter."

"What should I make of it?"

"Just wait." Joseph turned to Salim. "Take off your shirt so we can see your right shoulder blade."

"I most certainly will not. I refuse to be treated this way. This is an outrage," shouted Salim.

Pharaoh's face hardened. "Do as he says or I will have Potiphar do it for you," he said in his most commanding voice.

Salim whimpered as he turned his back toward the table and lifted his shirt. The symbol tattooed on his shoulder was clearly the same as the one on the note. Pharaoh rose from his chair and threw his glass at Salim. It shattered against Salim's back, and he cried out in pain as shards of glass exploded everywhere.

"How dare you!" shouted Pharaoh. "How dare you betray me. After all I have done for you. I spared your life, and this is how you repay me. I will have you killed for this."

Salim threw himself at Pharaoh's feet. "I can explain. It was Zuleika. She is the mastermind behind all of this. I swear. Please, you must believe me."

Pharaoh looked back and forth between Zuleika and Salim. Zuleika's tears had turned into hysterical wailing while Salim rocked back and forth in a prostrate position. Joseph could see the wheels turning in Pharaoh's head as he tried to make sense of everything. Salim reached for Pharaoh's foot, but Pharaoh kicked at him. "Do not touch me. You are the one behind all of this. You had access to the prisoner. I would not doubt for a second that you blackmailed this poor woman here and forced her to participate in your treachery. I will parade your head around Avaris on a pole. Your name will become a curse." Pharaoh had worked himself into a lather by this point.

"Have mercy, Your Greatness. Have mercy," cried Salim.

"You will receive the same mercy that you showed Joseph's brother," declared Pharaoh with disgust.

"Thank you," wailed Zuleika, and she wrapped her arms around Pharaoh. "Finally, I will be free of his conniving ways, his threats, his blackmail. Today I am released from my bondage."

Pharaoh gently patted Zuleika with one hand while he tried to pry himself from her firm grasp with the other. "You are most welcome, Zuleika. I am so very sorry—"

Potiphar rose from his seat, and all eyes shifted to him. "May I speak, Your Greatness?" He looked at his wife and shuddered. "My wife is guilty as well, and I cannot allow her to go free again by covering up her deceit. I made that mistake once, but I will not do it again."

Pharaoh was clearly perplexed, and Joseph waited with bated breath. "What exactly are you saying?" asked Pharaoh.

"I am saying that my wife hates Joseph and his wife with a fiery passion. It has been like this ever since the day that Joseph spurned her advances and chose Mariam over her. I kept this secret to protect her reputation, but it seems that I may have only served to empower her. The world has never seen a more jealous woman. I knew of her hatred, but until this moment I did not realize the depths to which she would stoop to seek her revenge. I have no doubt that she and Salim were equal accomplices. Should she be spared, then Joseph's life will continue to be in perpetual danger. I have sworn an oath to protect him, and I will uphold my oath."

"How dare you!" spat Zuleika. "My own husband has turned against me. I should have known. You have no spine. You—"

"Enough!" shouted Pharaoh, and for a second Joseph thought that he was going to strike her. "You will not insult Potiphar in my presence. I owe him my very life. He is anything but a coward." He turned to Joseph. "What do you make of this?"

Joseph took a moment to compose himself. "I believe that both parties are guilty. The evidence points to them having plotted and carried out the murder of my brother and the warden."

"Based upon the evidence and Potiphar's testimony, I agree with your conclusion. Since it is you they have wronged, what punishment would you recommend?" asked Pharaoh.

Joseph hadn't anticipated this. He looked at Zuleika, hissing mad like an alley cat, and Salim, curled up in a pathetic pile at Pharaoh's feet. In that moment, he knew what he had to do.

"Pharaoh, when I was younger, I was consumed by the desire for revenge after my brothers wronged me, but I learned that revenge is a cruel and unfulfilling master. It eats away at the soul and brings no peace. Even still I can hear it calling to me, enticing me. The desire for revenge is strong. To say otherwise would be a lie. Had this happened years ago, I would have demanded that these two criminals be whipped publicly and then killed. An eye for an eye, and a life for a life. But I have seen and I have learned much. I'm not the man I once was. I believe it's better to forgive than to hold a grudge. Better to love than to hate. I've seen enough death to last me a lifetime. I will not have more bloodshed on my hands. Instead, I choose to forgive and to extend mercy. I ask that you banish them from Avaris. Give them enough food and water for a week's journey. What they do and where they go is up to them, but let them have a second chance to redeem their broken lives."

Pharaoh looked at Joseph with admiration on his face. "You are a good man, Joseph— a better man than me. Let everything be as you have requested." He turned to Salim and Zuleika. "You have been shown mercy, a kindness I would not have extended were it my decision. Now, hear me well. You will be escorted directly to the city gate and given provisions. Once outside, you are never to return to Avaris. Should you try, you will be killed. Go, and know that each breath you draw is an undeserved gift."

"Don't let them do this to me, Potiphar. Please, if you love me, help me," wailed Zuleika. She threw herself at her husband, but he pulled away, and she fell to the ground next to Salim.

"My love for you died long ago. You cannot bat your pretty eyes and make this go away this time. At last your sins have caught up to you," said Potiphar. Then he turned his back on her.

"Guards, take these two away," commanded Pharaoh.

"I will escort them myself," said Potiphar quietly. "I want to ensure this is done correctly." He turned to the guards. "Gag the prisoners. I do not want to hear any more words from their poisonous tongues." Salim and Zuleika were marched out of the room with Potiphar close behind.

"If they are lucky, they might live," said Joseph.

"If they're lucky, they won't kill each other," replied Pharaoh.

"I don't know. I have a feeling they'll make it. They're survivors. The question is whether they will change."

Pharaoh put his hand on Joseph's shoulder. "You've given them the chance. What they do with it is up to them."

CHAPTER 36

Beloved Sons

A month later, the palace was filled with the sacred sound of a newborn baby crying as Mariam gave birth to a healthy boy. She was assisted by the oldest and wisest doctor in the city, who was now a free citizen of Avaris.

When Joseph held his son in his arms for the first time, tears streamed down his face. Everything about the boy was perfect. Joseph put his face right up next to his and whispered softly, "I love you."

Joseph felt a hand on his back and looked up to see Emmanuel. The old man's smile was a ray of joyous sunshine. "What are you going to name him?" asked Emmanuel.

Joseph looked at Mariam, and she nodded for him to unveil the big secret. "His name is Reuben Emmanuel. He's named after two great men."

Emmanuel's eyes filled with big, sloppy tears that ran down his wrinkly face. "Thank you," he whispered. Then he stretched out his delicate pointer finger, and baby Reuben grabbed a hold of it. "Welcome to the world, precious one."

A little over a month later, a messenger arrived at the palace with an important message for Joseph. He rushed to the main city gate to find Judah waiting for him. Judah told him everything that had unfolded after the brothers left Avaris.

"The going was slow. The wind and rain pounded us day and night, soaking us to the bone. We were nearly struck by lightning several times, and the skin on our feet peeled off in strips from the damp and wet. Each day we didn't make it to the bunker, we feared the worst."

Joseph shuddered, knowing all too well what that felt like.

Judah continued, "When we finally arrived at the bunker, we found Father lying on the floor of his room barely more than a skeleton, but he was still breathing."

Joseph's heart sank. "What happened?" he asked.

"He'd fallen and didn't have the strength to get up. He'd been like that for three whole days. It's a miracle he survived. He said he had a dream and that God told him we were coming. Whether it was God or a hallucination, I don't know, but it made him keep fighting until we got there."

Joseph smiled. "Looks like dreams run in the family."

Judah smiled too. "It looks like it. It took a couple of weeks to nurse him back to health, and he's still weak and in constant need of assistance. His eyesight is completely gone. His sense of humor has returned, though. He seems to think it's funny to keep telling us that now he can truly walk by faith and not by sight."

Joseph chuckled. "That sounds like Abba."

Judah just shook his head. "Anyhow, the return journey to Avaris was painfully slow because of Father. We made a stretcher to carry him up over the mountains. Benjamin held his hand almost the whole way. After the mountain trek, he needed time to recuperate, so I came ahead to let you know we were okay."

Joseph put his arm around Judah. "You've done well. Can you bring me to the camp where Abba is?"

"Yes, but a little food and water first would be nice."

"Of course. Once you have eaten, we will be off."

An hour later they were hurriedly hiking away from Avaris, accompanied by a retinue of armed guards, including Potiphar. He'd insisted upon personally overseeing Joseph's safety, and Joseph was wise enough not to try to stop him. They made good time, and by late afternoon they saw dots on the horizon moving in their direction.

"That must be them!" shouted Joseph. They doubled their speed, and the dots grew bigger and then slowly morphed into people. Joseph was a bundle of nerves and excitement as he thought about seeing his father again. It had been so long he didn't know what to expect.

As they drew close, the brothers called out in welcome, and Joseph couldn't stop himself from breaking into a full sprint to close the distance. His brothers let him pass until he came to Benjamin, who was sitting with an old man. The man's body was slender and hunched over, and what little hair remained was white as a sheep's fleece. So much had changed, but there was no question it was his father.

Joseph approached him cautiously. As he drew near the old man heard his footsteps and perked up. "Joseph, is that you, my son?"

"It is me, Abba." Joseph's voice cracked with emotion.

Abba gasped. "I know that voice. It truly is you. Praise be to God. Come to me, my son." Joseph kneeled and gently enfolded his father in his arms, and the smell of him brought back a thousand beautiful memories. Both men began to weep. Never had such a flood been seen in the desert.

When at last the tears had run their course, Joseph's father ran his hands over his son's face to get the measure of him. Then he pulled Joseph's head to his chest, and Joseph could hear his father's heart beating softly. They sat like that for a long time, trying to make up for all the years of separation.

When Abba finally regained his voice, he spoke as one standing on hallowed ground. "My beloved son, I thought this day would never come. Not a day went by when I did not mourn your death and blame myself for what happened. When I finally learned the truth about your brothers' deception, I burned with anger against them. But then I remembered your vivid dreams as a boy. Those dreams were a promise, a foreshadowing, and God has made good on his promise. I have come to see that what your brothers intended for evil, God has used for good. God heard my cries. He saved you from the pit. He blessed the work of your hands and has returned you to me. Now I may die in peace, for I have once again held you in my arms. My son who was dead is alive again."

Joseph took his father's hands in his. "I do not doubt that the Lord heard your cries. Even in the darkest of times God protected me. It took me a long time to realize it, but now that I have, I see his fingerprints everywhere, from the dreams of my youth to the people he placed along my path. I promise I'll tell you the whole story when we reach Avaris, but there's an even more important reason for us to get there."

"And what might that be?"

"You have a grandson," said Joseph proudly.

This revelation brought about more tears, and at last Abba declared, "We have wet the ground enough with our tears. Let us go so I can meet this grandson of mine and hold him in my arms. Surely the Lord has blessed me beyond what I deserve."

"He has blessed us both," replied Joseph.

Off they went, arm in arm, a father and his long-lost son. In the dwindling light, the outline of Avaris could be seen on the horizon. Joseph's brothers came around them, and together they headed toward the city. Their new home was waiting.

Epilogue

Joseph's family settled into life in Avaris, and Abba lived for three more years before he passed away peacefully in his sleep. He was buried next to Reuben, and his death was mourned throughout Avaris. Emmanuel lived long enough to see Mariam give birth to a second son, whom she lovingly named after her own father. Emmanuel passed away shortly after the birth and was buried next to Joseph's father. Though not by blood, Emmanuel was family.

Joseph continued to serve faithfully as the Commander of Avaris for more than two decades. By the time he stepped down, he'd served for well over thirty years and was credited with single-handedly saving Avaris during the terrible years of famine. His greatest joy was spending time with his beloved Mariam and their two sons.

Zuleika and Salim were never seen again, but years later traders from the south came with tales of a mysterious woman who had emerged from the desert and become a powerful warlord. They said her beauty was matched only by her ruthlessness, and she was known to always wear red. When this little piece of news made it to Cyasi, he brought it directly to Joseph. He'd been due for a shave anyway. The two of them discussed it for a long time, but they never could agree on whether it was Zuleika. In the end, they decided that some things are best left unknown.

ACKNOWLEDGEMENTS

I would like to say a special thank you to my parents for introducing me to the beautiful stories found within Scripture from an early age and for teaching me the value of holy imagination. I am forever grateful for the foundation that you built for me. Dad, thank you for being my first reader and for encouraging me to keep working on the manuscript when I was ready to give up.

To my wonderful wife, Alison, I love you with all my heart! Thank you for letting me disappear for hours on end to write. *The Dreamer* would be nothing more than a dream if it weren't for you and your support. To my incredible kids, Sam and Lydia, thank you for believing in me and for cheering me on each step of the way.

Lastly, a big thank you to Sarah and Charissa at Two Sisters Press. Sarah, thank you for your amazing work editing my manuscript. Charissa, thank you for your work to get *The Dreamer* out into the world. It's a joy to work with you.